Both Here And Gone

Michael Dante DiMartino

Cover design by Stuart Bache

First Edition

ISBN: 979-8-9904591-0-6

For Shoshana

So thoroughly and sincerely are we compelled to live,
reverencing our life, and denying the possibility of change.

—HENRY DAVID THOREAU, *Walden*

Chapter 1

The only thing worse than losing your memory is being forced to remember all the ways you've hurt the people you love. My friend Alyssa told me that after she came back from the dead.

I was eight the summer *Star Wars* came out. My parents and I had to wait in line at the movie theater for half the day because all the screenings were sold out. But it was worth it. For weeks after, I ran around the house, imagining I was Luke Skywalker, flying through space in my X-Wing and blowing up the Death Star.

I begged my parents for a *Star Wars*–themed party for my ninth birthday, which was coming up. October 11, 1977, to be exact. Mom searched the stores for decorations, but there wasn't anything *Star Wars*–related. So she got crafty and made her own decorations. She transformed cardboard tubes and paint into lightsabers, drew the *Star Wars* logo on a bunch of paper plates, and even baked a cake shaped like Darth Vader's helmet and slathered it with chocolate frosting. It looked pretty cool.

Alyssa, Trevor, and a few other kids from school came to my house for the party. Except my dad wasn't there. He'd just gotten this new job working for a computer programming company, and he had to travel a lot. He would fly to different businesses up and down the East Coast to set up their computer systems or something. I never understood what he did, exactly. All I knew was that he was busy all the time. And too busy to make it home in time for my party, even though he'd promised he'd be there. It was the first birthday of mine he'd ever missed. But not the last.

Anyway, he got back a couple of days after the party. As soon as he walked in the door, he was all apologetic about missing my big day and promised it wouldn't happen again. My throat tightened and all I could choke out was "It's not a big deal" even though, deep down, I knew I was lying. I guess I didn't want him to feel bad.

Dad handed me a present—a long box covered in space-themed wrapping paper. On the tag he'd scrawled, *To Jack. Let's explore the galaxy together. Love, Dad.* I remember being surprised because Mom was always the one who did the gift shopping. I figured he'd picked it up at the airport gift shop out of guilt. It was his attempt to show me he cared, but it felt more like a business transaction.

I'd barely finished ripping off the wrapping paper when Dad asked what I thought. Inside was a telescope.

"It's cool, I guess." I turned the box over in my hands. On the back was a picture of a boy peering into a telescope, his father standing next to him, pointing skyward, a smile on his face. Was that why Dad had bought it? So we could be more like the fake father and son on the box?

But guess how many times we explored together. Once. That night, he helped me set it up, and we went outside and spotted the Big Dipper and Orion and a bunch of other constellations I can't remember the names of. The telescope wound up abandoned on the back deck. Eventually Mom threw the telescope in the garage along with a guitar Dad had barely played and a tennis racket he'd used a couple of times. Mom always got mad at Dad for starting hobbies he never followed through on. I guess stargazing was one of those hobbies, too.

So years later, when he tells me he's leaving for six months to hike the Appalachian Trail, I figure there's no way he'll follow through on that, either.

———

THE APPALACHIAN TRAIL is this super-long path that goes from Georgia all the way up to Maine. It's more than two thousand miles. Most people only walk parts of it, but Dad had a grand plan to finish the entire thing. "A thru-hike," he called it. My dad was more comfortable programming computers than living out in nature, which was the other reason I didn't believe he'd really leave. The only times he showed his outdoorsy side were when he raked leaves or shoveled the driveway after it snowed.

But then one chilly February morning, he dragged me to the Army Surplus store to buy a bunch of stuff for his trip: a tent, a sleeping bag, first aid kit, rain gear, cooking supplies, clothes for cold and hot weather, and hiking boots. Panic struck me when Dad outlined his plan to carry it all inside his brand-new green camo backpack. His eyes filled with a wild determination I'd never seen before—he was dead serious about pursuing this insane dream of his. Mom began smoking again, which meant she was worried too. Uncertainty clouded my future.

Dad promised he'd be back in time for my fourteenth birthday. I told him I'd believe him when he walked through the front door, since he'd missed four out of my past five birthdays. A couple of weeks later, he quit his job. Dad told me he'd saved up enough money to cover groceries and pay the bills while he was gone. "You'll be fine," he assured me. But that was a bunch of crap, too, because our family wasn't fine. It hadn't been for a long time. Dad's leaving just made things worse.

Nine months later, Alyssa fell through the ice on Lake Trapper and was dead for twenty-three minutes.

———

TIME BLURRED after Alyssa's accident—or "the incident," as people started calling it. It was basically code for "that horrible day we'd rather not talk about." The days passed but I couldn't tell you what happened one to the next. All I remember was eating cereal for every meal since Mom had given up on cooking. I holed up in my room, numbing myself with sugar and marshmallows, sinking deeper into sadness. From my bed, I stared out the window, watching the New Year's Day snow slowly melt off the roofs of the neighborhood houses. The snowbanks shrunk until nothing remained but patches of gray slush. Whenever Mom paced up and down the hall past my door, I'd get a whiff of her stinky cigarette smoke and have to hold my breath until the air cleared.

Practically every hour, the phone rang. Relatives called to ask how we were holding up. What did they think? That Mom and I had turned into a couple of quaking buildings, about to collapse? Come to think of it, I guess we kind of were.

But I'd figured out a way to keep myself from completely falling apart. A foolproof strategy to block all the chaos in the real world from getting to me. I made my bedroom a fortress.

On a piece of poster board, I wrote KEEP OUT in big red letters and taped it to my door. For backup, I'd wedged my desk chair under the handle. I retreated to my bed and imagined the carpet was a moat of lava. Sure, it was childish, but it helped me feel safe. Like I was actually in control of something when just the opposite was true.

Then one night, Mom knocked on my door.

"Jack? Honey?" she said through the door. She'd just gotten off the phone with someone who I assumed was Aunt Beth. Even though she was Dad's sister, Mom talked to her all the time, ever since I was little. Mom was an only child, like me, and seemed to love being part of Dad's bigger family.

"Can't you read the sign?" I asked.

"Jack, this is serious. I need to talk to you now." When she tried to push open the door, my trusty chair defense blocked her from getting in. But it didn't make her go away. Mom kept shoving the door against the chair, barking at me to let her in or else.

"Or else what?" I barked back. The universe had already punished me. There was nothing she could do to make my life more miserable. She must have known that because her voice got calm.

"Please, honey. It's good news, I swear."

Good news had been rare since Dad walked out on us. But I was curious, so I scooted to the edge of the bed, stuck out my leg, and kicked over the chair.

Mom came in, smoke trailing from a cigarette between her fingers. She picked up the chair, dragged it next to the bed, and took a seat. That's when she got a good look at the mess she'd walked into. Mom scanned the room, her nose crinkling.

"It reeks in here."

How her sense of smell still functioned after smoking two packs a day, I had no idea. Still, she had a point. There was a mountain of dirty clothes in the corner that had been building for weeks. On my desk, I'd piled empty bowls that had hard lumps of cereal and dried milk in them. Mom sucked down the rest of her cigarette and tossed the butt in one bowl, where it fizzled out.

I'd never been a neat kid, but I used to clean up my room once in a while. After Dad was gone, though, I didn't really see the point. I didn't see the point of doing a lot of things. Like showering. Or brushing my teeth. Or going to school. Which explained why my breath stank and my grades tanked.

"When's the last time you ate a piece of fruit?" Mom asked.

I retreated to the head of my bed and pulled the covers over my legs. "I had Froot Loops for breakfast."

"And for lunch?"

I shrugged. "Captain Crunch?"

Mom shook her head and gave me this disappointed look, which meant she thought I was being a smart aleck. "And I suppose you probably had more sugary crap for dinner?"

"What else am I supposed to eat?" I said, adding an extra hit of smart aleck. "It's not like you cook anymore."

Mom didn't have a comeback, so she just glared.

"So why did Aunt Beth call?" I asked.

"It wasn't your Aunt Beth. It was Alyssa's mom."

Even though I was sitting down, the room started spinning. I yanked the covers up higher and hugged my knees to my chest.

Mom leaned forward, and for the first time in forever, she smiled. "Alyssa woke up. Isn't that incredible?"

"Incredible" barely described it. Alyssa had plunged into a freezing lake, came back from the brink of death, and then spent the past month in a coma. It was like something out of a movie, not real life. Especially not *my* life. I still couldn't wrap my head around what had happened.

"Mrs. Sawyer said the doctors moved her out of the ICU, which means she can finally have visitors." Mom made her voice sound all comforting, but it did nothing to calm my churning stomach. "Tomorrow morning you're going to take a shower, change into some clothes that don't stink, and you and I will go say hello. Okay?"

She probably expected me to leap out of bed like I used to on Christmas morning, but I wasn't excited. Just light-headed. All I did was sit there, frozen to the backboard, the room spinning. Finally the dizziness passed, and I got out a few words. "I . . . I doubt Alyssa even wants to be in the same room as me."

"Of course she does. Mrs. Sawyer said that when Alyssa woke up, you were the first person she asked about."

That might've been true. Or Mom was trying to get me to do what she wanted.

"I realize this has been a tough few weeks," Mom said.

I rolled my eyes. "Oh yeah, everything was fantastic before that."

"Okay, a tough nine months," she admitted. "But seeing Alyssa . . . it'll help."

"With what?"

"With not feeling so sad all the time."

"How do you know that?"

"I just do. Trust me, honey."

Mom had also assured me that going back to school would help. But she'd been wrong about that, too.

The only good thing that happened after "the incident" was getting to play hooky for a couple of weeks. And that was on top of Christmas break. But my first day back, the other kids in class looked at me like I had some kind of disease they were afraid of catching if they got too close. No one—not even any of my teachers—mentioned what had happened to Alyssa or brought up the reason I'd been absent. Since no one knew what to say, everyone acted like "the incident" had never happened. Living in denial felt weird at first, but after a couple days, I got used to it. Visiting Alyssa meant I would have to face a reality I'd been avoiding for weeks. And I wasn't ready to do that yet.

"Actually, I forgot I made plans for tomorrow already," I said.

"What plans?"

"With Trevor. I'm meeting him at the arcade."

"What am I supposed to tell Mrs. Sawyer? That you'd rather play video games than see her daughter who almost died?" Mom sounded pissed.

"Tell her I got the flu."

"You want me to lie to her?"

I didn't know why Mom sounded so shocked. She was good at lying to people. Especially Dad. Why couldn't she help me out just this once?

"Well, you can't avoid Alyssa forever, Jack. She's your best friend."

A best friend would have noticed something was off with Alyssa that day. A best friend would have made sure she didn't go so far out on the ice. A best friend wouldn't want her to stay in a coma just so he wouldn't have to face reality.

"Hiding in your room won't change what happened," Mom said.

"Maybe not, but I'm going to stay here anyway."

"Fine. Then I guess when the movers come, they can pack you up in a box and throw you in the back of their truck."

I was suddenly a million degrees. I flung off the covers. "What movers?"

That's when Mom dropped the bomb. "I'm selling the house, honey."

I jumped out of bed and got in Mom's face. "You just decided that without me? That's not fair!"

Mom touched my shoulder to calm me, but I shrugged her hand away and stormed to the window. She apologized, claiming she was out of options—bills were piling up, and Dad's savings were gone. In the reflection in the window, I could see her fighting back tears. If I had been a good son, or at least an understanding one, I might've said something kind or given her a hug. But all I could think about was how to stop her. Dad was gone. I'd almost lost Alyssa. I couldn't deal with losing the only home I'd ever known.

"What do you even know about selling a house, anyway? Dad always took care of that stuff."

"I know how to use a phone to call a Realtor. I'm meeting with one next week."

"Where are we going to go?"

"I still have to figure that part out."

"Who's crazy enough to buy this dump, anyway?"

"You're the one living in your own filth!" Mom stormed out, ripping down my KEEP OUT poster on the way. She slammed the door behind her.

Another wave of heat washed over me and, in a fit of rage, I kicked my desk. Not the best move, considering I only had socks on. Pain shot up my leg and I screamed. I hopped to my bed and collapsed onto it, cradling my aching foot, until the throbbing in my toes finally stopped.

Chapter 2

The next morning, while Mom was visiting Alyssa at the hospital, I went to the mall to meet Trevor at GameZilla. Usually the arcade is packed, but on Sunday mornings, when most of Ravensberg is in church, you have the place all to yourself. The only other people there were a couple of punks with leather jackets and mohawks, looking like they'd just stepped out of a Billy Idol video. Trevor and I beelined for our favorite game—Pac-Man.

We popped in two quarters and the bouncy, high-pitched theme music kicked in. Like always, Trevor picked "player one," and immediately went to work, moving the joystick with quick, precise gestures. His Pac-Man swept through the first board, avoiding the ghosts and gobbling up all the dots and fruit. I had given up hope long ago of ever winning a video game against Trevor, especially Pac-Man. He played like his life depended on it.

While he waited the few seconds for the next board to load, Trevor said, "So, I heard Alyssa is, like, a zombie now." He always made stupid jokes like that. Sometimes I laughed. But not that day.

"She's not a zombie," I said, raising my voice over Pac-Man's *waka waka waka*. He was on the move again.

"My dad's the one who gave her CPR, remember? He said she was dead for, like, twenty-five minutes after she fell in."

"Twenty-three," I corrected.

"Whatever, dude. The point is, she came back from the dead. Therefore—zombie."

"She is not!" I shoved Trevor's arm and his Pac-Man veered off-course, slamming right into Clyde, the orange ghost. Trevor glared at me, his face turning redder than his hair.

"What the hell? You know the rules."

Around the arcade, Trevor was a legend. Other players called him the Pac-Man Kid because he could make one quarter last for more than an hour. And since his initials filled the top eight out of ten slots on the high score screen, Trevor considered himself untouchable. Which meant he didn't want anyone touching him while he was playing, literally.

"Sorry," I said.

Trevor stepped aside so I could have my turn. The music kicked in and my Pac-Man materialized. I gripped the joystick. I'd only eaten a few dots when Trevor started criticizing every move I made.

"No, don't go up! Go through the tunnel! Get the power pellet!"

I told Trevor I didn't want his advice, but he kept giving it anyway. He'd read in some video game magazine about how the creators of Pac-Man had put a hidden pattern in the game, and if you followed it exactly, you'd eat a ton of dots, power pellets, ghosts, and fruit. Ever since learning that, Trevor had been trying to master the pattern, racking up higher and higher scores along the way.

"Come on, dude, how many times have we played Pac-Man

and you still haven't figured out the pattern? You can't let those gnarly ghosts get you."

Trevor knew a lot about being chased by ghosts. And not just the ones in video games.

Unlike me, Trevor hadn't always been an only child. He'd had a younger brother, Scott. Everyone called him Scotty. Scotty's two favorite things in the world were his Batman action figure and his big brother, Trevor. But three years earlier, Scotty had gotten sick. Like cancer sick. He was in and out of the hospital for a year doing chemo. The last six months of his life, he spent in a children's hospital in Boston. The doctors there were supposed to be specialists in treating leukemia. Toward the end of sixth grade, Trevor's parents took him out of school and they moved to Boston for Scotty's treatments. Mom, Dad, and I drove up one weekend. When we walked into his room, Scotty smiled, but just barely. He was bald and had dark circles under his eyes. He couldn't sit up to eat and had to be fed through tubes. No six-year-old should have to go through what Scotty did.

I never saw him again. He died sometime that summer. I'm not sure exactly when because the Donlans had arranged a private funeral with only their close family. The first day of seventh grade, Trevor was back at school. When I saw him in class, I didn't know what to say, so I said nothing. Trevor didn't talk about Scotty, either. Trevor and I went back to hanging out, but the Donlans were never the same after that.

"I don't need your advice," I said, focusing back on the game. "I'd rather just have fun and follow my gut."

I jerked the joystick up and my Pac-Man shot toward the top of the screen. All four ghosts closed in. I escaped to the corner of the maze and gobbled a power pellet. The ghosts all flashed blue and turned tail. Right away I ate two, then charged after the others. Feeling pretty proud of myself, I gobbled up the third ghost then chased down the last one—Pinky. But before I could reach her, she started flashing.

"Retreat, retreat!" Trevor shouted in my ear.

I ignored Trevor and kept going. The ghost turned back to pink. My Pac-Man slammed into her and fizzled out.

"Your gut really sucks at this game, you know that?" Trevor flashed a smug smile as he grabbed the joystick and took his turn.

"For a best friend, you can be a real dick sometimes, you know *that*? Worry about your own problems, not mine."

Trevor shot me a look. "What's that supposed to mean?"

I instantly regretted mentioning anything. "Nothing," I squeaked.

Trevor may have had the upper hand when it came to winning video games, but I knew something he didn't—his dad and my mom had had an affair.

It started after Scotty died, but I wasn't exactly sure when. I found out sort of by accident, but the signs had been there. I suspected something was up when Mom started coming home late, claiming she'd been at work. And whenever I was over at Trevor's house, his parents were always fighting. One night, when Dad was out of town, I heard Mom on the phone in her bedroom. I tried to mind my own business but couldn't help myself. I quietly picked up the kitchen line and listened in. It was Mr. Donlan. He and Mom talked about meeting up at a motel the next day. It was gross.

I hung up and went to bed, desperate to forget what I'd just learned. If I pretended the affair wasn't real, maybe the whole thing would just go away. I kept my discovery to myself and vowed never to mention it to anyone, especially Dad. I didn't want to be the reason my parents split up. But after that phone call, something in me shifted. I started avoiding Mom and spending more time alone in my room. At the dinner table, I stayed silent. Mom didn't have to ask if I knew about her and Mr. Donlan. My behavior said it all.

Dad eventually found out about the affair without me having to tell him, and after that, my parents' fighting got worse. Every night, Mom would cry herself to sleep while Dad crashed on the couch. After a couple of counseling sessions, Mom agreed to end things with Mr. Donlan, but tensions were still high. I couldn't say for sure if the affair was the main reason Dad chose to wander the Appalachian Trail, but it must have played a role.

Dad being gone left a gaping hole in my life. But that pain was nothing compared to the daggers I felt from Mom's eyes every time she looked at me. Even though she never accused me directly, the way she glared at me made it obvious that she blamed me for their marriage falling apart.

Even though part of me wanted to dump the awful truth on Trevor, I couldn't bring myself to do it. I'd convinced myself I was being a great friend by keeping him in the dark. He'd already lost his little brother. I wasn't about to be the one who shattered the rest of his world.

Neither of us spoke for the next half hour as Trevor cleared board after board. Finally, he messed up and one of the ghosts got him. I'd barely started my turn when I had this feeling of being watched. A second later, Mr. and Mrs. Donlan walked up behind us. Trevor hadn't mentioned he was meeting up with his parents, so their sudden appearance threw me off my game. My hands started sweating and I lost my grip on the joystick. A ghost gobbled up my Pac-Man.

"You about ready to go, Trevor?" Mr. Donlan said.

"I still have one life left," Trevor said, eyes focused on the screen.

"We'll wait," Mrs. Donlan said.

"It might be a while," Trevor said.

With Trevor occupied, Mr. Donlan turned to me. He looked as rigid as a statue, his tree trunk arms crossed over his broad chest. He was a tall guy, but that day he loomed larger than usual. "How've you been, Jack?"

"Okay," I said.

Mr. Donlan had played football in college, which is where he met Mrs. Donlan, who'd been a cheerleader. She was pretty. Like, movie star pretty. If you had to imagine the perfect couple, you'd think of them. And for a mom, Mrs. Donlan was pretty cool. Way cooler than my mom. Whenever I slept over at Trevor's, she'd let us order pizza and stay up as late as we wanted playing Atari. Why in the world Mr. Donlan had cheated on her with my mom was a mystery.

"We're going to the food court for lunch," Mrs. Donlan said. "You're welcome to join us." Her makeup was running like she'd been crying.

I was in no mood to drag out what was an already awkward situation. "Sorry, I have to go. My mom's about to pick me up." The truth was, she wasn't due for another half hour.

"Maybe next time," Mrs. Donlan said.

"Maybe."

"But you're gonna miss me break my high score," Trevor complained.

"I'm sure you'll tell me all about it later," I said, hightailing it out of the arcade.

Chapter 3

I rushed through the mall doors and gulped in the cold air. I zipped up my coat, put on my winter hat, and waited alone. Since I couldn't play Pac-Man anymore, I came up with my own game to pass the time. The curb became my balance beam, and I tried my hardest not to fall off. I made it pretty far, but then a rumbling engine distracted me. The sound got louder and louder, pounding my eardrums and I stumbled off the curb. An ancient-looking truck pulled up next to me. A classic Ford from the 1950s, I later found out. Red paint peeled off its body like dead skin, revealing patches of rust. Black smoke that smelled worse than Mom's cigarettes spewed from its tailpipe. A pile of scrap metal rattled around in the back. I was no mechanic, but it was obvious that the truck was in rough shape.

I'd seen the pickup around town before. Mom always eyed the truck's driver suspiciously and described him as "some creepy guy who lives alone in the woods." Creepy Guy was notorious around Ravensberg. People gossiped about him while waiting in store check-out lines and during church pot-lucks. I never got a great answer about why the guy was so terrible, but the community's message was loud and clear: keep your distance.

"Hey, kid," Creepy Guy called from the truck. I kept my eyes on the balance-beam curb and acted like I hadn't heard him.

Brakes squeaked, and the pickup stopped right next to me. Out of the corner of my eye, I could see Creepy Guy leaning out his window. He took a swig from a Coke bottle and wiped his mouth with the sleeve of his denim jacket. "You ignoring me on purpose?"

I looked up. He was close enough to reach out and grab me. I took a step back, studying him. He was hollow-cheeked with a leathery face, like he'd spent a lot of time in the sun. Shaggy brown hair sprouted from his worn John Deere cap. It looked like he hadn't shaved in a few days. He had on a blue flannel shirt under his jacket.

"You gonna say 'hi' or just stare at me?" he said.

I forced out a timid "Hey."

"That's better," he said, flashing a smile. "What's your name?"

"My mom's picking me up," I said, trying to scare him off. "She should be here any minute."

"How about I go first? Name's Renny Laforge." He tipped his cap.

I quickly scanned the parking lot. No sign of Mom yet.

"Now you know who I am, but I still don't know who you are," Renny said.

"I'm Jack." As soon as the words came, I regretted not giving him a fake name.

"Nice to meet you, Jack. I was driving past and noticed you out here all alone. Took it as a sign."

"A sign of what?"

"That we were meant to meet today. I thought you might

17

help me with something." Renny reached into his jacket pocket and pulled out a photo, holding it at arm's length so I could get a good look. It was a Polaroid of a black dog standing in a pile of leaves. "I'm looking for my dog. He likes to drive around with me in my truck, but he ran off when I was over at Reynolds Grocery. Goes by the name Seneca. Maybe you've seen him?"

I backed away, raising my hands, and let out a nervous laugh. My mind flashed to the faces of kidnapped kids on milk cartons. I didn't want to become one of them. "Missing dog? You think I'm stupid enough to fall for that trick?"

Renny chuckled. "I get it, kid. I'm just a stranger and this photo could be of anyone's dog. You're right to be suspicious. But you got nothing to worry about. I'm not planning to lure you into my truck and drag you off into the woods or anything like that. I'm just asking for your help."

"Which is exactly what a kidnapper would say to lure me into their truck."

Renny's jaw and neck tightened. "Whoever you think I am, you're mistaken."

"Well, I didn't see your dog," I said.

"You sure? Go on, take a closer look." Renny leaned forward, waving the photo at me.

Out of instinct, I snatched the Polaroid out of his hand and gave it a quick glance. "Nope. Didn't see him. Sorry."

Before I could hand the photo back, a man in a mall cop uniform walked up behind me and marched over to Renny. "Can I help you, sir?"

"Nope," Renny said. "Just talking to my friend Jack, here."

Officer Mall Cop turned to me. He had a gun and a mustache, just like the cops on TV. "Do you know this man?"

"No. He just drove up."

"Is he bothering you?"

All I had to do was say "no" and let Renny off the hook.

Instead, I made the situation worse. "Yeah, I think he's trying to kidnap me."

Renny scowled at me. Officer Mall Cop stepped closer to the pickup. "Let me see your license."

"No way in hell," Renny said.

Officer Mall Cop gripped his holstered gun. "Step out of the truck."

I flinched, my heart racing. A wave of guilt came over me. Renny was about to get arrested because of some stupid thing I'd said and I didn't even know why I'd said it. But before I had the chance to clear Renny's name, he solved the problem himself.

"You don't have any authority over me," Renny said. He was right because rather than drawing his gun, Officer Mall Cop pulled out a small pad of paper and a pen instead.

"Well, I am authorized to cite you for parking in a red zone," he said.

"All right, all right, I'm going." Renny sneered at me. "Thanks for nothing, kid."

The pickup chugged away, leaving behind a trail of black smoke.

Officer Mall Cop asked me if I was okay. I said I was fine and that my mom would be there soon. He waited with me for a couple of minutes, but then got a call on his walkie-talkie and had to leave.

Clutching the Polaroid of Renny's dog, I thought about tossing it in the garbage. But something caused me to stuff it in my pocket instead. I couldn't shake what Renny had said about us being destined to meet that day.

A few minutes later, Mom pulled up in our station wagon. When I opened the door, a wall of smoke hit me. The smell burned my nose and bit at the back of my throat, making me gag and cough.

Mom rolled her eyes and lit up another cigarette. "Is there something you want to say?" she asked.

I got in and kicked away the empty cigarette packs littering the floor. All I wanted to do was to tell her was how much I hated her smoking, and how it made us both sick. But the only words that came out were, "You're late."

"Barely." Mom rolled down her window a crack and blew out a puff of smoke. She pulled out of the lot and we headed home. "How was the arcade?"

"Fine," I told her.

"How's Trevor? I haven't seen him since . . ." She trailed off. "I haven't seen him in a while."

"He's fine."

"He wasn't waiting with you. Did Mr. Donlan pick him up?"

She didn't actually care if I had fun at the arcade, all she wanted was information about Mr. Donlan. So I told her that he and Mrs. Donlan had showed up, hand in hand, all smiles.

Mom couldn't hide her displeasure as she took a drag on her cigarette and practically choked on the smoke. "Oh yeah?" She acted like that news was no big deal, but I could tell it was eating her up inside. She changed the subject.

"Aren't you going to ask how Alyssa is?"

"No, because you're about to tell me, anyway."

"Well, she's doing great. The doctors say she'll make a full recovery."

"I'm glad."

But Mom wasn't done yet. "You really should visit her. Mrs. Sawyer looked disappointed that you didn't come."

Translation: Mom was disappointed in me.

"I already told you, I don't want to go."

"She's your friend, Jack."

"I know."

"You have a strange way of showing it."

Mom was a genius at pushing my guilt buttons.

"Mrs. Sawyer told me Mr. Donlan visits her every day," she added.

"He's a paramedic. Being at the hospital is part of his job," I argued.

"He doesn't have to visit Alyssa. He does that because he cares."

My stomach churned—not only from the cigarette smoke but also from Mom going on and on about Mr. Donlan as if he were some sort of saint.

On our way home, we drove past the Sawyers' house and its familiar, hand-painted sign on the front lawn declaring, "SAWYER FUNERAL HOME. SINCE 1942."

When I was younger, I didn't really get that Alyssa's house doubled as the family business and that her dad worked with dead bodies for a living. But once I understood, it was kind of eerie being there. It gave me chills knowing that Mr. Sawyer was down in the basement pumping corpses full of chemicals and putting makeup on them while Alyssa and I were hanging out upstairs.

THAT NIGHT, on the six-o'clock local news, a story came on about Alyssa. Mom called me into the living room to watch.

The TV screen flashed to Channel 5 reporter Dorothy Jackson, standing in the hospital lobby, her hair permed into blond waves, her bright blue blazer a jarring contrast to the sterile white walls.

"Tonight, a cheerful scene at Billings Memorial Hospital where, after spending nearly four weeks in a coma, fourteen-year-old Alyssa Sawyer is awake." The reporter's lips curled into a practiced smile. "Some are calling her 'The Miracle Girl.'"

I looked for the remote to flip the channel, but it was in Mom's hand. She turned up the volume.

The reporter described the details of the accident, even though everyone in Ravensberg already knew them. But I guess that's usually what the news is for: to state the obvious.

"It was a cold morning, the day after Christmas," Dorothy Jackson continued, "when Alyssa Sawyer went ice skating with her friends on Lake Trapper. Far from shore, she encountered a patch of thin ice, and fell into the frigid water for several minutes." The TV cut to footage of the lake shore still strewn with yellow police tape.

My throat constricted at the memory of Alyssa's scream, the desperate flailing of her arms as she went under. I dug my fingernails into my palms, trying to ground myself in the present.

By the time Dorothy Jackson got to the part about the "local hero" who saved Alyssa, I had made my way over to the TV and clicked it off. I stared into the dark void of the screen, able to breathe again.

A few seconds later, the TV came back to life, snapping me out of my trance.

"What the hell, Jack? I was watching that!"

I whipped around. Mom was aiming the remote at my chest, like she meant to zap me into oblivion. Her eyes flashed with irritation, lips pressed into a thin line. "Move. You're blocking the set."

I stepped aside as Mr. Donlan appeared on the screen. He

was the paramedic who gave Alyssa CPR and literally brought her back to life. Dorothy Jackson asked him what was going through his mind that day.

"I just couldn't let Alyssa die," Mr. Donlan said. "I had to do everything in my power to save her."

"It really is a miracle," Mom said, wiping a tear from her eye.

I remembered watching with a kind of numb horror as the firefighters pulled Alyssa to shore. I kept waiting for her to gasp, to cough, to open her eyes. But she just lay there, cold and still. When Mr. Donlan got to her, Alyssa didn't have a pulse. Her skin and lips were blue. But he kept pumping her chest, breathing for her. After what seemed an eternity, her heart started beating again.

Seeing him on TV, I felt a rush of gratitude and affection. Mr. Donlan had refused to give up on Alyssa. If only I could say the same.

The next part of the segment was actually news to me: Alyssa had lost some of her memories. Her doctor—Doctor Wexler—explained that while Alyssa's health was making "marked improvements," her brain had been oxygen-deprived for so long that she had developed a condition called "retrograde amnesia." She still had all of her long-term memories, but she couldn't recall anything about the weeks leading to her accident or the accident itself. The doctor couldn't predict how permanent her memory loss would be.

"Poor Alyssa," Mom said. "Can you imagine not being able to remember? It must be so frightening and disorienting for her."

Disorienting. The word resonated, and I rubbed a hand over my eyes. Alyssa wasn't the only one groping through a fog lately. In the time she'd been in a coma, I'd avoided facing the truth about what had happened. Now that she was awake, I feared I couldn't hide from it anymore.

My mind raced as I imagined my own interview with Dorothy Jackson:

"You were with Alyssa on Lake Trapper that day, correct?"

"Yes."

"Why didn't you stop her from skating out so far?"

"I didn't realize where she was until it was too late."

"You claim to care about Alyssa, yet you haven't visited her. Why is that?"

"What if she doesn't remember me?"

"Well, if you don't visit Alyssa, how can you expect to remain friends with her?"

The blare of a car commercial interrupted my fantasy before I could answer. But the guilt lingered.

My jaw clenched as I turned to Mom. "Fine. If I go see Alyssa this once, will you stop bugging me?"

She nodded and headed for the phone in the kitchen. "I'll call Mrs. Sawyer and tell her the good news."

Chapter 4

I hate hospitals. I mean, is there anyone who actually enjoys spending time in them? Especially a place like Billings Memorial—a giant, brick monstrosity that looks like it was built during the Civil War.

I followed Mom through the glass doors and into the bland waiting area where even blander music played over the speakers. Mom signed in with a woman behind the information desk who told us to take the elevator up to room 423. The elevator jolted and shook as it started to rise. Part of me hoped it would break down and trap us. Then firefighters would need to come to pry open the doors and by the time they freed us, visiting hours would be over.

Instead, the elevator ride ended uneventfully with a ding. The doors opened, letting in a whiff of disinfectant.

As we made our way down the hall, nurses in blue scrubs hurried past. Buzzers buzzed and phones rang.

Mom had told Mrs. Sawyer we'd be there at 6:30 on the dot but the clock on the wall read 6:50. When we got to the room, Mrs. Sawyer was waiting outside with her arms crossed, foot tapping impatiently on the linoleum. Even though she was annoyed, she pried a smile onto her face and waved.

Alyssa's mom had been practically living at the hospital for weeks, but you wouldn't have guessed it from her flawless perm and perfectly applied makeup. She wore a pristine white blouse with a button-down red sweater and prim dress. She was the image of the put-together mother, unlike my own mom, who had thrown on her frumpy sweater and jeans before rushing out of the house.

"I'm so sorry we're late, Gayle," Mom said. "I got stuck at the office, then I had to pick up Jack."

Mom worked as an assistant in an insurance office. She constantly complained about her boss, who kept piling paperwork on her desk and refused to pay her overtime.

"Oh, it's no trouble at all, Pamela." No one except Mrs. Sawyer ever called Mom by her full name.

Mrs. Sawyer and Mom hugged, then Mrs. Sawyer looked over to me and asked, "How are you doing, Jack?"

I answered with a shrug.

Mrs. Sawyer leaned in closer and looked me in the eye. "Just remember: God never gives us more than we can handle. You'll make it through this."

"Uh-huh," I murmured, even though I wasn't so sure I believed her.

That's another thing to know about Mrs. Sawyer. She's super religious. She went to Catholic school and wanted to be a nun before meeting Mr. Sawyer. In some ways, I was jealous of her faith. There used to be a time when I accepted whatever Father Murray and Bible stories told me to believe without thinking twice. But then Scotty got sick, and Mom cheated on Dad, and Dad left, and "the incident" happened. It all got me wondering: if there really is a God, why would he put our families through so much pain and suffering?

Mrs. Sawyer turned back to Mom. "If there's anything you need, anything at all, just let me know. Walter and I are here for you." She put a hand on Mom's shoulder. Mom placed her hand on top of it.

"Thank you, but we're fine, Gayle. Really. Besides, you're so busy taking care of Alyssa, and I know Walter has his hands full with work."

"That's right. The dead don't take a day off," Mrs. Sawyer said with a strained chuckle. I'd heard her use that phrase a million times before. Over the years, Mr. Sawyer had missed countless dinners, dance recitals, church events, and family get-togethers because he was busy preparing bodies for funerals. Mrs. Sawyer always tried to joke about their situation but I got the sense she didn't find her husband's constant absence very funny. I know Alyssa didn't.

It was Mom's turn to sound supportive. "It must be hard, not having Walter here with you."

"God only puts obstacles in our way that he knows we can handle," Mrs. Sawyer's said, which was basically the same thing she'd told me.

"That's one way to look at it," Mom said politely before changing the subject. "And the girls? How are they?"

"Happy being spoiled by my sister, I imagine."

A few days after "the incident," the Sawyers sent Alyssa's two younger sisters to live with their aunt in Rhode Island until Alyssa got out of the hospital. Mrs. Sawyer insisted that it was the best arrangement for everyone.

As Mom spoke with Mrs. Sawyer, I looked toward the closed door to Alyssa's room, feeling dizzy. Was I really ready to see her? What was I even going to say?

The doorknob turned and for a second I imagined it would be Alyssa walking out, feeling like herself again and ready to go home. We could all put the accident behind us and pretend it never happened.

Instead, it was Trevor's dad who stepped out. As soon as he spotted me and Mom, he froze.

"Hi, Jack," he said stiffly.

"Hey, Mr. Donlan."

His eyes moved past me to Mom. Her face flushed red, and she fought to hold back a smile. She said, "It's nice to see you, Steve."

"You too, Pam."

"I didn't realize you'd be here," Mom said, even though she knew that Mr. Donlan visited Alyssa every day. I started to suspect she'd left work late on purpose so she'd run into him. What she said next confirmed it.

"While Jack's visiting Alyssa, would you like to grab a cup of coffee downstairs?" Even though the affair had been over for a while, anyone could see she still had feelings for him.

I thought nothing could rattle Mr. Donlan. I mean, his job required him to go into dangerous situations and save people. But Mom asking him out to coffee in the hospital cafeteria made him sweat. Mr. Donlan cleared his throat and shifted his weight from one foot to the other, obviously uncomfortable with the invitation. For once, he was the one who needed saving, so I threw him a lifeline.

I looked right at Mom and said, "Didn't you already have, like, five cups of coffee today?" She gave me the look of death, like I'd just revealed her deepest, darkest secret.

To my surprise, Mrs. Sawyer added, "And the cafeteria coffee is terrible. I'd stay far away from it if I were you."

Mom got all pouty, like a kid who'd just had her favorite toy taken away. But I wasn't sorry I'd ruined her stupid plan for a coffee date.

"Sorry, Pam, I can't," Mr. Donlan said. "My shift's starting soon."

Mom barely hid her disappointment. "That's okay. Another time, maybe."

"Maybe." Mr. Donlan stared at the floor and Mrs. Sawyer looked away uncomfortably as an awkward silence filled the air.

Mr. Donlan quickly said good-bye and scurried toward the elevators. Mrs. Sawyer offered to take Mom across the street to a bakery called Norma's that she insisted had the best coffee in town. Mom said she'd settle for the cafeteria and told me to meet her in the lobby in half an hour.

"You're not coming in with me?" I asked.

"I don't want to overwhelm Alyssa with too many guests all at once," Mom replied before rushing into Mr. Donlan's elevator just as its doors were closing.

Mrs. Sawyer asked if I wanted anything from the bakery, but I was too nervous to eat or even think about eating.

"Are you sure it's okay if I go in by myself? What if Alyssa has a bad reaction or something?"

"It's fine. She asked that it just be you. And if there is a problem, you can always press the call button and a nurse will come right over."

"Is she really going to remember me?" I couldn't stop my voice from shaking.

"Of course, dear." But then Mrs. Sawyer leaned closer, her expression hardening. "However, there is one request I need to ask of you. Alyssa is aware there was an accident, of course, but not about everything that happened that day. So I would greatly appreciate it if you didn't mention anything. And if she asks, don't go into any details about . . . Well, you know. Let's not cause her any more distress. I've asked the same of her other visitors, including Mr. Donlan and your mother. Can you do that for me?"

If Mrs. Sawyer didn't want me to mention "the incident," that was fine by me. Honestly, it was a relief. "Yeah, I can do that."

Mrs. Sawyer nudged me toward the open door. "Now, go on in. She's going to be so happy to see you."

Before I knew it, Mrs. Sawyer was gone, and I was alone. The beep beep beep of the machines from Alyssa's room drifted into the hall.

Taking a deep breath, I stepped inside.

I CREPT FORWARD, one step at a time, my sneakers squeaking on the linoleum. A bead of sweat trickled down my spine, my body ready to run if it came to that.

Alyssa was lying on her bed, propped up against several pillows. Her eyes were closed and her skin was pale. She must have fallen asleep in the few minutes since Mr. Donlan left. Her dark hair was pulled back away from her face, and her hands lay limply by her sides. Tubes and wires snaked from her nose, her arms, and from under her hospital gown, connecting her to various medical machines.

I held my breath and stood totally still, afraid to make the slightest sound and wake her. After everything she'd been through, I didn't want to make things harder for her. I was about to leave while there was still a chance, but then Alyssa whispered a raspy "Hello?"

All I could say back was a quiet "Hey."

Alyssa opened her eyes and gazed straight ahead with this empty stare, like she was looking right through me. I stepped closer to her bed. "It's me. Jack."

She squinted for a second, trying to place me, then slowly

pushed my name out of her mouth like she was sounding out the word in another language. "Jack?"

"I live down the street from you in the two-story brown house with the white mailbox and the big pear tree in the front yard. We go to school together."

Alyssa rolled her eyes, the way she always did when I said something dumb. "Yeah, I know where you live, Banana Brain."

Hearing that nickname made my whole body relax. She gave it to me when we were in first grade. I'd been going through a phase where all I ate for lunch were bananas so she'd joked that my brain was going to turn to mush. Now I can't even look at a banana without wanting to puke.

"So . . . you remember me."

"Better than you remember me, apparently," Alyssa shot back. "I've been in this stupid hospital for weeks and today is your first visit? What were you waiting for?"

"Your mom said they didn't allow visitors in the ICU unless they were family." Alyssa didn't buy my weak excuse.

"But they moved me out of there two days ago. I thought maybe . . . maybe you were mad at me or something."

The guilt rose in my throat like bile. I swallowed hard and shook my head. "I'm not mad at you. I'm so sorry I didn't come sooner. I was . . ."

Cowardly. Selfish. A terrible friend. But I couldn't say any of that.

"It's okay." Alyssa squeezed my hand and smiled. "You're here now. That's what matters. It's good to see you."

"You too, Miracle Girl."

Her smile faded as quickly as it had formed. "Never call me that."

"Sorry . . . I didn't mean . . ."

"My mom won't shut up about what a 'miracle' all this is. But I don't feel very miraculous. I can't even remember what happened, and who knows when I'll get out of here and go back to being a regular kid." She could recall almost everything—her parents, her sisters, even the name of our elementary school gym teacher, Mr. Koviak, who would give us rocket rides on our birthdays by throwing us up in the air. But she couldn't remember celebrating any of the holidays, going back to Halloween. It was like "the incident" had formed a black hole in her mind that had sucked in three months of memories.

As I looked at Alyssa in her hospital bed, I hated her for being blissfully ignorant of it all as I stewed in resentment and grief. At the same time, I envied her. I wished my memory of that day had been erased, too. How messed up was that?

Eventually, Alyssa got around to asking me the question I'd been dreading. She was curious about "the incident." She'd put together bits and pieces from conversations between her mother and her doctors when she was in the ICU, which she swore she'd overheard even though she'd been in a coma. She knew we'd been out skating on Lake Trapper and that she had accidentally fallen through a patch of thin ice, and that Mr. Donlan had saved her.

Since waking up, Alyssa had asked her mom a bunch of times about "the incident." And each time Mrs. Sawyer urged Alyssa to rest and assured her that her questions could wait. So, Alyssa turned to me to fill in the blanks. I did what Mrs. Sawyer had asked and simply repeated the story she already knew.

"But there has to be more," Alyssa insisted. "Please, tell me."

My legs trembled, like they were about to give out. I sat on the edge of the bed. "You don't understand, that day was the worst day of my life . . . Honestly, it's all kind of a blur. Can we not talk about it?"

I held my breath, waiting for her to push me for more information. Her head fell back on the pillow and her gaze drifted toward the window. "Okay."

"Thanks."

It was strange, sitting in silence with Alyssa, both of us lost in our own thoughts. Usually, when we hung out, you couldn't get us to shut up. Even though we didn't talk much that day, there was something comfortable about just being together again. Despite the time we'd had apart, our connection still held.

When Mrs. Sawyer and my mom finally came back, I got up to leave.

Alyssa turned to me and smiled. "Thanks for coming."

"Of course. I'll come back again in a couple of days. Okay?"

"Next time bring a chessboard," Alyssa said.

"You sure you'll be up for it?"

She laughed weakly. "Don't worry, I haven't forgotten how to beat you."

"We'll see," I said, chuckling.

It was as if we had never lost touch at all. And it seemed for the moment that our friendship had found a new beginning.

WHEN MOM and I got outside, she immediately lit a cigarette. I didn't feel like standing out in the cold, dark parking lot while she slowly killed herself, so I told her I'd meet her at the car.

"You'll need these," she said, tossing me the keys.

We had pulled up to the hospital in such a hurry I didn't notice where Mom had parked. So I started walking up and down the rows of cars, looking for our station wagon, but couldn't find it anywhere.

I was about to give up the search when I spotted a rusty Ford pickup with peeling red paint parked under a streetlight.

Suddenly the pickup roared to life and I jumped back. It pulled out and headed in my direction.

Renny was behind the wheel, and I had a choice: wave hi to

him or hide. I didn't want him yelling at me for trying to get him thrown in mall jail, so I did what any coward in my situation would have done—I dove between two cars and hid. My heart raced as he drove by and I stayed put until the roar of the engine faded away.

What had Renny been doing at the hospital? He struck me as a guy who didn't believe in doctors. Like, if he cut a finger off, he probably knew how to sew it back on himself. I convinced myself it was just a weird coincidence. He was probably visiting a sick friend, too.

Mom started yelling for me. "Jack! Jack, where the hell are you?!"

I popped up from behind the cars, and spotted Mom seething at me from a few rows away, standing beside our station wagon. I cautiously approached her and handed back the car keys. "I'm right here."

"Don't scare me like that. You need to answer me when I call for you. I thought you'd run off or something."

"Well, I didn't."

Mom watched me from beneath her furrowed brow, her cigarette clamped tightly between her frowning lips. "Don't do it again." She flicked the smoldering butt on the pavement and ground it out with her heel before unlocking the car door with a click. She didn't say another word to me on the ride home or the rest of the night.

Chapter 5

All my grumbling about selling our house hadn't changed Mom's mind about moving. To prove it, she went on a cleaning rampage. The whole last week of January, she'd get home from work, change into old clothes, then clear out closets and cabinets and throw the mess into piles in the garage. Mostly, it was stuff that had built up in the years since my parents bought the house after they got married. Mom's plan was to have a garage sale and sell what she could. Anything left over would end up at the town dump.

Every nook and cranny held reminders of my dad—a pair of his old boots, a broken typewriter, a bag full of his worn out winter clothes, boxes full of yellowing college papers . . . all stuff that Dad should have gotten rid of a long time ago but had hung on to for some reason.

Mom kept complaining that the cleanup would go a lot faster if I helped. But I didn't want to give her the idea that I was going along with the house sale, so I shut myself in my room. I claimed I had homework to do, which we both knew was a lie because I'd stopped doing homework ages ago. But once

Saturday morning came, Mom stopped accepting my homework excuse.

"It's the weekend, Jack. You can help me pack for a few hours." She was kneeling on our shag carpet, taping cardboard boxes together. "I'll start in my bedroom. You start in yours. Whatever you don't want, throw in a garbage bag." She held out a roll of flimsy black plastic.

I sat on the couch, arms crossed, unmoving. "I can't. I'm going to the mall to meet up with Trevor."

Mom sliced through a strip of packing tape with a box cutter. "You're not going anywhere. You're staying here and helping me."

"Why?"

"Because the Realtor said this place needs to feel inviting for the open house. Does any of this look inviting to you?"

She gestured to our living room, which had become ground zero for the mess of our lives. Newspapers and magazines that had collected over the past nine months were stacked next to the couch. Dust covered every surface like newly fallen snow. Cigarette butts stuck out of an ashtray like tiny grave markers. Mom always complained about my room being a disaster zone, but ever since Dad left, she hadn't done much to keep the rest of the house clean.

"What's the point of packing when you don't know where we're moving to?" I said.

Stacks of empty boxes were piled up around Mom like she was building a fort. "I found some apartments in the classifieds that sound promising. I left messages for the landlords to ask if there are any still available."

"You want us to move into some tiny apartment?"

"This house has more space than we need now."

"We won't have a yard."

"What do you care? You never play outside anymore," Mom

said. "Which reminds me, we should get rid of your old swing set and do a few plantings. We need better curbside appeal."

Mom had never used the term "curbside appeal" before.

"Since when did you become an expert on selling houses?" I joked.

Mom didn't look amused. She got up and dropped a box in my lap. "Enough with the wisecracks. Just get to work."

I stared into the empty void of the box and said, "I don't feel like it."

"And you think I do? You think this is fun for me?"

I shrugged. "I don't know . . ."

"Well, it isn't. But if we don't clean up this place, we can't get the painters in here. And without a fresh coat of paint, the Realtor will postpone the open house."

"Good."

Mom sighed and sat next to me on the couch and lit a cigarette. "C'mon, Jack. Work with me, here. Please?"

Her desperation only made me dig in my heels more. I wasn't going to let her kick me out of the home I grew up in. "Why should I?"

"Because we're supposed to be a team." She offered me a deal. If I cleaned up my room and packed, she would take me to Burger King for lunch. "I'll even buy you a Happy Meal," she said in a singsong way that made my whole body cringe. "Wouldn't that be fun? You used to love Happy Meals."

I glared at her, like she'd just made the most ridiculous statement a human being could utter. "First of all, you get Happy Meals at McDonald's, not Burger King."

"Really? Are you sure?"

"Yeah. And second, I haven't had a Happy Meal in forever. I'm not a little kid anymore, you know."

Mom blew smoke upward. "Then quit acting like one . . ." she muttered under her breath.

"You're the childish one," I muttered back.

Mom flinched. "Excuse me?"

"Nothing."

"No. Go ahead, say whatever it is you want to say to me."

"When we were at the hospital, why'd you ask Mr. Donlan to coffee?"

Mom took a long drag. "I was just being polite."

"It was embarrassing. I mean, he couldn't get away from you fast enough."

Until that point, Mom had been playing nice, but I'd pushed the wrong button. Which is what I was trying to do, I guess.

Mom's face flared red and she shot to her feet. "Fine, forget it! If you won't help me, I'll do it all myself! I swear, you're worse than your father." She grabbed a box and stormed away into her bedroom, slamming the door.

A few seconds later, I heard an explosion of crying and yelling, followed by a huge crash. I figured Mom had broken a lamp or threw an ashtray at her mirror. She usually kept her cool, but once in a while something would really set her off and she'd snap and smash something. I could feel the rage radiating from Mom's room. The last time she'd gotten that mad was with Dad, right before he left. He'd brought up Mr. Donlan in that argument, too.

My feet dragged down the hallway, toward her room. I tried to convince myself that apologizing and packing my stuff would be for the best. But halfway there, I hesitated. Giving in might make it seem like she won. So I whirled around, grabbed my coat, and ran out to the garage. With my heart pounding, I jumped on my bike and pedaled away as fast as I could, feeling like something inside me was broken.

When I was six, Dad took me to the store to pick out my first two-wheeler bike—a red Schwinn with chrome fenders and a white banana seat. It was called a Lil' Tiger, which I thought sounded cool. I imagined myself whizzing up and down the street, popping wheelies like the older kids in the neighborhood.

I hoped Dad would teach me how to ride it, but he had to leave on one of his work trips, so the job fell to Mom. The first thing she wanted to do was attach training wheels. I begged her not to put them on. It was going to ruin the whole look of the bike and what if the older kids saw them and laughed at me? But she refused to let me ride without them, saying I wasn't ready.

To prove her wrong, I hopped on my bike and coasted down our driveway. I picked up speed down the slope and, for a second, I felt totally in control, like nothing could stop me. But the next thing I knew, the world tilted, and I hit the pavement hard. My elbow was bleeding, but I held back my tears. I got back up and tried again. A few more falls later, I gave in and let Mom attach the training wheels. I kept them on for an entire year after that.

By the time I turned ten, my legs were too long for the Lil' Tiger so I got to trade up to a ten-speed.

Ten speeds for ten years, Dad had written on my birthday card—he wasn't there to make his dumb joke in person.

That was the bike I rode after the fight with my mom. My plan was to meet Trevor at the mall, which was a few miles away from my house. Most of the snow had melted, which made it easier to navigate the roads.

I took a shortcut down Widow's Creek Road, which was about halfway between my house and the mall, when I spotted a black dog trotting down the yellow line in the middle of the road, heading my way.

Out of nowhere, a car flew past me and swerved around the

dog. The driver blared the horn, but the dog didn't even react. It just kept trotting along, its tongue lolling and its tail wagging, oblivious to the danger it had barely avoided.

During my rides around town, I'd come across plenty of road kill—mostly squirrels, sometimes opossums or raccoons, and once, a pet cat.

I squeezed my breaks and pulled off the road. "Hey! Move it, dog!" I shouted, waving my arms to get its attention. "You're gonna get run over!"

The dog's ears twitched at the sound of my voice, but its gaze stayed focused on the yellow line no matter how loudly I shouted. It seemed like the dog had a death wish.

As the dog got closer, a shiver shot through me, but not because of the wind. The dog looked just like the picture of Renny's black lab. No way I'd randomly found Renny's missing dog a week after he'd gone missing. But I had to be sure. I pulled Renny's Polaroid out of my jacket pocket and compared the dog in the picture to the dog in front of me. Same breed, black fur, collar with tags. The main difference was that the real-life dog looked a lot mangier. Its fur was all matted and muddy. To make a positive ID, I had to check the tag on the dog's collar.

I hopped off my bike and propped it up against a fence post. I checked both ways. The coast was clear. I stepped into the dog's path and held out my hand so it could sniff me and know I was friendly. The only pet I'd ever had was a goldfish, but I'd been around Trevor's golden retriever a bunch.

I put on my friendliest voice. "Hey, buddy, are you lost?"

The dog just walked right on past me, like I wasn't even there.

I followed him. "Hey! I'm talking to you, dog!"

Still no response.

A silver Cadillac zoomed over the rise, definitely breaking the speed limit. The driver must've not seen me or the dog because the car didn't slow down. I moved to the side of the road and yelled at the dog to follow, but it kept on ignoring me.

There wasn't enough time to rush back into the middle of the street and pull the dog to safety. Plus, if I tried, there was the very real possibility that the dog might freak out and bite me. I stayed put.

Renny had told me his dog's name, but with the Cadillac speeding closer and my heart racing, I couldn't remember it. Then, as the horn blared and brakes squealed, the name popped into my head.

"Seneca, come!" I shouted, like a Jedi using mind control. The dog turned his head and bounded in my direction. When he reached me, I ordered him to sit, and he obeyed, tail wagging. He licked my trembling hand, coating it in a warm slobber. Now I was 100 percent sure I'd found Renny's lost dog.

The Cadillac honked again and cruised past. The driver was this wrinkly old guy. He leaned out the open window and yelled, "Get your damn dog out of the damn road!"

Before I could explain it wasn't my dog, the old guy shot me the middle finger as he sped away. He was a dickhead for sure, but he had a point. I needed to get Seneca somewhere he wouldn't get run over.

I checked Seneca's tag, which confirmed I'd gotten his name right. On the back was an address—50 Old Mill Road. I knew how to get there, but it was a few miles away from where I was. Biking out there meant I'd get home really late and Mom would start wondering what happened to me.

I'd heard stories about dogs who had an instinct for finding their way home. I wanted to believe that Seneca was one of those dogs, but considering he'd been wandering the streets of Ravensberg for almost a week, it seemed unlikely. I knew Mom would get madder the longer I stayed away from home, but something in my heart wouldn't let me leave Seneca behind.

41

I didn't have a leash or any rope, so I got back on my bike and started pedaling slowly, calling Seneca's name as I went. Thankfully, he followed, trotting beside my back wheel, panting and wagging his tail.

During the ride, I thought about my chance encounter with Renny that day at the mall. It was starting to seem like more than just a coincidence. Was finding his dog just a stroke of luck? Or was there a greater power at work, drawing us together?

Chapter 6

It took me almost half an hour to ride out to Old Mill Road, which is really just a dirt path that leads from the main road into the woods. I'd passed it in the car a bunch of times before, but I never imagined someone actually lived out there. As soon as I turned onto the dirt road my front tire dropped into a giant rut and I lost control and almost flew over the handlebars. I hopped off and pushed my bike the rest of the way. Seneca bounded ahead. I let him take the lead since he knew the area better than I did.

Overgrown grass blew in the wind. In the ditch, old refrigerators and stoves lay open like gutted carcasses, along with black garbage bags full of who-knows-what. *Renny really seems to like junk,* I thought.

A few minutes later, Seneca and I reached a rusty metal gate. I didn't see a house beyond it. A barbed wire fence extended to either side, surrounding the land. Nailed to a post was a NO TRESPASSING sign that reminded me of my KEEP OUT sign that Mom had ripped off my door. Maybe Renny and I had more in common than I'd first thought.

"You sure we're in the right place?" I looked down at

Seneca, who was obediently sitting and waiting. He pawed at the gate, which I took as a "yes."

I propped my bike against a fence post and unlatched the gate, which didn't have a lock on it. I pushed the handle and the hinges groaned. Seneca slipped through the opening.

I said "See ya" and started to close the gate, but Seneca came back through and sat next to me.

"What are you doing? Go on home." I waved my arms, hoping Seneca would leave, but he didn't budge from my side. I pulled at his collar and tried to lead him through the gate, but he stayed put, and, since he was a big dog, I couldn't drag him very far.

"Fine, I give up. You're on your own from here." I grabbed my bike and headed back down the road, but Seneca followed.

"Shoo!" I shouted. "Go home!" I pointed toward the woods.

Seneca just stood there, panting and looking all cute and innocent. My gut told me that if I left, Seneca would follow me back home. If I wanted to get away dog-free, I needed to deliver Seneca to Renny's front door.

"All right," I grumbled. "Come on." I walked through the gate, hoping Renny would be so happy I'd found his dog that he'd forgive me for trespassing on his land and for trying to get him arrested by a mall cop.

The path leading into the woods didn't have as much junk. Well, it was a different kind of junk. Every twenty feet stood these tall, abstract metal sculptures made of old cars parts and twisted hunks of scrap metal. They looked pretty awesome, like the relics of an ancient, alien civilization.

A couple of minutes later, Seneca and I reached a clearing. Renny's red pickup was parked outside a cabin, so I knew we were in the right place. I was surprised. I'd seen plenty of creepy old shacks in horror movies and I guess that's what I was expecting, but Renny's cabin was nice. Like a postcard. There was a fenced garden area to one side and neat stacks of firewood to the other. A few more abstract metal statues stood among the trees. An American flag fluttered from a pole that stuck out from the cabin's front porch. Another flag hung below it. It was black with white letters that spelled POW-MIA. I'd seen the same kind at the Army Surplus store and knew it meant: Prisoner of War-Missing in Action.

When I got closer to the cabin, I spotted an entrance to a cellar—two metal doors lying on top of a concrete wedge. But the weird part was, it was separate from the main house, off on its own.

I didn't have time to investigate further because the next thing I knew, there was this loud bang and tree bark was pelting my arms and face. I hit the ground fast and scurried behind one of the metal statues for cover. My ears were ringing and my heart was pounding. I didn't see Seneca anywhere. A second bang rang out. Dirt exploded a few feet away.

I peered through a gap in the twisted metal and made out the barrel of a long gun sticking out the front door of the cabin. "Can't you read?!" Renny yelled from inside. "The sign at the gate says, 'No Trespassing!'" So much for him forgiving me.

I was lying on the ground, breathing hard. If I tried to make a run for it, Renny would shoot at me again. But staying put made me a sitting target.

Another bullet pinged off the metal inches away. A second later, I felt something warm and wet on my leg. I thought for sure I was bleeding, but it was just Seneca licking and nuzzling me, his body trembling. He was as freaked out by the gunshots as I was.

Finally, after what felt like an eternity, I worked up enough courage to yell out, "Stop! I found your dog! I found Seneca!"

Renny poked his head out the front door. "Where is he?"

"Right next to me! I'll bring him out if you stop shooting. Deal?"

Renny stayed quiet for a few seconds and then said, "Deal."

I walked out from behind the statue, hands up. Renny shouldered open the cabin door and stomped across the porch, shotgun lowered. He squinted, eyeing me. As I got closer, a spark of recognition crossed Renny's face. "Hey, you're that kid from the mall."

"Yeah, it's me, Jack. Listen, I'm sorry about trespassing and for what I said to that mall cop, but you don't have to shoot me over it." I was nervous, but tried not to let my voice wobble.

Renny still looked annoyed, but my apology—and the fact that I had found his dog—seemed to win him over. "Don't get all testy. Those were just warning shots."

"You almost killed me," I protested.

"Nah." He patted the gun barrel. "I can barely hit the side of a barn with this thing. My eyesight ain't what it used to be. I'm supposed to wear glasses, but they keep breaking and I can't keep track of them anyway."

"You could've at least asked who I was instead of opening fire," I complained.

"Sorry, but I get all sorts of riff-raff around here. Hunters, people dumping junk, and teenagers up to no good."

Renny lowered his shotgun and whistled. Seneca ran up the porch stairs to Renny, who crouched down and scratched him behind his ears. "What kind of trouble did you get up to this time, fella?"

"So your dog's run off before?" I asked.

Renny nodded. "More than a few times."

"You should probably keep him on a leash, don't you think?"

Renny winced, like I'd spat in his face. "Why the hell would I do that?"

"Uh . . . so you don't keep losing him?"

46

Renny stood and stared off into the woods, letting out a long exhale. "Sometimes the things you love run off and they don't come back," he said. "That's just the way of the world."

Like Dad, I thought.

Renny disappeared into his cabin. A few seconds later, he returned without his shotgun but holding a set of keys. He jingled them in front of my face. "I'll give you a lift home. Hop in Big Charlie over there." He nodded toward his rusty pickup. Considering Renny's eyesight wasn't so hot, I didn't want to take my chances.

"That's okay. I left my bike at the gate. I can ride back."

Renny walked past me and got in his truck. "You brought Seneca home, safe and sound. Least I can do is return the favor."

"Really, it's fine."

"Get in the damn truck," Renny said gruffly.

Since Renny felt like he owed me, I thought of a different way he could repay his debt. "How about you give me a reward and we'll call it even?"

Renny scratched at his beard. "A reward? For what?"

"For finding your lost dog."

"I never offered a reward."

"But if it hadn't been for me, your dog would be dead on the side of the road."

"That's just speculation."

"A car almost hit him!"

"But it didn't!"

"Yeah, because I got him out of danger!"

"You trying to hustle me, kid?"

"Hustle you?"

"Grift, cheat, pull a fast one over . . ."

"I know what it means, and I swear I'm not trying to do any of those things."

"Then get in the damn truck," Renny said again, more

forcefully. He leaned across the front seat and popped open the passenger door. He shoved the key in the ignition and Big Charlie's engine roared to life, rumbling like an angry beast.

Suddenly my energy drained away as the postadrenaline crash set in. My legs felt weak from all the bike riding, I was starving, and Mom was probably starting to wonder where I'd run off to. The sooner I got back home, the better, even if that meant trusting Renny to drive me there.

As BIG CHARLIE drove down the bumpy path, I got a good look at how beat up he was. He had a cracked windshield, a rusty dashboard, and ripped seats. I stuck my fingers through a hole next to my leg and got poked by a spring sticking out, like a snake guarding its den.

"How old is this truck, anyway?" I asked.

Renny patted the steering wheel. "Big Charlie, here, is a 1952 Ford F100. He's the real deal. Not like the automatic junk they make nowadays." He glanced my way. "You drive?"

I gave him this look like his question was crazy. "I'm only fourteen."

"My father taught me how to drive when I was ten," he said.

"I can't even get a learner's permit for another year."

Renny shrugged. "Life doesn't give out learner's permits. You learn what you need when you need to."

When we pulled up to the gate, Renny hopped out to open it. He grabbed my bike and threw it in the truck's bed, where it landed with a clunk. I winced, hoping the frame or the wheels didn't get bent.

Renny got back in all out of breath, like he'd just run a mile.

"You okay?" I asked.

"Fine." He shifted into gear and Big Charlie rattled down

Old Mill Road until we reached the paved street. Renny clicked on the radio and leaned back in his seat, one hand on the wheel. A gravelly voice sang over a blues riff.

"I like this song," I said.

Renny glanced over. "You know who's singing it?"

"Yeah, Bob Dylan."

He nodded and flashed a smile. "Good for you. Kids nowadays only listen to that Top Forties crap."

"My dad had a bunch of his records. Technically, I guess they're my records now."

"Your old man's not in the picture anymore?"

"Not exactly."

"He split on you?"

"Something like that."

"Yeah . . . that can be tough."

I didn't feel like getting into my dad's story, so I changed the subject. "Did you build your cabin?"

"My grandfather did, many moons ago. After he died, my aunt and uncle moved in. They didn't have any kids, so when they passed, they left it to me. I moved in after I got back from the war."

"Which war?"

"What do you mean, 'which war'? The Vietnam War. How old do you think I am?"

"I don't know . . . fiftysomething?"

Renny burst out laughing. "I guess living alone in the woods hasn't done wonders for my appearance. I'm only forty-three."

"So does that mean you're a war hero?"

"Not to the people of Ravensberg, it doesn't. I notice the suspicious looks I get and hear them whisper about me after I pass by. Most folks don't want anything to do with me, same as you, the day we first met."

Guilt ate away at me. "Sorry."

"It's all right. I'm used to being an outcast." He claimed it didn't bother him but he sounded bitter.

"What was Vietnam like?" I asked.

"Like hell wrapped inside an inferno topped with napalm," he said.

I didn't know what napalm was, but I guessed it was pretty bad. "It sounds awful."

"Yeah, a lot of the guys I knew made it out alive but wound up real sick from all the toxic chemicals our government dropped. But being there taught me one thing."

"What?"

"That you gotta live every day like it's your last and be grateful for the people you still got."

"That's two things," I said.

"Smart aleck."

"Hold on," I said, realizing something. "Is that why you were at the hospital the other day?"

Renny gripped the steering wheel tighter. "What were you doing there?"

"Visiting a friend. She had a bad accident, but she's okay now. Well, not entirely. It's a long story." I wasn't ready to dredge everything up, so I moved the conversation back to Renny. "Were you visiting a friend, too?"

"What friend?"

"At the hospital. You said a lot of guys you knew got sick."

"Oh, yeah . . . turns out, one of them got cancer."

"Is he going to die?"

Renny's voice got softer. "The doctors are only giving him a few months. So . . . looks that way."

I wanted to tell Renny I was sorry, but that didn't seem like enough, so I kept quiet. I just stared out the window, watching the trees whizz past, letting the sadness fill me.

BIG CHARLIE SQUEALED to a stop at the end of my street. I had Renny drop me off there because I didn't want him pulling up in front of my house where Mom might see him. The last thing I needed was her interrogating me about where I'd been.

We got out of the pickup and Renny lifted my bike out of the back and handed it to me.

"Take care," he said, tipping the brim of his hat.

"You, too."

We both stood there, facing off like gunslingers in one of those old Westerns, waiting for the other to make the first move. Renny didn't get in his truck and I didn't get on my bike. This empty feeling came over me. Renny hadn't left but I was already missing him, which was strange. I mean, putting aside the fact that he'd shot at me, there was something about him I kind of liked. He had this cool, no-nonsense way about him. And after getting to know him a little, he didn't seem so creepy, like everyone in town believed. He'd just been through a lot. Was that any reason to treat him like an outcast?

As I was about to ride off, Renny called after me. "Hey, listen, kid, if it's money you need, I could give you some work to do around the cabin. It wouldn't be easy, but it'd be a job. And at your age, it's good to learn some responsibility."

His offer was tempting, but something held me back from saying yes. Sure, he'd gotten me home in one piece, but I still didn't completely trust him. "Thanks, but I don't need any money."

Renny eyed me for a second, then shrugged. "Coulda fooled me." He walked around the pickup and opened the door. "Anyway, if you change your mind, you know where I live."

We said our good-byes, then Renny took off down the road, exhaust spewing from Old Charlie's tailpipe.

When I walked into the house, Mom was sitting at the kitchen table with an ashtray full of cigarette butts and a glass of red wine in her hand. Her eyes were red and puffy.

"Hey, Mom," I said, sounding totally casual, even though inside I was bracing myself. I figured she was about to chew me out for being gone so long. But Mom just stared at me and took a sip of her wine. "Next time leave a note, okay?" Her voice was icy. Distant.

"Okay," I said, noticing a pile of bills on the table with red PAST DUE stamps on them. I went to my room and shut myself in for the night.

Chapter 7

The next day, Mom had a meeting with the Realtor. On her way, she dropped me off at the hospital. I brought my chess set with me, like I'd promised Alyssa. It was Dad's set from when he was a kid and it still had all the original wood pieces.

Dad had taught me and Alyssa how to play when we were six. It was one of the rare times when Mom was out somewhere and I was home with just Dad. Alyssa had come over like she usually did on weekends, and most of the time Dad sat in the kitchen, face buried in the paper, while Alyssa and I played hide and seek. At one point, I found her hiding in my parents' closet holding the chess set box. I told her to put it back because I didn't want Dad getting mad that we'd gone through his things, but Alyssa ignored me. She ran into the kitchen and set the game on the table. Dad peered over the top of the newspaper with a sour look. He didn't like people bothering him.

"Where did you find that?" he asked.

"In your closet," Alyssa confessed. "How do you play?"

I braced myself. Dad was usually a quiet guy, but when something pissed him off, he could explode like a volcano. I couldn't believe it when he folded the paper, put it aside, and smiled.

"I haven't played chess in years. Jack's grandfather taught me."

Then he lit up in a way I hadn't seen, at least not for a long time—before or after.

He showed us where each piece went on the board and how they moved. It wasn't as easy as the games we usually played, like Uno or Yahtzee. But once Alyssa and I got the hang of it, we played all the time.

When I walked into the room, a nurse was checking Alyssa's blood pressure. Mrs. Sawyer wasn't there. Alyssa said she'd been spending most nights in a chair next to the bed, so she'd gone home to shower and put on some fresh clothes. The nurse took away the tray with Alyssa's half-eaten lunch, leaving the two of us alone.

"Ready to lose, Banana Brain?" Alyssa said, pointing to the chess set tucked under my arm.

I opened the box and set it on the hospital bed table where her tray had been. "Just because you were in a coma doesn't mean I'll go easy on you."

"I don't want you to."

I clenched a white pawn in one hand and a black one in the other and held my fists out to Alyssa. She picked the hand with the white pawn, which meant she got to make the first move. As we set up the pieces, Alyssa put her knights where the bishops were supposed to go. Once I set up my knights, Alyssa realized her mistake, but acted like she'd meant to do it. "I was just seeing if you remembered how to set up a board," she joked, then quickly switched her knights with her bishops.

Alyssa moved her pawn to e4, and I slid my queen's pawn out to meet it. After a few moves, we'd traded pawns and knights. After that, the game got . . . interesting.

Alyssa brought her queen out earlier than usual and put it out in the open, right where one of my bishops could have easily taken it. It was an obvious blunder, but Alyssa didn't seem to notice. Normally, I would have jumped at the chance to take Alyssa's queen, but it didn't feel right. I moved one of my pawns instead. A dozen moves later, Alyssa put me in checkmate.

"Good game," I said.

"No, it wasn't. You blundered, like, three times," she said.

"I guess I have a lot on my mind." I didn't have the heart to tell her I'd let her win on purpose.

"Sorry . . . I haven't even asked how you're doing, you know, with everything."

I told her about Mom deciding to sell the house without even asking me. "It's like she's trying to put all the bad stuff behind us as fast as she can."

"Like she did with your dad?"

The air suddenly got sucked out of the room. It took me a second to get my words out. "What . . . what do you mean?"

"After he left you guys to walk the Appalachian Trail, you told me she got over it really fast."

"Yeah," I said, catching my breath. "That's what I was talking about."

Alyssa squinted, like she was working on a really hard math problem. "But it's weird . . . I remember when he left because you were so upset about it. But when did he get back?"

I let the question hang, unsure how to answer it. I remembered Mrs. Sawyer's request not to upset Alyssa. But if I didn't offer some kind of an answer, she'd keep giving me the third degree. Finally, I forced the words out of my mouth. "He disappeared. My dad's gone."

"Gone? I don't understand."

I kept the story light on details. My dad had been sending postcards from the trail every week or so, updating me and my mom on his progress. As the months wore on, he fell way behind schedule. He didn't think he'd make it back in time for my birthday like he'd promised. Then somewhere around Pennsylvania, the postcards stopped coming.

It was the truth, more or less.

Alyssa stared at me, blinking rapidly, trying to process what she'd just heard. "How could he have just vanished like that?" she asked. "Did the police or anybody search for him?"

"Yeah, but they never recovered his body."

"Are you saying your dad is dead?"

I nodded.

Alyssa hung her head, her eyes filling with tears. "I'm sorry, you probably told me all that before. But I don't remember."

"It's okay."

Alyssa and I played chess until Mrs. Sawyer got back and it was time for Mom to pick me up. Alyssa beat me twice more, this time fair and square, but I was glad for the distraction.

On the ride home from the hospital, I didn't ask Mom about her meeting with the Realtor, and she didn't ask about my visit with Alyssa, which was fine by me.

———

THAT NIGHT, I headed to the kitchen to get a glass of water and a snack. Mom was in the living room, putting a video in the VCR, a cigarette dangling from her mouth. I tried to sneak past, but I guess I wasn't quiet enough.

"I rented a movie. Want to join me?" Mom sat on the couch and patted the seat next to her.

It had been a while since Mom and I had watched a movie together. It had been our thing, something fun we did whenever Dad left town for work. We'd drive to the video store and debate which movies to rent, then Mom would pop a big bowl of popcorn and we'd stay up late. I actually liked most of the black-and-white movies Mom picked out. But we hadn't rented any movies since Dad left for the trail.

"What did you get?" I asked.

"*Sunset Boulevard.* It's a classic."

"I don't know. I'm tired."

"I'll make popcorn."

I gave in and stayed. I wanted things between me and Mom to feel normal again. And for a moment they did. We got cozy on the couch under a blanket and the popcorn tasted the perfect amount of buttery and salty. In my mind, "the incident" had never happened. I told myself that Dad was just gone for a few days on business and he'd be back soon. But the fantasy vanished once I hit play on the remote.

The movie begins with a dead man lying face down in a pool. And the man is narrating, like he's a ghost.

I glanced over at Mom. *What had possessed her to rent this movie?* I wondered. *Did she really think this was the best thing to watch after everything that had happened?* Her gaze was glued to the screen, so I kept my mouth shut.

It turns out the dead guy was a Hollywood writer named Joe who was running from the cops when he ends up in this mansion where this famous actress named Norma Desmond lives. She hasn't made a movie in years. Everyone's forgotten about her, but she still acts like she's some big movie star. She's totally delusional about it. She even convinces Joe the writer dude to write a movie for her to star in. Joe goes along with Norma's plan because he needs a place to hide out—and the money.

I cringed every time Norma appeared onscreen. She was so desperate to get things back to normal. And I hated how the people around her played along with her fantasies. It was gross.

Halfway through the movie, I gave this enormous yawn and

told Mom I wasn't feeling so good. She put her hand on my forehead.

"You don't feel warm."

"I just want to go to bed."

"Don't you want to see how it ends?" she asked.

"I already know how it ends. The Joe guy ends up dead in the pool. They gave everything away at the start. It's a stupid movie."

"No one forced you to watch it," Mom said, sounding annoyed.

I said good night and went to my room. I buried myself under the covers, but I couldn't get the image of Norma Desmond's creepy, wide-eyed stare out of my mind.

WHEN DAD WAS STILL AROUND, the only times I worried about money was when he was late with my allowance. So all week, I kept mulling over Renny's job offer. I thought about it during school, while I visited Alyssa, and while I was watching Trevor rack up higher and higher Pac-Man scores. But I couldn't figure out the best play. Sure, Mom and I needed money, but I wasn't thrilled about the idea of going to work for a guy who almost shot my head off.

Then one night, in the middle of my dilemma, I found Mom sitting at the dining room table, bills spread out in front of her, a cigarette dangling from her lips. She rubbed her temple like she had a headache. She told me there was some leftover pot pie in the fridge if I was hungry. I wasn't.

My eyes passed over the bills. I didn't know how much Mom owed, but judging by all the red stamps on the envelopes and cigarette butts in the ashtray, I guessed it was a lot. Before Dad left, Mom smoked a couple of cigarettes a day. Once he was gone, she went up to a pack a day. Then two. Pretty soon she'd be sucking down three.

"How bad is it?" I asked.

Mom picked up one bill and waved it around. "If I don't pay this one, our water will get shut off." She grabbed another bill in her other hand. "But if I don't pay this one, we lose electricity. Plus, there's the phone bill and the mortgage payments . . . I think we have to say good-bye to cable."

"Then what am I going to watch?"

"Free TV, like most people." Mom lit up another cigarette.

"Or you could stop smoking and use the money to pay the bills," I blurted out.

Mom gave me this an absolute look of death, then just took a long drag and started stacking up the bills. "All our problems will disappear once the house sells."

I didn't believe her. From where I was standing, our problems were only getting started. She crushed her cigarette butt in the ashtray and shook her head, like she wasn't entirely convinced either.

Only one person was to blame for the situation we were in—Dad. He cared more about walking that stupid trail than his own family. And since he wasn't around anymore to help, Mom's cash problems had officially become my cash problems. Luckily, I had a solution.

———

THE NEXT DAY AFTER SCHOOL, I rode my bike out to Old Mill Road again. When I walked up the path to Renny's cabin, I announced my arrival, loud and clear.

"Hello, it's Jack approaching! Jack Finn! The kid who found your dog! Don't shoot me!"

Seneca bolted out of the woods and ran over. He jumped up

on me and slobbered all over my face. I wasn't expecting to be so happy to see him, too, but I was.

"Over here!" Renny shouted. I found him in the work shed next to the cabin. He had goggles on and was blowtorching two pieces of metal together. That's when I realized he had made all the strange sculptures around his property.

"I didn't know you were an artist," I said.

"Gotta keep my hands busy, you know?" He put the goggles on top of his head and shut off the blowtorch. "But I'm assuming you're not here to buy one of my sculptures, so what can I do for you?"

I asked Renny if his offer to hire me was still on the table.

He shrugged. "Depends."

"On what?"

"How hard you're willing to work."

"As hard as you need me to, I guess."

Renny nodded. He seemed satisfied with my answer. "And what are you looking to get paid?"

I'd never had a real job before, so I told him what I got paid for my allowance. "Five dollars."

"An hour?" Renny crossed his arms and cocked his head. "You got some nerve, kid. Minimum wage is only three dollars, thirty-five cents."

I'd meant five dollars a week, but Renny didn't need to know that.

"Then I'll take minimum wage. I just need to earn enough to pay some bills."

"Fair enough. You got yourself a deal."

Renny immediately put me to work sweeping his porch. Then he had me climb a ladder and dig leaves out of the gutters. And after all that, I washed the cabin windows, which were filthy. A couple of hours later, the sun had set and I was exhausted, but I was six dollars and seventy cents richer.

Chapter 8

After dreading it for a week, I finally returned to Alyssa's hospital room. My chest tightened as I pushed open the door. I had no idea what I was walking into, but I knew I wasn't ready.

When I entered, Alyssa and Mrs. Sawyer were talking to Doctor Wexler, who I recognized from his interview on TV. He was in the middle of discussing Alyssa's brain scans. As soon as he noticed me, he gave me this long, piercing look, like he was scanning *my* brain and reading all the thoughts I'd kept to myself about Mom, Dad, Alyssa—everything. I quickly looked away, trying to break his hold on me.

I told them I'd come back later, but Alyssa flashed me a welcoming smile and waved me back in the room. While I retreated to the corner and kept quiet, Doctor Wexler continued updating Mrs. Sawyer on Alyssa's progress. He was encouraged by what he saw on her latest scans. Also, Alyssa's physical and occupational therapies were going well. His only concern was Alyssa's insomnia. Apparently the nurses had been giving her something at night to help her sleep.

"I keep reminding her she needs to get her rest," Mrs. Sawyer told the doctor.

Alyssa said, "I'll sleep better once I'm in my own bed."

"You'll get your wish soon," Doctor Wexler said.

Mrs. Sawyer's face brightened. "When can I bring her home?"

Doctor Wexler wouldn't make any promises, but he said if Alyssa continued to show improvement, he could discharge her in a couple of weeks. A nurse poked her head in the room and told the doctor he was needed immediately. He hurried out.

Mrs. Sawyer said hi and asked if everything was all right with me. "You look as exhausted as Alyssa."

"I'm fine," I said, forcing a smile. "I've been sleeping like a baby."

Mrs. Sawyer shook her head, doubtful. "And you're skinnier than you were last week. Have you been eating?"

"All the time," I said. "Mom made pancakes this morning."

All I'd had that day was half a bowl of Frosted Flakes.

Mrs. Sawyer grabbed her purse and slung it over her shoulder. "I was about to go to Norma's. I'll buy you a sandwich. You like turkey, right?"

"Yeah."

"One turkey sandwich, coming up. Be back soon." Mrs. Sawyer kissed the top of Alyssa's head and Alyssa flinched. "Love you, sweetheart."

As soon as Mrs. Sawyer had left, Alyssa sat up in her bed, looking more energetic than I'd seen her in any of my previous visits.

"I'm glad you're feeling better," I said.

Alyssa ordered me to shut the door because she had something important to tell me. The look in her eyes was serious.

I walked over to the door and swung it closed. "What is it?"

Alyssa said there was a reason she hadn't been sleeping well. Every night since she woke up from her coma, she'd been having the same nightmare. A nightmare about the accident.

A wave of coldness washed over me. "What happens in it?" I asked, even though I didn't really want to know the answer.

Alyssa described her nightmare. In it, she's skating across the lake when, suddenly, the ice under her melts away. She plunges into the freezing water where a thousand icy needles stab her body. She thrashes, desperate to swim to the surface, but her soaked winter clothes become like heavy anchors dragging her down, deeper and deeper. Her arms and legs go limp with exhaustion as she fights an unwinnable battle for survival. With one last gasp, the icy water floods her lungs and the life goes out of her . . .

It sounded horrific, and probably close to what she'd experienced that day, but that wasn't even the scariest part.

As she's sinking, she sees someone else underwater with her. It's a man. She can't see his face. She reaches out and touches the man's hand, which is as solid as ice. She thinks he's dead, but then his eyes snap open. And that's the moment when she always wakes up, panting, her heart monitor beeping superfast.

If I'd been hooked up to my own heart monitor, I would have broken the thing.

"What do you think it means?" she asked.

I stepped back from the bed, distancing myself, like if I got too close to Alyssa, my memories of that day would rub off on her. After a few breaths, I said, "I have bad dreams all the time. Don't read into it."

"I've had nightmares before. This one is different. It feels so real."

"You were comatose for weeks. Plus, you've been taking drugs to help you sleep. Your mind's probably just a little mixed

63

up. Now I get to call *you* Banana Brain." I chuckled when I said the last part.

"This isn't a joke!" Alyssa's monitors beeped and her heart rate numbers climbed higher and higher.

"Okay, sorry. Don't give yourself a heart attack."

Alyssa's breathing was fast and shallow. A nurse rushed in to make sure Alyssa was all right. She adjusted the pillows and had Alyssa lie back down. "She needs calm and quiet," the nurse reminded me.

After a minute, the beeping slowed. Alyssa told the nurse that she was fine and asked me to stay, but I took it as an opportunity to duck out early. Before Alyssa could argue with me about it, I headed for the door. But as I ducked out, I could see the disappointment in her eyes. Alyssa had always been there for me, and now I was leaving her to face her troubles alone. But in that moment, it was all I could think to do.

ONE NIGHT, Mom got a call from the Realtor. Her name was Mrs. Licht. When Mom had first told me about her, I thought she said "Mrs. Lick." After that, every time I heard her name, I kept imagining a woman who liked to lick things—envelopes, spoons, door handles . . . you name it. Anyway, Mrs. Licht told Mom that the open house was going to happen the first weekend of March.

As soon as she hung up the phone, Mom headed straight into the garage to sort stuff into piles for the garage sale.

"I can't believe you're really going through with this," I said.

"According to Mrs. Licht, it's a great time to put a house on the market."

"So you just go along with whatever this Lick lady says? What if she's trying to hustle us?"

Mom shot me an annoyed glance. "Mrs. *Licht* has been a Realtor for years. She sold the Walters' house down the street for over the asking price. She gets results."

I can get results too, I thought. There was still time to stop Mrs. Licht from destroying my life.

———

THE FIRST COUPLE of weeks working for Renny were intense. Every afternoon after school, I'd rush outside and unlock my bike from the bike rack before Trevor had a chance to ask where I was going. If I told him, he'd probably blab to his dad, who would end up spilling the beans to Mom. And if she found out I was working for "the creep who lived in the woods" she would probably ground me for weeks.

It usually took me about twenty minutes to ride out to the cabin. As soon as I arrived, Renny would barely give me a second to catch my breath and get a sip of water before he put me to work, stacking wood or hauling scrap metal for his sculptures. After a couple of hours, my arms and legs dangled like limp noodles. My reward was a bottle of Coke and another six dollars and seventy cents to add to my earnings. Before I left, I'd fill Seneca's food and water bowls, then I'd throw my bike in the back of the pickup and Renny would drive me home. I'd have him drop me off a couple of blocks away since Mom usually came home from work by six thirty. Then I'd ride the rest of the way. If Mom asked me why I was so late, I'd tell her I was hanging out with Trevor. She never questioned my alibi.

After a few weeks of this, I ran into a problem—I'd made almost a hundred bucks, but I had no way to use the money. When I told Renny about my predicament, he suggested embezzling the cash.

"Isn't that illegal?" I asked while I was sweeping the porch.

Renny leaned against the railing, taking the last swig of his Coke. "Sure, if you're a huge business or the government or something. But I doubt the cops are going to come after you because you diverted a few bucks into your mom's pocketbook."

"What if she notices?"

Renny wiped his mouth with his sleeve. "You're a smart kid. Figure out a way to do it without her knowing."

And that's when it hit me—I could use the upcoming garage sale to my advantage.

Chapter 9

I wish I could say I was helping Mom out of the goodness of my heart but that's not quite true. My main goal was to slip her the money during the garage sale without her noticing. That way, she'd have some extra to cover the bills that were due. The side benefit was that Mom would think I was being cooperative and she'd get off my back, at least for a little while.

On the big day, I helped Mom set up folding tables in the garage and put out all the stuff she planned to sell—a stack of mystery paperbacks, my baby toys, a toaster that popped up on only one side, a box of tarnished silverware and mismatching plates, and some of Dad's records, but not the Bob Dylan ones. I was keeping those. There was a bunch of other stuff, too. The whole time we were getting ready, Mom kept giving me suspicious looks. She couldn't figure out why I was suddenly on board with the whole garage sale thing, but since I was pitching in, she didn't complain.

When I questioned if people would actually show up, Mom told me about these bargain hunters who go to garage sales every weekend. It's like a hobby to them. I hope my life never becomes so boring that I end up buying other people's junk for fun.

Anyway, it turned out Mom was right. The garage sale was supposed to start at 8:00 a.m. By 7:45, a few people were already lurking at the end of our driveway. One guy was nerdy-looking, wearing glasses and a bow tie. An older couple stood behind him. The husband and wife both had short white hair.

"Our first customers!" Mom said cheerily. She checked to make sure everything was in place, then flung open the garage door and welcomed the early birds. The people didn't even say good morning. They marched up the driveway, all business, and glanced over everything on the tables. The white-haired couple paid for a stack of plates and four teacups. My chest tightened when they also bought Dad's old transistor radio from college. But it wasn't like he was around to use it anymore. I let it go. Then the couple was off to the next garage sale, carrying a little piece of Dad with them.

I'd been so focused on the old couple, I hadn't noticed Bow Tie Guy pick up my stamp collector's book. Mom must have dug it out of the back of my closet during her cleaning spree. The pages made a crackling noise as Bow Tie Guy flipped them. I remembered when Dad took me to the post office to pick it out, along with a few books of stamps. Each page had faint illustrations showing where to put the real stamps. Dad had promised we would fill up the book together. Most of the pages were still blank.

"This is in excellent condition," Bow Tie Guy said, then offered Mom three dollars for it, instead of the four she was asking for. They met in the middle and the man left a happy customer.

Mom got all giddy. "We already made seven dollars." She slipped the money into a cash box that was really an old shoebox.

No one else came until about 8:30, when a tan Volvo with a bent antenna pulled up to the curb. Trevor and his dad weren't there to buy anything. I'd invited Trevor to come hang out for the day, partly because I felt bad for avoiding him all week, but mostly because I didn't want to be stuck alone with Mom. Trevor was happy to be anywhere other than around his parents.

As soon as Mr. Donlan showed up, Mom got all perky. She checked her reflection in a cracked mirror that was for sale and adjusted her hair. She told me to keep an eye on things while she said hi to Mr. Donlan.

That's when I saw my chance.

I pulled out a wad of ones and fives from my pocket and thought about shoving it all into the cash box at once, but I stopped myself. It was still early, and I didn't want Mom getting suspicious. So I only dropped ten dollars and some change into the shoebox at first. I planned to slip in a few bucks at a time throughout the morning, whenever Mom wasn't looking, until I'd emptied my pockets.

Trevor moseyed up the driveway, hands in his jacket pockets, head down. Mom stood next to the car, practically leaning into the driver's side where Mr. Donlan had his hands on the steering wheel. The car was still running. I couldn't tell if he was happy to see Mom or if he was getting ready to speed off. They ended up talking for a while, so I guess he wasn't in any big hurry.

Trevor said, "Hey" but looked at the items on the tables rather than me.

"Hey," I said back.

I waited for him to make some joke about the stuff we were selling but he didn't really say anything. He just sat on a folding chair, sulking, which wasn't normal for Trevor.

When Mom got done talking to Mr. Donlan she came back in the garage and went over to Trevor. "I'm sorry about your parents, honey."

Trevor shrugged.

"What happened?" I asked.

Mom looked to Trevor and waited for him to explain. He didn't, so Mom answered for him. "Trevor's father just told me that he and his mother have decided to separate." I swear she smiled for a second when she said it.

"It's just a trial basis," Trevor added.

"Right," Mom said. "Of course."

A customer showed up and Mom walked away to help them.

"I can't believe it," Trevor said, shaking his head. "My parents were going to counseling and everything. They promised they'd work it out."

"That sucks" is all I said.

We hung out in the garage while shoppers came and went. It was a mix of people browsing and buying. By noon we had more than eighty dollars in the shoebox. Mom was surprised. I didn't let on that half of our haul was thanks to my money laundering scheme. She took some of the money inside for safekeeping.

Not long after, a father and son walked into the garage. The boy, who looked six or seven, checked out all the stuff we were selling, then got all pouty. "They just have baby toys!"

The father turned to me. "Do you have any toys for older kids?"

I told him we didn't. But then, two seconds later, the boy said, "What about this, Daddy?"

In the corner of the garage, the boy had taken a box off the shelf and he was pulling out my telescope—the one Dad had bought me for my ninth birthday.

"That's not for sale," I said.

"I'll give you ten bucks for it," the father said.

"Put it back!"

Mom came into the garage to see what was happening. The father upped his bid to twelve dollars and before I knew it, Mom had the money in hand. The boy hugged the telescope— *my* telescope—and headed out of the garage.

I snapped and grabbed the telescope out of the boy's hands. The boy lost his balance and fell on his knees. He started crying and screaming.

"Jack Marcus Finn!" Mom only yelled my full name when she was furious.

I froze. The father picked up his son, glaring at me the whole time. His fist clenched. If Mom hadn't been standing right there, I bet he would have smacked me for hurting his kid, even though I hadn't meant to. After his kid was back on his feet, the father opened his fist and held out his hand to me. "Give me the telescope. It belongs to my son now."

I looked over at Mom, silently begging her to intervene. But she took the man's side. "Jack, you haven't touched that telescope in years. Time to let it go."

But I couldn't bring myself to hand it over. So what if Dad and I had only stargazed that one time? That didn't mean I had to let some random kid use my telescope to stare at the night sky with his father.

The next thing I knew, I had hurled the thing onto the concrete as hard as I could. Glass shattered. Metal squealed. Mom yelled at me to stop. The kid started crying again. The father grabbed his money out of Mom's hand and shouted something about how she should get her son's head examined. Mom didn't argue the point. The father and son stormed away and drove off.

Mom grabbed my shoulders and shook me hard. "What's wrong with you? You're out of control!"

Trevor had watched the whole thing unfold from the

sidelines, not saying a word. He looked scared of me, to be honest.

Mom made me clean up the mess. I got rid of the telescope's carcass in the garbage and swept up all the glass and broken bits of plastic and dumped those in the trash, too. Mom called Mr. Donlan to come pick up Trevor and after he left, Mom sent me to my room for the rest of the day while she finished the garage sale. Which was fine by me. I didn't want to be around her, anyway.

That night, I had a nightmare that I was watching the night sky through the telescope when the stars blinked out, one by one, until the heavens turned pitch black. When I looked around where I'd been standing, everything else was gone, too. The telescope, my house, my neighborhood, all of Ravensberg— until I was alone, floating in a dark, empty void, unable to breathe.

I startled awake, gasping for air. I tried to force myself to fall back to sleep by telling myself the same thing I'd said to Alyssa. *Don't read into it. Don't read into it.*

TREVOR DEALT WITH HIS PARENTS' separation the same way he'd dealt with his brother's death—by spending more and more time at GameZilla. He went every day after school, plus on the weekends. It had become his second home. When Trevor focused on the Pac-Man screen, his hand on the joystick, navigating maze after maze, he forgot about his family situation. It didn't take long before he'd doubled his highest score ever. Word around school was the Pac-Man Kid had become unstoppable.

So when the local news came looking for a player to interview for a story about the popularity of arcade games, the arcade manager pointed the reporter in Trevor's direction. "That's the kid you gotta talk to," he said. It turned out the reporter was Dorothy Jackson, the same woman who had done the news story on Alyssa. As she made her way over, I imagined myself being questioned by her for a follow-up interview.

"A lot has happened since we last spoke. You're now working for the town outcast but haven't told your mother. How long do you think you'll get away with that?"

"As long as I need to."

"And your mother isn't the only person you've been deceiving. What about Trevor?"

"I'm not lying to him."

"You haven't informed him about the affair between his father and your mother, correct?"

"I'm just leaving out a few facts."

"To hide the truth?"

"If I tell him the truth, he'll only get more upset. He's sad enough as it is."

Trevor's victorious whoop brought me back to reality. He stretched his fingers, waiting for the next board to load. Dorothy Jackson introduced herself and said she'd like to ask Trevor a few questions. Luckily, she had no idea we were Alyssa's friends or she might have started grilling us about "the incident." Usually, Trevor hated when people interrupted him while he was playing, but I think he liked getting some attention. I think he needed it.

"What do you want to know?" Trevor asked the reporter, eyes glued to his Pac-Man who was being chased by three ghosts.

"I hear they call you the Pac-Man Kid," Dorothy Jackson said.

"That's right."

"How long have you been playing?"

"A couple of years."

"And what's your secret to success? How have you gotten so good?"

"It's like any sport. You gotta dedicate yourself."

Onscreen, the ghosts surrounded Pac-Man. With a flick of the joystick, Trevor slipped away. He gobbled up a power pellet and started chasing them. Dorothy Jackson nodded, impressed. She instructed her cameraman to get some footage of Trevor playing.

The cameraman filmed for the next half hour until Trevor's last Pac-Man was gone. He didn't get his highest score that day, but he didn't seem too disappointed. Especially after Dorothy Jackson asked if he would be interested in being interviewed at home with his parents. "I'd love to know what they think of your hobby."

I could practically hear the gears turning in Trevor's head, like he'd just found a hidden power-up and was figuring out how to make the most of it.

Trevor gave Dorothy Jackson his phone number and address. He said his parents were big fans of hers and that they'd love to sit down with her and answer some questions.

I had my own set of questions for Trevor.

"WHAT'S YOUR PLAN?" I asked him afterward, while waited outside the mall for his mom to pick us up.

"My plan with what?" Trevor shoved his hands in his pockets and shifted back and forth, acting like he didn't know what I was talking about.

"With letting that news lady interview your parents. You really want them in the same room right now?"

"It'll be fine."

"What do you think is going to happen? That they'll be so proud of your Pac-Man skills they'll forget all their marriage problems and get back together?"

Trevor got quiet for a second, then said, "You think you know everything about my family, but you don't."

I could've said it right there. Told him everything and proved how much I really knew. But I chickened out. "I'm trying to save you from walking into a disaster."

"You're the one who's a disaster, dude. You, like, completely lost it on that kid at the garage sale over a dumb old telescope."

He was right but I wasn't about to admit it. "Well, don't be surprised when your stupid plan backfires."

"Whatever. I have the situation under control."

When Mrs. Donlan pulled up in her car, Trevor sat up front and I got in the back.

"How are you boys doing?" she asked all cheerily, like her life wasn't falling apart. Adults love to act like they have their lives figured out, but most of the time they're just as confused as teenagers.

"Fine," Trevor said.

"Fine," I repeated.

Chapter 10

After a few weeks of being Renny's handyman, I thought I knew what to expect when I showed up at his cabin after school. But one afternoon, instead of handing me a shovel or an ax and barking at me to "get to work," Renny led me to his pickup and told me to hop in.

"Where are we going?" I asked.

"To pick up some supplies."

"What supplies?"

"You'll find out when we get there."

"Get where?"

"Enough questions."

"Why are you being all secretive?"

Renny shoved his key in the ignition and Big Charlie sputtered to life. "I promise this'll be a lot easier than what you usually do. Unless you'd rather stay here and chop more wood?"

My sore muscles screamed mercy, so I quit asking questions and got in the truck. Looking back, I should have stayed behind and chopped wood.

Big Charlie rumbled down the road and into town. I

assumed "picking up supplies" meant going to the hardware store or Reynolds Groceries. I assumed wrong.

When Renny pulled into the parking lot of the Army Surplus store, my stomach turned. The last time I'd been there had been with Dad when he bought supplies for the hike. I got lost in a flood of memories so hadn't noticed Renny park the truck and get out. When he realized I wasn't following him, he called back, "What's the holdup?"

I rolled down the window. "I'll just wait out here if that's okay."

"No sitting down on the job. You're on the clock."

"Then I'm quitting early and you don't have to pay me for today."

Renny strode up to my window, his face stern. "You want to tell me what's going on with you, kid?"

My throat tightened and I mumbled, "Not really."

"Does it have anything to do with your friend in the hospital? You didn't mention she was the one who fell into Lake Trapper back in December."

"How . . . how did you know?" I asked, suddenly feeling exposed.

"I'm no detective but I can read a newspaper and put two and two together."

My breath caught in my chest. "I don't want to talk about it."

Renny gave me a sympathetic nod. "Fair enough. A man's business is his own. I'm not gonna pry."

I let out a big sigh of relief. "Thanks."

"But that doesn't mean you're off the hook," Renny added. "You can feel sorry for yourself all you want but it's no excuse for avoiding your responsibilities. Come on."

Every bit of me wanted to stay in the pickup, but what Renny'd said about avoiding responsibility was jabbing me like the pointy end of a stick. I wasn't anything like Dad and wanted to prove it to myself.

I flung open the door and marched past Renny. "Let's go," I said.

Stepping inside the store was like walking into an old person's musty closet. The strong smell immediately brought me back to being there with Dad. Before the memories could overwhelm me, I sucked in a breath and grounded myself, focusing on what was right in front of me—a mannequin dressed in a camouflage jacket wearing a gas mask, a wall lined with bows and arrows, and the man behind the counter. It was the same guy who'd been working the day I came with Dad. I recognized his long, white hair and mustache and his denim jacket covered in eagles and American flag patches. He greeted us with a nod and said, "How you doin', Renny?"

Renny tipped his hat and said, "Hey, Dave. I've been better."

"I hear that."

Denim Dave, as I called him in my head, glanced at me. I looked away. I didn't want him to recognize me and start asking questions about Dad and how he'd fared out on the trail.

Renny and Denim Dave talked for a couple minutes, mostly about the weather and guys they knew from the war. I assumed they had been in the same unit in Vietnam, but Renny set me straight. "Every soldier's like a brother," he told me later. "It doesn't matter if you fought side by side, or on the same battlefield."

Renny ordered me to grab a cart, and I followed him down the first aisle. He filled half the cart with cases of canned beans and meat and soups with bland, industrial labels.

"You know, you can buy real food at the grocery store," I said. "It's a lot tastier."

"But it won't last near as long as what's in these cans."

Renny's response threw me off. "So, you're not planning on eating any of this stuff?"

"Only if there's an emergency."

"What kind of emergency?"

"The kind you don't see coming."

We moved on to the other aisles where Renny picked out water purification tablets, rope, toilet paper, cans of Sterno, boxes of matches, and a transistor radio. Dad had bought some of the same supplies.

My heart raced. Sweat tricked down my back. At first, I blamed it on the cart being so full and hard to push. But then my vision got cloudy, and the room swayed.

"Are we almost done?" I asked.

"In a minute," Renny said. "I just gotta grab one more thing." He disappeared down an aisle.

I turned the corner, and that's when I saw him. Or that's when he appeared to me, I should say. My dad was standing in the aisle, trying on a green backpack.

"Are you okay?" Dad asked.

"Please don't leave," I said. "Please don't walk the trail."

"Excuse me?" he said, frowning.

"I don't want you to go," I pleaded more forcefully.

"I think you might have mistaken me for someone else, young man."

Everything went blurry. I squeezed my eyes shut and when I opened them again, the illusion had vanished. Another customer stood in Dad's place, wearing the green backpack. He stared at me with a very confused and concerned look.

"Are you here with anyone?" the man asked. "Do you need help?"

I tried to breathe but no air was getting in. The next thing I remember was bolting past Denim Dave at the front counter and out the door. I gulped down the fresh air.

A few minutes later, Renny found me sitting in the truck's bed, curled up like a baby. Renny pulled open the tailgate and shoved a bag of supplies next to me. "Once we get back to the cabin, I'll need your help unloading all of this."

I was miserable and all he seemed to care about was his stupid cans of crappy food. "I told you I didn't want to go inside!" I snapped.

"But you did it. So give yourself some credit."

I pulled myself up to sitting and felt the tightness in my chest loosen. I could breathe again. "I just want to go home."

"We still got plenty of sunlight," Renny said. "And some physical labor will take your mind off whatever's messing with your head."

I knew Renny was right. I'd been starting to notice how much better I felt after a hard day of work. It seemed to help unload some of the heaviness I'd been carrying around. I climbed out of the truckbed and helped him finish unpacking the cart and loading it into the truck.

WHEN WE GOT BACK to the cabin, Seneca was lying on the porch. At the sound of the truck, he perked his head up and trotted down the steps and came over to meet me. I scratched him behind his ear the way he liked. I think it comforted me as much as it did him.

Renny hollered at me to quit petting his dog and help him unload the truck. I kneeled down and looked Seneca in his eyes. "Sorry, Buddy. We'll play later, okay?"

Seneca whimpered and wandered back to his spot on the porch. Renny tossed me a bag and grabbed another for himself. I headed for the cabin, but Renny stopped me.

"This stuff doesn't go in the house," he said.

"Then where does it go?"

"In the bunker."

"What bunker?"

Renny nodded in the direction of the strange metal hatch sticking out of the ground and headed toward it. I followed a few steps behind, hesitant about where he was leading me. Renny grabbed the handles and yanked. The doors opened with an ear-piercing screech. I peered past Renny into the opening where cement stairs led into the earth.

I stared into the darkness, my heart and thoughts racing. Maybe I should've trusted my first instincts about Renny. What if he had been acting friendly just so he could lure me into his bunker and trap me there forever? What if I went down there and never came out? My bike was leaning against a tree nearby. I could make a run for it and race back home and forget I ever met Renny.

I told myself to stop being ridiculous. If Renny had wanted to lock me up in his secret bunker, he'd had plenty of chances over the past couple of weeks. I stuck around, curious to see what secrets Renny was keeping underground.

Renny flicked a switch on the cinderblock wall. A bare bulb came on, lighting up the stairway. I followed him down. At the bottom we reached another metal door, which looked a lot thicker than the hatch doors. Renny unlocked it with a key from his keyring and pushed it open with his shoulder. The same smell from the Army Surplus store wafted out. It was musty, like opening a tin of stale crackers.

Renny hit a switch, which triggered a loud hum. Fluorescent lights flickered to life. "This place has its own generator in case the main grid goes out," he explained.

I stepped in. The space was about the size of my living room. It had a couch and a coffee table and a bookcase full of books. The small kitchen had a sink and a few cabinets. Bunk beds were against the back wall. The rest of the space was full of shelves stocked with cans and boxes similar to the ones Renny had bought earlier.

"I built it all by myself," Renny said, a proud smile on his face. He told me how he'd dug out the pit with a backhoe, stacked and cemented the cinderblocks, and hooked up the water and power. "What do you think?"

I had to admit, it was a lot nicer than I expected. "It's pretty cool for an underground house."

"More like an underground fortress," Renny corrected me. "It's got four-foot-thick concrete walls, sixteen-gauge steel-reinforced doors, and recycled air flow. Nothing's getting in here."

"Do you live down here sometimes?"

"Haven't yet."

"Then why'd you build it?"

"You can never be too prepared."

"What are you preparing for?"

"The world plunging into chaos," Renny said, like it should've been obvious to me. "If there's a nuclear winter, I can survive down here for at least five years."

"And why would there be a nuclear winter?"

"Because of the Russians dropping nukes."

At first, I assumed Renny was just messing with me, but he looked dead serious. "Could that really happen?"

Renny shrugged. "One thing's for sure—if the Commies bring on the apocalypse, you'll want to be down here when it happens. Trust me, this'll be the safest place in town. Probably all of Massachusetts."

We took a couple of trips back up to Big Charlie to unload, then stacked the supplies on the empty shelves. I couldn't get the image of nuclear Armageddon out of my mind.

"Do you really believe the Russians will drop atomic bombs on us?" I said.

"What do you know about the Cold War?" Renny asked.

I remembered hearing the term once, when Mom and Dad were watching the news. "It's, like, when there's a war, but there aren't any battles."

Renny looked impressed that I'd gotten the answer right. "The United States and Russia have been jockeying for world dominance since I was a kid. And neither one wants to start a full-blown conflict. So they use spies and propaganda to promote their agendas, you get me?" Renny started getting worked up, his voice filling the tiny space we shared.

"But one of these days, Russia might decide that propaganda isn't enough. So the Kremlin gives the order to drop the 'big one' on America. It'll be Hiroshima all over again, but on our soil. Let me tell you, Hiroshima was a damn bloodbath. People screaming in the streets, entire towns burned to the ground. Over a hundred thousand dead. Horrifying. So no one should be surprised when the chickens come home to roost. And they will."

Stunned, I stared at Renny. He must've sensed my discomfort because he softened his voice.

"All I'm saying is . . . the world can go haywire at any moment. And if it's not a nuclear bomb, it could be an asteroid, or a plague, or a flood, or your house catches fire. People think bad things won't happen to them, but nobody is immune to life's miseries. All we can do is prepare ourselves as best we can, so when the hard times hit, we can weather the storm."

Renny's words stayed with me as we finished stocking the shelves. I was jealous that he had somewhere to go if the world blew up and started wishing I could move into the bunker. *I'd be safe here*, I thought. But I later learned, not even concrete walls and steel-reinforced doors can keep out all the pain and suffering.

Chapter 11

After leaving things with Alyssa on a sour note, I avoided going back to the hospital. But after a few weeks, my guilt had bubbled back up until I couldn't take it anymore. Hoping to find some relief, I went to visit her.

Nervously, I slunk into her room, expecting her to give me the cold shoulder or tell me to get lost. I was surprised to find her relaxing, watching Saturday morning cartoons with her mom and laughing together. It felt like Alyssa was almost back to her old self, and when she smiled and said she was glad to see me, I assumed things were alright between us.

But that feeling of "normal" didn't last long. Minutes after my arrival, Alyssa asked her mom to get her something to eat. The second Mrs. Sawyer closed the door behind her, Alyssa looked me in the eye, super serious. Tension filled the room. "I need to tell you something," she said.

"Okay . . ." I sat in the chair next to the bed, bracing myself for the worst.

"My mom's lying to me about something."

"Lying? About what?"

"I'm not sure, exactly."

Alyssa explained how she woke up from a nap earlier that morning, and heard her mother whispering on the phone to her father. She kept her eyes closed and listened in on the conversation. Mrs. Sawyer said a letter addressed to Alyssa had arrived at the hospital. It was from a man who claimed to understand what Alyssa had been through and who wanted to talk with her. Mr. and Mrs. Sawyer agreed it would be best if Alyssa never saw the letter, then her mother tucked the envelope in her tote bag.

Mrs. Sawyer's directive came back to me: *Let's not cause her any more distress.*

After Alyssa finished her story, I slumped back in the chair, pulling my knees to my chest. "I wouldn't worry about it. It's probably nothing."

"If it's nothing, why is my mom hiding it from me?"

"She's just trying her best to take care of you."

"Why are you taking her side?"

"I'm not," I insisted, even though that's exactly what I was doing.

"Then prove it. Hand me my mom's bag." Alyssa pointed to a COFFEE GETS ME STARTED, JESUS KEEPS ME GOING tote bag on the floor.

"I'm not going through your mom's stuff," I said.

"You don't have to. Just bring me her bag. I'd get it myself if I didn't have all these stupid wires attached to me."

I didn't want her getting angry with me like last time, so I grabbed the bag and dropped it in Alyssa's lap. She dug her hand in and rooted around. She pulled out a pink sweater . . . a folded-up newspaper . . . a Bible . . . and finally, she found what she was looking for—an envelope with her name on it. Inside was a typewritten letter.

As Alyssa read it out loud, her eyes widened and she let out little gasps. The letter was from a man named Aldous Watts, who was some kind of researcher from New York City. He'd come across a newspaper article about Alyssa surviving the accident. Aldous Watts wanted to speak with her because he had written a book about near-death experiences, which he called NDEs. Since she'd been clinically dead for twenty-three minutes, he suspected Alyssa may have had one. But to be sure, he needed to hear more details about her story. He asked her to write him back, if she was so inclined.

Alyssa tucked the letter back in its envelope and stared off into space, trying to make sense of everything she'd just read. "Do you know what this means?"

"Don't open letters from strange men," I said.

She shot me a look. "I'm being serious. If I had a near-death experience, it might explain why I keep seeing the same man in my nightmares, or give me a clue about who he is."

"But what about your retrograde amnesia? Even if you had one of those NDE things, you can't remember it."

Alyssa let out a disappointed sigh. "Yeah, that's the problem." Then all of a sudden, she perked up. "But Doctor Wexler said it's possible to recover some memories over time."

"Forget about that letter," I urged, grabbing it from Alyssa and putting it back in her mom's tote bag. "This researcher guy sounds like a nut. What kind of name is Aldous, anyway?"

"I want to read his book at least. Maybe learning more about NDEs will jog some memories about what happened when I was dead. Do you think you could check out a copy for me from the library?"

The thought of Alyssa reading that book sent a chill through me. I was terrified to hand over the very thing that might tear her world—and mine—apart. But the desperation in her eyes dredged up all my guilt. I didn't want to let her down like I had before, so I gave her the answer she wanted.

"Okay, I'll go."

"Promise?" Alyssa's gaze drilled into me.

"Promise," I said.

I returned the tote bag to its spot next to the chair and slunk out of the room, knowing if I didn't return with Aldous Watts's book, I shouldn't bother coming back at all.

———

ON THE MORNING of the open house, I hid in my room as long as I could. After several warnings to "get my ass ready or else," Mom barged in at about noon, her eyes blazing. She yanked the blanket off me before grabbing my arm and dragging me out of bed.

I got dressed and stumbled into the living room, where a woman with caked on makeup and wearing a red blazer with huge shoulder pads scanned the area with her beady eyes. It was Mrs. Licht, in the flesh.

"Everything appears to be in order," she commented as she placed a vase full of pink and purple flowers on the table by the entryway. The last time I'd seen flowers in our house was a few years before, when Dad had remembered to buy Mom some roses for Valentine's Day. "A little pop of color always brightens a buyer's mood," Mrs. Licht said in a way that implied our house was dull and depressing. Which I guess it was.

Finally, Mrs. Licht noticed me leaning against the wall. "And you must be Jack," she said, her bright red lips forming into a smile. "It's nice to finally meet you. Your mother told me a lot about you."

Did she tell you how much I hate the idea of selling our house? I thought.

Mom said, "Put on your shoes, honey. We're going."

"Where?" I asked.

"I already told you. We have to look at apartments."

"And it's customary for the seller not to be present during an open house," Mrs. Licht added.

"I don't want anyone going in my room," I grumbled, tying my sneakers.

Mrs. Licht said, "I'll be here the whole time, if it makes you feel any better."

"It doesn't."

Mrs. Licht went wide-eyed and slack-jawed.

"Jack, don't make this harder than it needs to be," Mom said. "Get your jacket and let's give Mrs. Licht some space so she can do her job."

As we headed out to the car, Mrs. Licht waved to us from the front door. When Mom wasn't looking, Mrs. Licht flashed me a smug smile, acting like she owned the place.

THE FIRST APARTMENT Mom took me to wasn't even in Ravensberg. It was a couple of towns away, which meant if we moved there, I'd have to switch schools. Which also meant I probably wouldn't hang out with Trevor or Alyssa anymore. Already I hated it.

The landlord was this old man who smelled like he hadn't showered in weeks. The apartment stunk worse, like rotten fish and old farts. The place looked like someone had died in it. Turned out, someone had. An elderly widow with six cats had recently keeled over from a heart attack. The landlord was very matter-of-fact about it, like that kind of thing happened a lot to his tenants. He assured us the old woman's daughter would clean out the place before we moved in.

For the first time in a while, Mom and I agreed: we'd rather live out of our car than be stuck in the apartment of death.

The other places we toured weren't much better. They

featured lovely details such as stained carpets, peeling wallpaper, leaky faucets, and a variety of strange smells I couldn't place. Honestly, Renny's bunker was nicer. Bigger than a couple of them, too.

As a reward for being such a good sport, Mom took me to McDonald's for an early dinner. I was actually hungry, so I got a quarter pounder with cheese, fries, and a vanilla milkshake.

"What about that last place?" Mom said, sipping a Diet Coke. "I could picture us living there."

"I couldn't." I nibbled a fry, already losing my appetite.

Mom pressed her case. "You'd still have your own room. And the landlord was a lot nicer than that first one. He promised to repaint and clean the carpets."

"He should pay *us* to live in his crummy apartment."

"That's not how this works, Jack." She reached into her purse and pulled out a pen and the application the landlord had given her. "I should at least fill this out. You never know."

Mom wrote her name and our address. With each letter and line she completed, my world crumbled. Without thinking, I grabbed the application and tore it up.

Mom's face got so red I thought her head was going to explode. If we hadn't been in public, she probably would have slammed the table and screamed at me. But she gritted her teeth and kept her cool. "Why the hell did you do that?"

I just sat there, staring at my food. "I don't know."

"Finish eating and let's go."

"I'm not hungry anymore."

Mom shook her head with a look of disgust. "You're unbelievable. Well, I'm not letting all this food go to waste." Mom grabbed my tray and wolfed down my burger and fries like she hadn't eaten in days. She slurped the rest of my shake on the way out to the car. She didn't say another word to me.

The first thing Mom did when we got home was to ask Mrs.

Licht if someone had bought our house. She shook her head. "A few people seem interested," she said, "but I'm not expecting any offers."

For the first time that day, I could relax. But not Mom. She paced the room, trying to understand what it all meant. "What if no one ends up buying? Don't tell me I'm going to be stuck here forever."

Mrs. Licht assured Mom that there was nothing to worry about. The house had only been on the market for a week. "I've never listed a house that didn't sell," she said, sounding pretty sure of herself.

I took that as a personal challenge. I could become the one to break Mrs. Licht's perfect record.

AFTER THE OPEN HOUSE, I put in some extra hours at Renny's and slipped the cash into Mom's pocketbook when she was in another room. Combined with the money I'd secretly transferred to Mom during the garage sale, she'd been able to pay off the bills, at least for January and February. If I could do the same with March and April's bills, Mom might eventually give up on moving altogether. That fantasy didn't last long.

The following weekend there was another open house, which meant for us another tour of depressing apartments run by shady-looking landlords. When we got back, though, Mrs. Licht said she had some good news.

"I met a lovely young couple this afternoon, the Petersons, and they are very motivated to buy." She stood in the living room with this big, lipstick smile. "They're from out of state and the husband just got a job at the university. They have a six-year-old son and a baby on the way. I have to wait for the official offer to come in, but it sounds like they'll pay full asking price.

Assuming the inspection goes smoothly, the house would be theirs in thirty days."

Mom looked like she was about to burst into tears of happiness. Meanwhile, I was tensing every muscle, trying not to explode.

"What about the bills?" I said.

Mom looked at me. "What about them?"

"I thought you paid them all."

"Yeah, but just barely."

That's when it hit me—all the hours I put in at Renny's, all the money I'd made—none of it had made a difference. Nothing I did would ever make a difference.

Mom turned back to Mrs. Licht, who gushed over the couple's plans to remodel the kitchen, add a large bay window, and create a second bedroom. "A complete transformation," she called it, as if she were talking about some generic office building, not the house I grew up in. The house we used to live in with Dad.

"Are they really allowed to do that?" I asked.

"They'd need to get the correct permits," Mrs. Licht explained, "but once they take ownership of the house, it's theirs to do with as they please."

"Then we won't sell it to them."

"Why don't you go to your room," Mom said politely while glaring at me.

I didn't budge. "I don't want to sell. I never agreed to this."

I expected Mom to chew me out, but it was Mrs. Licht who spoke next. "This isn't your decision to make, young man. It's your mother's."

It was one thing for Mom to lecture me. She gave birth to me, so that was her right, even if I hated it. But Mrs. Licht was nobody to me. Less than nobody. She was just a creepy old vulture circling my home, picking it apart until there was nothing left.

"Get out!" I screamed. "Get out of my house!"

Mrs. Licht flinched. I doubt anyone my age had ever yelled at her like that. And she didn't look too happy about it. Her face twisted up into a mix of confusion and fury. She yelled back, "Do not speak to me in that tone, young man!"

That was it. I couldn't keep from erupting any longer. I grabbed the closest thing to me, which happened to be the vase of flowers Mrs. Licht had put out for the open house. "Get out!" I screamed again.

I remember what happened next in snippets: Mom yelling at me to stop. Mrs. Licht grabbing her purse and running for the door. Me hurling the vase at her. Mrs. Licht slamming the front door as the vase shattered against it. Bits of glass scattering everywhere. Flowers lying in a pool of water on the floor. Mom grabbing my arm hard and yanking me back. Her shoving me down the hall, screaming at me to stay in my room.

Later, I overheard Mom talking to Aunt Beth on the phone. "I don't know what to do with him. He's completely out of control," she said. "He's acting like a little asshole." Her anger turned to hopelessness, and she started sobbing.

Usually, when Mom would call me names, I'd get angry, but this time it felt different. I knew deep down that it was true. I had been acting like an asshole and I didn't know how to stop. My life had been thrown into chaos, and it was getting harder and harder to deal with. I was scared that if I didn't figure out a better way forward, I'd be destroying more than telescopes and vases.

Chapter 12

The next day at the cabin, I was quiet. Quieter than usual. Renny could tell something was up, but true to his word, he didn't pry. But he also didn't go easy on me.

"There are a couple of rotting boards on the porch that need replacing." Renny brought me over to his workshop and pointed to a long piece of wood propped between two sawhorses. "Cut that down into four-foot lengths. Think you can handle that?"

"Sure," I said.

Renny tossed me a tape measure and I started marking the board every four feet. Meanwhile, he propped a ladder against the side of the cabin and climbed up to the roof, where he went to work fixing some old shingles.

Renny had set out a handsaw for me to use. The metal blade was as long as my arm and it wobbled when I picked it up. Even though I'd told Renny I could handle the job, the only time I'd ever cut wood before was once when I made a birdhouse in shop class. But for that, I'd used a small handsaw, not a giant steel blade.

I lined up the handsaw with the first mark and pushed. Right away, the blade got caught. I yanked it out of the wood and tried again, but the blade kept getting stuck. I'd been helpful with cleaning and stocking shelves, but for a job that required actual skill, I was apparently useless. And Renny didn't mind letting me know it.

"What the hell are you doing?" Renny called down from the top of the ladder. "Have you ever held a saw before?"

"Not like this one. Do you have an electric one?"

"You think Thoreau used an electric saw when he built his cabin?"

"Who?" I asked.

"Henry David Thoreau."

I had no idea who he was talking about. "Is that a friend of yours?"

Renny shook his head and groaned. "What the hell do they teach you kids at school nowadays?" He explained that back in the days before electricity, Thoreau had lived not too far away, in Concord, Mass. During the 1840s, he built a cabin in the woods next to Walden Pond. "Thoreau stayed there for a couple of years, living off the land. He wrote all about it in a book called *Walden.*"

"How's that information supposed to help me cut this stupid piece of wood?" I asked, growing more frustrated.

Sensing I needed help, Renny climbed down. The ladder wobbled, and I held my breath, worried he was going to fall. But he steadied himself against the side of the cabin and kept moving. Back on solid ground, Renny took the handsaw and nudged me aside. He moved the blade back and forth and cut through the wood like butter. "You can't force it," he told me. "You gotta let the wood guide you."

I nodded like I understood and gave it another shot. The blade moved a few inches, then got stuck again. I grunted and pushed harder, which only made things worse.

Renny hollered at me to stop. "You keep that up and you're

liable to lose a finger or two," he said. "I don't want to end up in the emergency room with your severed digits in an ice bucket. So open your ears and listen up."

He told me to think of the saw as an extension of my arm, and breathe in and out with each stroke of the blade. I tried to follow his instructions, but the saw kept getting jammed.

"Screw this!" I shouted, because what else do you say when a piece of wood gets the better of you?

Renny hung his head. "Time to take a break."

I gripped the handle tighter. "No, I'll get it. Let me try again."

"You're not in the right mind-set." He patted me on the shoulder. "Fixing the porch can wait. C'mon. We're taking a walk." Renny headed up the path toward the woods.

"Where are we going?" I said, catching up to him.

"To get a dose of nature."

I followed Renny along the trail. Seneca bounded ahead, sniffing at trees and peeing on every one. Renny didn't talk, not at first. He silently led me through the forest until the trail disappeared and we were creating our own route through the dead brush between the trees. Even without a clear path, Renny walked with a purpose, like he knew exactly where to go. I wished for that kind of confidence.

I caught up to Seneca, who stayed by my side as we headed farther into the woods. I was glad for the company. It's easier to be around a dog than around other people. A dog won't lie to you or run out on you or sell your childhood home right out from under you. As long as the dog gets food and shelter and walks, it'll give you back love and protection.

Eventually we came to a small clearing where Renny eased himself down on a rock. "Let's take a breather," he said with a groan.

"Are you okay?"

Renny didn't say. He just nodded to a rock next to him and said, "Have a seat."

I did. A gust sliced through the trees, invading the warmth of my jacket. "What are we even doing out here?" I asked.

"Just being."

"Being what?"

"Being a part of this." He gestured to the surrounding woods.

"Why?"

"See, this is your problem. You ask too many damn questions instead of just existing. I guess I can't blame you, though. Most folks are the same. They're too busy running around, driving here and there, working themselves to the bone. They've convinced themselves they don't have time to sit still for a few minutes. But that ain't true." Renny closed his eyes and took a deep breath. He told me to do the same. I inhaled cold air into my lungs and blew it out.

"You feel that?" Renny asked.

"Feel what?"

"Nature's energy. It flows through every living thing."

I couldn't help but laugh. Renny opened his eyes and scowled. "What's so funny?"

"You're talking about the Force."

"What force?"

"From *Star Wars*."

Renny gave me a blank stare.

"The movie," I said.

Renny hadn't been to the movies in years, so he knew nothing about *Star Wars*. He was probably the one person in the world who hadn't heard of it. "There's this old Jedi dude named Obi Wan Kenobi," I explained. "He believes in a kind of energy called the Force, which binds the whole galaxy together. And eventually, he teaches this skeptical farmboy named Luke Skywalker to believe in it too."

"Forget all that made-up galaxy crap." Renny insisted that if I really wanted to understand how to connect with nature, I was better off reading *Walden*. "It's all about living in harmony with nature, spirituality, and self-reliance. It's basically a guide for how to be a Transcendentalist."

I'd never heard that word before, so Renny filled me in. Transcendentalism was this really cool philosophical movement that developed during Thoreau's time. Its followers believed that we get knowledge about ourselves and the world through intuition, instead of from the things we can see, hear, and touch. But to tap into that wisdom, you have to take a step back from society so you can get in touch with yourself and see the bigger spiritual picture. It sounded like a philosophy Obi Wan would have believed in. And it explained a lot about what made Renny tick.

But the part about Thoreau and the Transcendentalists that really struck a chord with me was how they didn't count on prayers or God for answers. Instead, they found the divine in everyday life.

When Renny finished, I joked, "I hope you won't test me on this. Because I'll probably fail."

Renny chuckled. "No, this is just good stuff to know as a human being." He got up and started off. "Let's keep moving."

As we walked, I tried to practice what I'd just learned. I took in my surroundings. In the dirt, I spotted crisscrossing deer tracks; I heard a woodpecker's distant hammering; The scent of pine filled my nostrils; I tasted the sweet sap from a tree and felt its stickiness on my fingers.

All of a sudden, I experienced something really weird. My body tingled and I sensed a powerful presence, like the earth and sky were breathing together. It was a peaceful feeling that lasted only a second because, right then, I stepped out of the forest and saw where we were. And the peaceful feeling turned to terror.

I stood on a slope, staring out over Lake Trapper, still half frozen from winter. Across the water, I spotted an empty parking lot with ribbons of yellow caution tape fluttering from the trees. The sight transported me back to the day of "the incident." Suddenly I was out on the ice, shouting at Alyssa to stop, helpless to save her. I didn't let my mind linger there long.

I willed myself back to the present and got ready to bolt, but when I turned around, Renny and Seneca were blocking my way. Renny's eyes locked with mine and asked if I was okay. Now it was my turn to dodge the question. But it didn't matter. Renny was an observant guy, and he'd figured out why I was acting so strange.

"I'm guessing this must be close to where they pulled your friend out of the water."

My fingers and toes went numb. I shivered, stumbling back, the memory of that day whipping me like the wind off the lake. The idea of Alyssa drowning was too horrible to contemplate, and yet it had happened. I'd let it happen. My mouth went dry, and my heart started pounding. The watery deep loomed ahead, calling, wanting to pull me in. I was frozen with fear and indecision. I couldn't speak. So I did what anyone would do under the circumstances: I ran like hell.

My legs pumped. My head pounded. I raced through the woods until my lungs burned. I tried to keep up my pace, but after a while my legs gave out. My sweat-soaked hair fell into my eyes, blurring my vision. By the time I slowed down to catch my breath, I was all turned around. I wandered in circles, trying to find the trail that would lead to the cabin, but eventually I had to accept facts—I was lost. My heart sank and, exhausted, I collapsed onto the ground and hugged myself tightly. A sense of impending doom crept over me.

I don't know how long I sat there, but at some point I heard barking in the distance. Seneca came bounding through the woods and attacked me with his warm, slobbery tongue.

"Thanks for finding me," I whispered.

A few minutes later, Renny showed up and pulled me to my feet. I wiped my drippy nose on the sleeve of my jacket and followed him through the woods back to the cabin. After a long silence, he started telling me one of his war stories.

Before the army shipped Renny off to Vietnam, they put him through boot camp. It sounded horrible—a drill sergeant would yell at Renny and his fellow soldiers as they crawled through mud and climbed walls. "Get comfortable being uncomfortable!" the drill sergeant shouted, over and over.

Eight weeks later, Renny stepped off a plane somewhere in Vietnam and was thrown into the chaos. "Me and my platoon had to march miles and miles through the jungle to reach an outpost in the middle of nowhere. It was hot, humid, and dense with the stench of blood and sweat and burning diesel." Along the journey, he and the others had to fight off enemy Viet Cong soldiers and bugs the size of baseballs. Renny claimed he wasn't exaggerating about the bugs, but I'm not so sure.

One day, Renny was wading through water up to his waist, getting shot at and eaten alive. "I'd never been more uncomfortable in my whole life," Renny said. "I wanted to drown myself so I could put an end to the pain."

That's when the drill sergeant's words came back to him. Renny realized he could either fight the discomfort or surrender to it. And since he couldn't control if he got bitten by bugs or hit by an enemy bullet, Renny surrendered.

"In war, a soldier knows that any day could be their last,"

Renny said. "So I started living each moment as it came and being grateful for the one that followed."

"I'm not a soldier in a war, though," I said.

"Doesn't matter. Life's full of discomfort and it's always uncertain. If you don't figure out a way to live with that reality, it'll drive you nuts."

I followed Renny back to the cabin, a knot of emotion building in my chest. He was becoming the kind of guide my father never was able to be, like my very own Obi Wan. I wanted desperately for Renny to stay that way. But considering what he had just said about life being uncertain, I knew deep down that each day we spent together could be our last. At any moment, Darth Vader could crash into our lives with his lightsaber and cut Renny down.

Chapter 13

Mom and I spent another Saturday touring crappy apartments and arguing about where to live. Meanwhile, time was running out for me to stop the Petersons from getting their hands on our house.

After we got home, Mom popped open a bottle of wine, plopped herself on the couch, and tuned into the six-o'clock local news. That's when the story about Trevor came on.

"Jack, get in here!" Mom shouted. "Trevor's on TV!"

When I walked into the living room, there was footage of Trevor playing Pac-Man with me standing next to him.

"Look! There you are!" Mom smiled proudly at the Jack on the screen like he was some kind of celebrity. She didn't even glance at the real me sitting right next to her.

Dorothy Jackson described how Trevor was "the teenager to watch in the local arcade scene" and talked about his high scores. Then the story cut to Dorothy Jackson standing outside the mall. The tone of her voice got serious, and the report took a turn. "But some in the community view video games as a dangerous pastime for young people."

It cut to some old couple standing in the mall who complained that video games were corrupting the minds of America's youth. Next up: a woman in a brown sweater with a pouty face who was a child psychiatrist named Lydia Jenkins. According to her, a study done in Germany claimed that prolonged exposure to video games might stunt brain development in children. In her own practice, she noticed an uptick in children who confused fantasy with reality. And those children played a lot of video games. She wasn't suggesting a direct correlation, but the trend concerned her.

But what did they know? I mean, had any of those people ever set foot in an arcade? I doubted it. They were just talking nonsense. And who did Dorothy Jackson think she was, anyway? She'd acted nice, like she was genuinely interested in Trevor when her actual goal was to make kids who played video games look bad. She'd used us.

Trevor's interview finally came on. He was sitting on his blue-checkered couch in his living room, where I'd slept a bunch of times for sleepovers. Trevor sat between his parents, hamming it up for the camera, putting on this big fake smile. Mr. and Mrs. Donlan had these somber looks on their faces, like they were being held against their will.

Trevor never told me exactly how he'd convinced his parents to talk to a reporter, but it probably involved a lot of begging and nagging. When there was something Trevor wanted from his parents, he'd keep bringing it up until they gave in.

During the interview, Mr. and Mrs. Donlan pretended like their family was fine and that they were super supportive of their son's interests. "No, we're not concerned about any harm it might cause," Mr. Donlan said. "He gets excellent grades," Mrs. Donlan added. But they didn't look comfortable and their voices were full of bitterness.

"What's so funny?" Mom asked. I realized I'd been smiling to myself.

"Nothing."

When the news story was over, the weatherman came on, blabbing on about how the rest of March was shaping up to be unseasonably warm, which meant spring temperatures would arrive sooner than expected. I wandered into the kitchen and waited by the phone for Trevor to call. But the minutes ticked by without any word from him. What was he waiting for? His plan for a happy family reunion had obviously backfired, just like I'd warned him. He owed me an apology.

Finally, when I couldn't take it anymore, I decided to make the call myself. He answered on the fourth ring.

"Hello?"

"Hey, Trev. I saw the interview."

There was a long silence.

"That psychiatrist lady was so full of crap," I said.

Trevor stayed quiet. I thought he'd hung up on me, but I could hear him breathing.

"Trev? You still there?"

"Yeah."

"What did your parents think of the story?"

"They didn't see it."

"Why not?"

"Is that why you called? To rub it in?"

"Rub what in?"

"You'll be happy to know that after that reporter left the other day, my parents were pissed. They told me I couldn't fix it. That their marriage wasn't some video game I could figure out how to beat. Now they're *officially* separated. Mom and me are staying in the house and Dad just moved into a crummy motel. They agreed I'll be with him on the weekends."

"Oh." I started feeling bad for him, but I was still waiting for him to say sorry. To admit I'd been right.

"That's all you have to say? Why'd you even call, dude?"

"You should have listened to me."

"Some friend you are, Jack."

"I told you it was going to be a disaster."

"Screw you, Jack. I don't want to hear your stupid voice ever again."

The line went dead. I hung up the phone, stunned. Trevor had never spoken to me that way before. We joked around, called each other dumb names. But it was always in fun.

I turned and saw Dorothy Jackson sitting at the kitchen table, pen and pad at the ready.

"Would you care to elaborate on what just happened between you and Trevor?" she asked.

"No comment."

"Don't you think it's time he knew the truth?"

"No comment," I repeated.

By MID-MARCH, I had to accept that helping Mom pay the bills wouldn't save our home. This drained my motivation to keep working for Renny, but I felt guilty about abandoning him, so I still stopped by a couple of times during the week. He didn't appreciate that I'd changed my work schedule without running it by him first.

"I need to know I can count on you," he said.

"Of course you can," I said, but I was lying. The same way I'd lied to Alyssa when I promised I'd get her Aldous Watts's book.

In my defense, I tried. I went to the local library and when I couldn't find the book in the card catalog, I even asked the librarian behind the check-out desk for help. But when she placed the book in my hands, I started having second thoughts.

Aldous Watts stared at me from the back cover. He wore a black turtleneck and had a pencil-thin mustache, square glasses, and dark hair with gray at the temples. Under the author's photo was more info about the book. *In* Both Here and Gone, *you will encounter actual case histories that reveal there is life after death. Over the years, Mr. Watts's research has helped hundreds of people tap into their memories and understand the meaning of their near-death experiences.*

Did that mean if Alyssa read the book, she would remember everything about "the incident?" It wasn't worth the risk. I convinced myself that Alyssa was better off without the book. I told the librarian I'd forgotten my library card and that I'd come back another time.

WHEN I SHOWED up at the hospital empty-handed, Alyssa let out a heavy sigh and collapsed into her pillows. "You promised, Jack!" she said.

"I promised I'd go to the library. I did."

"Then where's the book?"

"They didn't have it."

Alyssa stared at me with a stony expression. It was clear she didn't believe a word I'd just said. "I called the library yesterday. The librarian said it was on their shelf."

I angled myself away from Alyssa and stared out the window. It had been getting harder to look her in the eyes, knowing I was lying to her. "I guess someone checked it out before I got there."

"Why are you acting like this?"

"Like what?"

"Like you're hiding something."

"You're the one lying to your mom and going behind her back."

"You said you'd help me."

I glanced over at her. "Why don't you start helping yourself? Unless you want to spend the rest of your life in a hospital bed."

Alyssa winced. I hadn't meant to hurt her feelings. Or maybe I had? I was so confused. Was I actually mad at her, or just at myself?

After a long silence, Alyssa said, "Do you think I'm having fun here? Being poked and studied like some freak of nature?"

I shrugged and mumbled, "I don't know."

Alyssa choked on the words as she explained how empty and lifeless she felt since waking up—like one of her father's embalmed bodies, preserved and displayed for people to visit. As a little girl, Alyssa had studied those dressed-up corpses, with their faces caked in makeup and their lips molded into faint smiles. She'd even practiced mimicking them, lying on her bed, arms across her chest, pretending to be dead. She imagined lines of mourners coming by to pay their respects.

Now she used the same trick to fool her mother, her doctors, and me into thinking that she was okay. But she wasn't. Part of her still felt dead inside. She was confused and hurting. She wanted answers about what she went through. Aldous Watts's book might unlock those answers. And I was the jerk who had hidden the key.

She didn't say that last part out loud, but she didn't need to.

"Maybe I should go," I said.

"Maybe you should."

I left the hospital that day, not knowing when I'd see Alyssa again. She didn't seem to want me to visit, and I was in no rush to go back. On the bike ride home, it hit me that I'd distanced myself from Renny, messed things up with Trevor, and

107

sabotaged my friendship with Alyssa. And I didn't know how to fix any of it.

———

MOM HAD GIVEN me strict instructions to make myself scarce during the house inspection with the Petersons. She handed me two bucks and told me to go play some video games with Trevor, not realizing we weren't on friendly terms. I pocketed her bribe, but I didn't follow her instructions. After school, I headed straight home to see with my own eyes the family that was plotting with Mrs. Licht to take away my home.

I parked my bike in the garage and walked right through the front door, acting surprised that a bunch of strangers were standing around my living room. There was a guy wearing a white button-down shirt with a plaid tie. The woman had on a purple dress that stretched tight over her pregnant belly. Another woman—older, with a giant perm that looked like a cat was on her head—stood nearby.

"Uh . . . what are you all doing in my house?" I said. I'd taken drama at school, so I was pretty convincing.

The Petersons looked at each other, confused. They asked Perm Lady what was going on. She put on a big grin and told them there must have been a mixup. She walked over to me, smile fading.

"Hi, sweetie," Perm Lady said in a nasal voice. "Are you Mrs. Finn's son?"

I looked her straight in the eye and said, "Who's asking?"

That stopped her in her tracks. She looked offended, and wouldn't tell me her name, only that she was the Petersons' Realtor. She informed me I wasn't supposed to be there "because of the home inspection currently being conducted."

"I guess my mom forgot to tell me." I shrugged when I said it, to really make it extra convincing.

"Is there someplace you can go for a few hours until we're done? Perhaps a neighbor's?"

I shook my head. "The neighbors aren't very friendly."

The Petersons looked worried. Perm Lady sensed their tension and flashed them an oozy smile, reassuring them we were in one of the most desirable neighborhoods in town. "Last month, I sold a house to a lovely couple just down the street. Wonderful people."

The Petersons looked relieved.

"I'll just be in my room," I said. "You won't even know I'm here."

That's when an older man with a potbelly and a tool belt waddled out of the kitchen. "Hold up, young fella. I still gotta inspect the bedrooms."

I hated being treated like a trespasser when it was the Petersons and Perm Lady and Mr. Inspector who were doing the trespassing. "Then I guess I'll just wait here until you're done."

"Whatever suits you." Mr. Inspector marked a paper on his clipboard and turned to the Petersons. "By the way, I found a dead outlet in the kitchen."

I saw an opportunity, so I took it. "Oh yeah, my mom never bothered to get that fixed," I said. "Actually, you have your work cut out for you, sir. There's a ton of stuff in the house that's busted."

The Petersons' worried expressions returned.

Perm Lady shot me a look of death. "Can you wait in the backyard? The Petersons' son is out there. I bet he'd love to play with you." She looked to the Petersons for their approval.

"Sure," Mrs. Peterson said.

"Good idea," Mr. Peterson added.

"Fine." I stomped through the kitchen and out the back door.

The Peterson kid was in our yard, kicking around a half-deflated soccer ball to nobody. It was kinda pathetic. As soon as he saw me, he waved and said "hi."

"Hey," I said.

"I'm Todd. What's your name?"

"Jack. I live here."

"Cool. What grade are you in?"

"Ninth. You?"

"First."

"Cool."

I had expected to hate the Petersons, but after meeting them in person, they seemed harmless. Just a nice, normal family like mine used to be. I wondered if I'd been making too big a deal out of Mom selling the house. Maybe she was right and it was time to move on.

But then Todd kicked the ball to me and I realized it wasn't just any soccer ball, it was the soccer ball Mom and Dad had gotten me when I turned six. The soccer ball Dad and I used to kick around together after he got home from trips. I hadn't seen it in forever and had completely forgotten about it.

"Where did you find this?" I planted my foot on the ball. It squished under the pressure. I didn't kick it back.

"Under there." Todd pointed to an area under the back porch Mom had forgotten to clean out.

"Oh. Well, I hope the rats didn't get you." I don't know why I said it. We didn't have rats. But Todd didn't know that.

He took a quick glance at the porch, then back at me. "Rats?"

"Snakes, too. Poisonous ones."

"Really?" Todd covered his mouth like he was watching a scary movie.

I should've stopped there, but I couldn't help myself. Todd had stumbled into my trap, and I smelled blood.

"Yeah, my brother got bit by one when he was playing out here. Right where you're standing, actually. He was about your age."

Todd stepped to the side. "Was he okay?"

"No, he got really sick and he . . . he died," I said, trying to sound sad.

"Like, *dead* dead?"

I moved close, lowering my voice to a whisper. "Sometimes, at night when I come out here . . . I see his ghost."

Todd turned white. "For real or pretend?"

"Oh, it's real. Once in a while his ghost comes into my bedroom, where you'll be sleeping. When a house is haunted, it's really hard to get rid of a ghost, but if . . . " I trailed off and waited to reel Todd in.

"If what?" he asked.

"If your parents don't buy this house, then my brother's ghost can't bother you. Or your new brother or sister."

Todd bolted back inside, screaming to his parents that he didn't want to live there.

Perm Lady marched out and glared at me from the porch. "What did you say to that poor boy?"

"Nothing."

———

By the time Mom got home from work, she'd gotten a call from Mrs. Licht, who heard from Perm Lady, who found out from the Petersons exactly what I'd said to their son.

"You weren't supposed to be here, Jack. I told you not to be here." Mom was putting boxes of Chinese takeout on the

111

kitchen table. "And what possessed you to make up a story about a dead brother?"

"I was just joking."

"It's not funny. And you terrified a kid half your age."

"He's old enough to know I was kidding."

"The Petersons are getting cold feet now. Are you doing this deliberately?"

"Doing what?"

"Don't play dumb. You've been trying to sabotage this house sale from the moment I told you about it. But I never thought you'd take it this far." Mom sat down and stuffed an egg roll into her mouth. "I swear, Jack, if this sale doesn't happen . . . " She didn't finish her sentence, but she didn't have to. If the Petersons backed out, she was going to blame me. And she'd never let me live that down.

Chapter 14

The day after the inspection, I rode out to Renny's cabin. As soon as I hopped off my bike, I sensed trouble. Renny was outside working, but he was limping. Badly. Seneca stayed by his side like he wanted to help but didn't know how.

"Oh, so now you show up," Renny griped. He unscrewed a dead porch light and replaced it.

"Sorry, my mom needed me for something yesterday," I said. "What happened to you?"

"Fell off the damn ladder is what happened." He explained that he'd been finishing the roof repairs and was coming down the ladder when he lost his balance. The ladder tipped, taking Renny with it.

A wave of guilt came over me. I should've been at the cabin holding the ladder for Renny, instead of at home, scaring Todd Peterson with ghost stories.

"Not that you asked, but I'm fine," Renny said. "My knee, on the other hand . . . " He bent down to pick up another lightbulb, wincing and groaning as he clutched his right knee.

"Maybe you should see a doctor?" I said.

Renny shooed me away like I was an annoying fly. "Nah,

I've seen enough doctors for a lifetime. Nothing they can do to help me at this point."

"At least take it easy and put some ice on it or something."

"For the last time, I'm fine. Now, move out of the way." Renny pushed me aside and stubbornly carried on fixing things here and there around the cabin, attempting to hide his pain. While I swept the porch, the sounds of his suffering filled the air. I couldn't bear to hear him cursing and howling, but there was nothing I could do except mind my own business. If Renny didn't want my help, I couldn't force him to take it.

But then Renny's knee gave out. It was like his entire leg had suddenly turned to rubber and his body just crumpled right there on the cabin steps. Renny wailed in unbearable agony. I froze midsweep.

"Get your ass over here and help me up!" Renny shouted.

I dropped the broom and went to Renny. I pulled him up by the arm, but as soon as he tried to stand on his bad leg, he fell right back down.

"Guess I'm gonna need to see a doctor after all," Renny said.

"I'll call an ambulance."

"I don't have a phone, remember?"

I tried not to panic, but I started sweating and hyperventilating. Renny said, "Get a grip, soldier. Help me over to Big Charlie."

"You're in no shape to drive."

"I know," he said. "That's why you're taking the wheel."

"Me? I don't know how to drive!"

"I told you, when you need to learn, you learn."

"What if . . . what if I bike back home and call for help from there?"

"That'll take too damn long." Renny grabbed my wrist and looked me in the eye. "Jack, I need you to do this. That's why I hired you."

114

"You knew something like this could happen?"

"Not this exact situation, but yeah. Please, I'm counting on you."

I'd let down Mom, Trevor, Alyssa . . . I wouldn't let Renny down, too. Especially since it was kinda my fault he got hurt in the first place.

There was no way I could carry Renny on my own, so he taught me a technique he'd learned in basic training—the human crutch. I crouched down, and he wrapped his arm around my shoulder. I got up nice and slow, and Renny used his good leg to hold himself up. Grabbing his wrist with one hand and his waist with the other, I helped him hop over to the truck. His skin was cold and damp. My stomach turned at the sight of his injured leg, which hung like a scarecrow's limb, all floppy and twisted. I turned my gaze toward our destination—Big Charlie.

It took all my strength, but I managed to get him in the passenger's seat. Maybe it was the adrenaline, or all the muscles I'd built up from working at Renny's, but for a second I felt like Superman.

Seneca came running over and tried to jump in the truck's bed. I pulled him away and assured him we'd be back soon. He whimpered in understanding, but I don't think he was happy about it.

I got in and slumped back against the driver's seat, wiping sweat from my forehead. Renny fished the keys out of his jacket pocket and handed them over. My hands were shaking so much that it took me a couple of tries to get the key in the ignition.

My feet wouldn't reach the pedals unless I perched right at the front edge of the seat. It was awkward being in that half-sitting, half-standing position, but it did the trick. I put one foot on the gas and the other on the brake.

I'd ridden in Big Charlie a bunch of times, so I knew I had to press the clutch and use the gear shifter to drive, but I wasn't exactly sure how it all worked.

"Just do what I say . . . you got this . . . " Renny said through labored breaths.

I had my doubts, but if I wanted to get Renny to the hospital, I needed to ignore them. "Okay."

"First, turn the key," Renny said.

I did, and Big Charlie roared to life. "Now what?" I asked.

"I'll shift. You gotta work the pedals."

"And the steering too?"

"Yup. That's all you."

I had played Pole Position, so I understood how driving a car was supposed to work. But Big Charlie wasn't some vehicle in an arcade game and if I crashed him, I wouldn't be able to pop in another quarter and try again. It might be game over for me and Renny.

Renny gripped the shifter. "Okay, keep your right foot on the brake and when I say so, press the clutch all the way down with your left. Big Charlie's as stubborn as a bull, so you're gonna have to put some muscle into it."

I took a deep breath.

"Now," Renny said.

I slammed my foot on the clutch while Renny jerked the shifter into first.

"Okay, ease up on the brake."

When I did, Big Charlie lurched, then started rolling forward.

"Now let off the clutch and push on the gas."

I followed Renny's instructions and Big Charlie started picking up speed, a lot faster than I expected. The cabin grew smaller and smaller in the rearview. As Charlie rattled down the dirt road, I clutched the wheel, trying not to get thrown out of the seat. It was like Charlie knew I wasn't supposed to be in the driver's seat and was doing everything in his power to buck me off.

"What now?"

"We're gonna shift into second. On my mark, take your foot off the gas and press the clutch again."

But I jumped the gun and stepped on the clutch before Renny could shift and the engine stalled out. The pickup lurched to a stop.

"Go again!" Renny barked.

After stalling out a couple more times, Renny and I found our rhythm. And once we reached the main road, Big Charlie didn't seem to mind so much that I was behind the wheel, not Renny. As we barreled down the dusky road, I could hear my heart beat, the rush of blood through my ears, the tires against the pavement, and the wind rushing past the window.

It was a strange sensation, driving for the first time. Leaning into the curves, the engine strained against me. I gripped the wheel, my knuckles turning white. Renny kept reminding me to keep breathing. I focused my mind on the road ahead. Eventually the world melted away and me and Big Charlie were one. In a strange way, it was the calmest I'd felt in months. Go figure.

I don't remember much about the rest of the drive, except that by the time we got to Billings Memorial, Renny had passed out, probably from all the pain. Since I'd lost my shifting partner, I couldn't really slow down, so I just sped through the parking lot and slammed the brakes outside the emergency entrance. Big Charlie let out a squeal and jumped the curb, startling a security guard who was standing nearby. I hopped out of the driver's side, shouting for help.

"Please! This is an emergency!"

The security guard ran into the hospital and quickly

returned with a couple of nurses in blue scrubs. They rushed over and pulled Renny out of the pickup and onto a gurney.

"What happened?" one nurse asked.

"He fell off a ladder and busted his knee really bad," I said.

"What's his name?"

"Renny."

"Is he your father?"

I'd spent enough time at the hospital to know that nurses and doctors always treated family members differently. So I figured it would just make things go easier if I went along with what the nurse had already assumed.

"Yeah, he's my dad." It surprised me how easily the words came out.

"Come with us," the nurse said. "We're going to take good care of him, don't you worry."

The nurses pushed the gurney into the ER. I looked down when a hand grabbed mine. Renny gazed up at me with half-lidded eyes.

"You're a hell of a driver," he said weakly.

I smiled. "And you're a great teacher."

I SAT in the waiting room for an hour, flipping through old copies of *Rolling Stone* while the nurses took Renny to get X-rays and a bunch of other tests. Finally, a doctor with long black hair came out to talk to me. She asked me if I was Jack Laforge and I told her I was and she said her name was Doctor Lakshmi. She explained that my "father" had torn his ACL, which she said was like a big rubber band that connected his shinbone to his thighbone.

"Typically, I would recommend surgery to fix the injury," Doctor Lakshmi said. "But because of the advanced stage of his disease, I want to discuss all the options with your father's other doctors."

My body went numb. *What disease? How advanced was it?* I didn't want to raise any suspicions, so I played it safe and didn't ask any questions. She told me a bunch of other stuff I don't remember because the whole time she was talking I kept wondering what was wrong with Renny and why he'd never mentioned it.

Doctor Lakshmi brought me to Renny's room. He was sitting up in bed with his knee in a huge brace. The nurses had hooked him up to an IV and a heart monitor. When Renny saw me, he gave me a wink.

"Good to see you . . . *son*."

"How are you feeling, Dad?"

"Alive and kicking."

In all the time I'd known Renny, I'd never seen him so relaxed. Doctor Lakshmi mentioned that they'd given him something for the pain. Another doctor came in. An older guy with gray hair and glasses. He narrowed his eyes, studying me.

"Mr. Laforge never mentioned he had a son," the doctor said.

My mouth went dry. "Oh, he didn't?"

"Sorry, must've slipped my mind, Doc," Renny said.

The man introduced himself as Doctor Edmund, and he was an oncologist. He explained what that meant, but he didn't need to. I knew exactly what kind of doctor he was because of Trevor's brother Scotty. He'd had a whole team of oncologists working to save his life, but the cancer still got him.

That's when it became painfully obvious that Renny had lied to me about having a friend in the hospital with cancer. There was no friend. Renny was the one who was dying.

Doctor Edmund kept talking, but his voice sounded muffled. Then the room went blurry as fear surged through me, making my heart race faster than ever before. All I wanted was to run and escape, but a firm grip on my wrist held me in place. I looked into Renny's determined gaze.

"Stay, Jack. You need to hear this."

I took a deep breath and my senses got clearer. "Okay."

The doctors took turns explaining the situation. Typically, it took six to eight weeks to recover from ACL surgery, but Renny didn't have that kind of time left. Renny didn't see the point of having the surgery. The doctors didn't disagree.

"We can transfer you to an assisted living facility if you'd like," Doctor Lakshmi said.

"That sounds like a good idea," I said.

"Hell, no," Renny said. "I can still take care of myself well enough. Just give me a few aspirin and crutches and I'll get out of your hair."

"We need to at least monitor you overnight," Doctor Lakshmi said. "To make sure there aren't any further complications."

"Yeah, let's do that," I said.

Renny crossed his arms and muttered under his breath, "This isn't your decision, Jack."

I glared at him, rage burning through me. "You should've told me what was really going on with you."

"It wasn't any of your business."

"You lied to me."

"I spared you the truth. That's different."

"You can't just give up. The doctors can help you get better."

"They already tried. There's nothing more they can do at this point. It is what it is."

I couldn't believe what I was hearing. "How can you act like this?"

"Like what?"

"Like you don't care that you're leaving me!"

And there it was. The thing I never got to say to my real dad, just my imaginary one.

"You think I don't care?" Renny said. "Of course I do, but there's no use denying it. Right now, time is passing and you and I are both inching toward the end, me just a little quicker. There's no avoiding death. It's the cost of living."

I collapsed into the chair, my chest aching.

Seeing how upset I was, Renny softened. "But if staying in the hospital makes you feel any better about it, then fine. I'll stay. But just the one night."

"Okay," I said.

"I'll fill out the paperwork," Doctor Lakshmi said, looking glad to have an excuse to leave the uncomfortable situation. Doctor Edmund hurried out behind her.

Renny and I were alone. It was quiet for a while, then Renny said, "The cancer's all over my damn body and the treatments would just make me sicker. I'd rather live the little time I have left not feeling like crap. Make sense?"

"Yeah, but it's not fair."

"Who the hell ever promised you life would be fair?"

I didn't have a good answer.

"Best you head home, Jack."

"What about tomorrow?" I asked.

"What about it?"

"You'll need help getting home."

Renny said I'd done enough for him and that I wasn't obligated to stick around. "Caring for a man dying of cancer wasn't exactly in the job description."

"Are you firing me?"

"You kinda quit on me."

"I guess I did. Sorry."

"There is one thing you can do."

"What's that?"

"Check on Big Charlie. Make sure he's parked in a safe spot for the night."

"Will do."

We came to an agreement that I'd come back the next day, but only if I promised not to say another word about cancer treatments or following doctors' orders.

I can't exactly explain what made me want to keep helping Renny, knowing he was dying. I guess of all the crappy things that were going on in my life, Renny was the one thing that wasn't so crappy. His weird wisdom had grown on me, and I enjoyed being around him. Seneca, too. I couldn't live with myself if I turned my back on him when he needed me the most.

Plus, I'd left my bike out at the cabin and needed to get it back.

Chapter 15

By the time I left Renny's hospital room, it was dark outside. I looked around the parking lot for Big Charlie but he wasn't there. According to the lady at the information desk, the pickup had been towed away. I dreaded telling Renny the bad news, but it would have to wait until morning. Since I didn't have a way home, I called Mom to come get me. I told her I'd been visiting Alyssa and had lost track of the time.

"What happened to your bike?" she asked.

"It got stolen."

"Where?"

"From the bike rack outside the hospital."

"Did you report it to the security guards there?"

"I'm sure it'll turn up."

"You don't sound too upset about it."

"Someone probably just took it for a joyride."

"I'm not buying you another one."

"I'm not asking you to."

Mom sighed and said she was on her way.

Fifteen minutes later, she pulled up in front of the hospital and I got in. The first thing out of her mouth wasn't "Hi, Jack" or "How are you?" No, she wanted to let me know that my little scheme had failed. "Thankfully, the Petersons decided to buy our house after all."

A lump formed in my throat, and I swallowed it. "So, we're really moving?"

"Escrow closes in two weeks. We need to be out by then."

"Two weeks? They can't just kick us out of our own house."

"I'm sorry, Jack, but it's not going to be *our* house anymore. And if we're still living there when the Petersons move in, they can call the cops on us for trespassing."

"Fine, then I guess I'll get arrested."

"That's not funny."

"I'm not joking."

"I know you don't like this, but we're moving. End of story."

"We don't have an apartment yet."

"We'll get a motel room until we find one. Supposedly, the Treetop Motel is half-way decent and not too expensive."

"I don't want to live in some crummy motel!"

"Why do you keep acting like this, Jack?"

"Like what?"

"Like reality doesn't exist. You're barely passing at school, you're making up stories about having a dead brother who haunts our house, you keep disappearing on your bike to God-knows-where, doing God-knows-what, and mystery money keeps showing up in my pocketbook every week. I'm not an idiot, you know. Where'd that money come from, huh?"

"That's classified information."

"Quit it with the smart-aleck comments. I'm trying to have a serious conversation. I get that this past year has been really, really hard. On both of us. That's why I tried to give you some space, but now I'm at a loss. I don't know what to do. I don't know what you need."

And I couldn't give her an answer. All I knew was I was a

jumbled mess of emotions, and I didn't want to feel any of them. I was like a TV on the fritz. So I shut myself off.

———

THE NEXT MORNING, I waited until Mom left the house to run some errands, then called a cab to pick me up and take me to the hospital.

When I got to Renny's room, a nurse stood at the side of his bed pumping a blood pressure cuff. Renny smiled when he saw me. The nurse released the bulb, and the cuff made a sighing sound. Renny's blood pressure numbers were normal and everything else checked out. Once the doctor signed the discharge papers, Renny was free to go home. The nurse handed me a couple of small pieces of paper with some scribbles on them.

"These are prescriptions your father needs to get filled. Okay?"

"Sure," I said. Apparently no one had bothered to check out if I was really Renny's son or not, so I kept playing the part.

"And make sure your dad uses those." She pointed to a pair of crutches leaning by the head of the bed. "He needs to keep weight off his knee as much as possible."

"Got it."

"Someone will be by soon with a wheelchair to take him to the lobby," the nurse said on her way out.

I slowly made my way to Renny's bedside.

"Good of you to come by," Renny said. "Now give me those." He snatched the prescriptions out of my hand and tore the papers into bits.

"But the nurse said—"

"Yeah, I heard her. They gave me a bunch of drugs in here,

125

but it doesn't mean I have to take them once I'm home. I've dealt with worse pain than this."

"But—"

"I thought we had an agreement."

"We do." I didn't question him after that. He was a grown man. If he didn't want to follow the doctor's orders, what business was it of mine?

A few minutes later, an orderly came to the room and wheeled Renny to the elevators. I followed, carrying his crutches. When we got to the lobby, the orderly asked if we needed to call a cab. Renny said, "I got my pickup. My son will pull it around."

I had to break it to Renny that Big Charlie had been towed.

"Well, goddammit." Renny looked up at the orderly. "Guess we'll be needing that ride after all."

The lady at the information desk called for a cab and gave Renny the name and address of the tow yard where they'd taken Big Charlie. I wheeled Renny outside to wait, and guess who came walking by? Alyssa's mom.

I turned away as fast as I could, hoping Mrs. Sawyer wouldn't notice me. No luck. She steered herself more in our direction, wearing her usual warm smile. But as soon as she saw Renny, her face got all tight and wrinkly.

"Jack? Is everything all right?"

I froze, fearing my entire house of cards was about to come crashing down.

Renny said, "How do you do, ma'am," and held out his hand to Mrs. Sawyer. She didn't shake it. "Name's Renny Laforge."

Mrs. Sawyer's lips tightened. "Yes, I'm aware of who you are. What are you doing with Jack?"

"He's been helping me out."

Mrs. Sawyer turned to me, eyebrows raised. "Your mother didn't mention anything about this arrangement."

"Yeah, it's a new volunteer program they have at the hospital where they pair you up with people who don't have family or anyone to help," I said.

"That's very saintly of you." Mrs. Sawyer placed her hand on her heart. "Give, and God will give back to you."

"Uh-huh . . . " I said, looking for a way to end the conversation. Thankfully, our cab pulled up. "Well, there's our ride. I have to get Renny home. Tell Alyssa I'll come by another time."

"I'm happy to say, you don't have to visit her here anymore."

"I don't? Why not?"

"Because she's finally coming home!"

My stomach dropped. "She's all better? Did she get her memory back?"

"No, not yet. But Doctor Wexler says she's on her way to a full recovery. Praise the Lord."

"That's . . . that's great," I said.

Alyssa going home also meant that her sisters were coming home, too. Mrs. Sawyer invited me and Mom to dinner the following weekend to celebrate. "I'll give your mom a call and let her know. Next Sunday. Seven sharp."

"Next Sunday . . . " I repeated, panic already creeping up on me.

Mrs. Sawyer gave Renny a polite nod good-bye, then disappeared into the hospital.

Renny nudged me. "So, am I your father or just your buddy now? Because I'm getting really confused."

I wasn't sure what he was to me and I didn't feel like talking about it. "Let's get you home, okay?"

I opened the door of the cab and helped Renny slide into the backseat, then I got in on the other side. When the cabdriver asked "Where to?" I told him, "Ray's Tow and Salvage on Pine

Road." But Renny said he needed to stop somewhere else on the way.

"You know that minimall up on Garrison?" he asked the driver.

The cabdriver nodded, and we were off. Fifteen minutes later, we pulled up in front of a place called Lee's Donuts.

"You need a sugar fix?" I asked Renny.

"Wait in the cab. I have to tend to some business."

"At the donut shop?"

"At my lawyer's office." Renny pointed to a storefront next to the donut shop. The sign said: LAW OFFICES OF LINCOLN EMERSON.

Renny struggled with his crutches as he got out, and I ran around to help him get on his feet. I offered to help him inside, but Renny said he could manage on his own. He hobbled his way to the building and disappeared through the front door.

I sat wondering why a guy like Renny had a lawyer. Was he in some kind of trouble? Even though I'd known him for a couple of months, Renny was still a big mystery to me.

A half hour later, he hobbled back to the cab, awkwardly slid back in, and didn't say a word about his lawyer or what they had talked about. And I knew better than to ask.

Our next stop was the tow yard, a rundown place on the edge of town surrounded by a chain-link fence and barbed wire. The cab drove past the gate and into a dirt lot full of cars and trucks in every state, from shiny new ones to mangled old ones that reminded me of Renny's sculptures.

Renny paid the cabdriver, and we got out. The cab drove off, spewing mud from its tires. A tall, scrawny man with a soggy-looking cigar in his mouth sauntered out of the garage, where a radio blared classic rock.

"Help you?" he said, chomping his cigar. When the smell reached me, I almost gagged.

"Sure can," Renny said. "See that handsome fella over there?" Renny pointed to his red pickup, which was parked between two gray trucks. "He belongs to me."

Fifty bucks later, Renny had the keys in his hand and we were back on the road.

Since Renny couldn't put any pressure on his knee, I had to drive again. Cigar Guy gave me a funny look as we pulled out of his lot, but I ignored it and focused on what I was doing. Honestly, for only my second time driving, I did pretty well. Renny and I had our rhythm down. He'd shift as I stepped on the clutch. We only stalled out twice and made it back to the cabin in one piece. If Renny had asked me to, I felt like I could've driven all the way to Boston.

When we pulled up, Seneca ran out of the woods to greet us. As Renny got out of the truck, Seneca circled him, wanting to help. Renny crutched himself up the stairs and into the cabin where he dropped into his recliner, propping his bad leg on a stool. He had me bring him his radio and a bottle of Coke. He pulled out his wallet and gave me a one-hundred-dollar bill.

"What's this for?" I asked.

"I owe you. For today."

"Not this much."

"Consider it a bonus."

"For what?"

"A job well done."

"My job's not over yet. I can come back tomorrow to check on you."

"Probably best if I take it from here."

What Renny really meant was, *I don't want you around to watch me die.*

I slipped the one-hundred-dollar bill into my back pocket. I wanted to give Renny a hug good-bye, but something held me back. Our parting felt too real, and that scared me. So I pretended like it was like any other workday. I refilled Seneca's food and water bowls. On cue, he came running into the kitchen. I kneeled down and scratched his head. "Take care of him, okay?" I whispered. Seneca whimpered in understanding.

I said good-bye to Renny and walked out the door.

I grabbed my bike off the porch and headed home. The entire ride, I couldn't stop thinking about Renny sitting in his recliner, waiting for the end, all alone.

Chapter 16

The dreaded day finally arrived—moving day. First thing that morning, four burly guys stomped through the house with a cold efficiency, packing and loading everything into the back of their truck. By noon, they'd cleared out every last box and piece of furniture from our home. All that remained were my mom's and my suitcases filled with clothes and personal things we'd need at the motel. My stomach knotted as the moving truck drove away to the storage place—where our things would sit until Mom and I could agree on somewhere more permanent to live.

When it was all over, I stared out over the desolate landscape that used to be our living room. On the floor where the couch and bookcase and TV stand had been, rectangles of dust had formed. With the curtains gone, the walls revealed long-forgotten memories: crayon scribbles from when I was three, and a spot where Dad had kicked a hole during a fight with Mom. He'd insisted on patching it himself, even though he was terrible at home repairs. It looked like a scar that had never healed.

Mom was outside, shouting at me to hurry up. My throat

tightened, but before I let myself get too choked up, I walked out the front door and closed it behind me for the last time. I'd done everything in my power to save our house, but it hadn't been enough.

When I got to the station wagon, Mom was cramming my bike into the back, contorting it around the boxes and suitcases. There obviously wasn't enough room, but Mom was determined to make it fit. In the end, she had to use a bungee cord to keep the trunk closed.

Mom took one last look at the house before getting into the car. "We had a lot of wonderful memories here. Now let's go make some new ones."

I laughed. "And you think that's going to happen at the Treetop Motel? Don't get your hopes up."

"At least try to keep an open mind," Mom said.

And just like that, we drove away from our old life.

As IF THE day wasn't hard enough, Mom made it worse by announcing that she'd made an appointment for me.

"Like a doctor's appointment?" I asked.

Mom's hands squeezed the steering wheel tighter. "Sort of. It's with a psychiatrist. Her name's Lydia Jenkins."

It took me a second to remember where I'd heard that name before—Trevor's news story. Lydia Jenkins was that idiot who claimed video games rotted kids' brains.

"Why would you make an appointment for me with a shrink? I'm not crazy!"

"I'm not sure how to help you right now, honey. But Mrs. Jenkins might. She talks to lots of kids your age in similar situations."

"So you just decided without me like you did with the house?"

"I asked around. Mrs. Jenkins comes highly recommended. She has an opening Monday afternoon."

"Who's going to bring me? Don't you have work on Monday?"

"I got the afternoon off."

"Where's the money to pay for it? I thought we were broke."

"Insurance should cover most of it."

"Well, I'm not going."

"It's not up for discussion."

"Nothing ever is with you! You're such a bitch!"

As the words came out, I felt a knot in my stomach. Mom stiffened and jerked the wheel. For a second, I was afraid that she would swerve off the road and wrap our car around a telephone pole. I guess that would've put us both out of our misery. But no one died that day. The car just barreled into the Treetop Motel's parking lot, bouncing over some bumps. Mom slammed the brakes as we skidded into a parking spot. My body flung forward, but I caught myself on the dash. Mom held back tears.

"You need help, Jack. Professional help."

She got out and sucked down a cigarette before heading to the lobby to check us in. I needed some air, so I paced around the parking lot, getting a lay of the land.

Whoever built the Treetop Motel designed it to make people feel like they're staying in a real cabin. It's got dark wood siding, white shutters, and these big stone chimneys. But it's all for show. I mean, the chimneys don't even work. The only thing good about moving there was that it was within walking distance of the mall. Normally, I would have been psyched about being so close to the arcade, but I wasn't in a rush to bump into Trevor, since we still weren't speaking. Not even a *Hey, how's it going?* when we passed each other in the hall at school.

Mom came out of the lobby, so I headed across the parking lot to meet her and that's when I passed an all-too-familiar tan Volvo with a bent antenna.

Mom approached, jingling the key to our new home. "We're in room two-oh-four."

I nodded toward the Volvo. "Did you know Mr. Donlan was staying here?"

Mom glanced over at his car, as if she hadn't noticed it. "Well, isn't that a coincidence?"

And in another amazing "coincidence," Mr. Donlan just "happened to appear" on the second-floor balcony, in front of room 205.

"Hey, Jack! Looks like we're going to be neighbors!" he called down.

"What are the odds of that, huh?" I said.

Mom waved up at Mr. Donlan and said hi with this stupid giggle, like she was a ten-year-old with a crush. It was obvious from the way they talked that running into each other at the motel was no surprise. I didn't have solid proof, but I would've bet a lot of money that Mom and Mr. Donlan had conspired to move in next to each other. I still cringe thinking about it.

Mom unlocked the door and I walked into the room, a wave of mustiness hitting me. There were two beds with stained comforters, shag carpeting, and peeling, flowery wallpaper. A faded painting of a river with trees hung over one bed. A dead deer's head loomed above the other. Since everything else about the motel was phony, I assumed the head was too, but I wasn't taking any chances, so I threw my suitcase on the bed under the painting. Mom took the one with the deer's head. She didn't even argue about it.

After we unpacked the car and got settled, Mom washed up

and put on earrings and lipstick. She casually dropped that she and Mr. Donlan were going to grab a bite to eat at the diner across the street. Not that I wanted to go, but she didn't invite me to join them.

"Whatever," I said, flopping onto my bed. "I'll just be here gnawing on a dead deer's head."

"Don't be gross. I'll you bring back some takeout, okay?"

"Sure, have fun. Just don't stay out too late."

"What is that supposed to mean?"

"I'm not stupid. I know what's going on."

"Nothing's going on." Mom checked her hair in the mirror and undid the top button of her blouse. "I'm just getting dinner with a friend."

I tried to keep my mouth shut, but I couldn't. "What do you think is going to happen? Huh? That after a romantic meal at a greasy diner, you and Mr. Donlan are going to get back together and we'll all live happily ever after at the Treetop Motel?"

Mom glared at me in the mirror. "Boy, Mrs. Jenkins sure has her work cut out for her."

"Maybe you're the one who should talk to a shrink, not me."

Mom was speechless. She grabbed her pocketbook and slammed the door on her way out.

She didn't get back to the room until three hours later, her cheeks flushed, holding a take-out box. She dropped it on the table and disappeared into the bathroom. I took one look at the cold hamburger and soggy french fries that was supposed to be my dinner and threw it all in the trash.

Chapter 17

The night after we moved into the motel, Mom and I headed over to the Sawyers' for Alyssa's welcome home dinner. I rang the doorbell and braced myself. I wasn't ready to see Alyssa again. Thankfully, it was her little sister Allison who greeted us. I hadn't seen her since before the accident.

"Jack!" she squealed, exposing a gaping hole in her top row of teeth.

"Hey, Allison. Looks like you lost a tooth there."

"Yeah! And this one's about to fall out next! See?" She jiggled the loose tooth with her tongue.

Mom and I walked in. Alyssa's other sister, Althea, was helping Mrs. Sawyer set the table. She was the middle child, and the spitting image of her mother.

"Welcome!" said Mrs. Sawyer with a big smile. "Hope you're both hungry!"

"Are you making lasagna?" I asked, catching a whiff of tomatoes and onions.

"That's right. I've been cooking all of Alyssa's favorite foods since she came home." I hadn't had a home-cooked meal in months, and the only thing I'd eaten that day was a bag of chips from the motel vending machine. So at the very least, I'd get some decent food out of the visit. Mom thanked Mrs. Sawyer for inviting us, then disappeared into the kitchen to give her a hand. I helped Althea and Allison finish setting the table. When we were done, I paced around, looking at the Sawyer family photos on the walls as if I hadn't seen them a million times already. Althea told me Alyssa was up in her room if I wanted to say hi.

"I can wait until she comes down."

"Don't be silly!" Allison said. "She's going to be so excited to see you!"

She grabbed my hand and pulled me up the stairs, shouting, "Jack's here!" Alyssa had shut her door and wasn't answering it. "Alyssa, did you hear me?! Jack's here!"

"Go away." The door muffled Alyssa's voice. I wasn't sure if she was talking to her sister or to me. Probably both.

"She's been acting this way ever since she got home," Allison whispered. "She barely comes out of her room. Okay, bye!"

She dashed down the stairs like a little sprite. I was about to leave, but the door opened a crack and Alyssa's eye peered out, checking to see if anyone was still there. When she saw it was just me, she opened the door a little wider and let me in. She was wearing a fuzzy pink nightgown, her hair all tangled. She retreated to her bed and pulled the poofy comforter over her.

I entered her room, carefully stepping across the carpet like it was thin ice that could swallow me up at any second. Alyssa stared at me, waiting for me to talk first.

"How does it feel to be home?" I asked.

"Different, I guess."

"Different how?"

"I don't know . . . everyone keeps acting like nothing's changed, like the past three months never happened. Dad still works all the time, and Mom keeps busying herself with cooking and cleaning the house so it looks perfect for all the people who come over. Now you walk in here acting like everything's fine between us."

"I think everyone's just ready for things to get back to normal," I said.

"You don't get it. None of you do. Normal doesn't exist for me anymore."

That's when I spotted Aldous Watts's eyes peering at me from behind Alyssa's pillow. My heart pounded in my head.

"Is that . . . "

Alyssa reached behind her pillow and pulled out a copy of *Both Here and Gone*.

"How'd you get that?" I asked, eyeing the book like it was radioactive.

"Mr. Donlan," she said. "He visited me the day before I got out of the hospital. He's been really nice to me."

"You tricked him into getting the book out of the library for you?"

"I didn't trick anybody. I asked nicely. And he was glad to help. I think he's looking for answers, too."

"About what?"

"About what life after death is like. Heaven, the hereafter, whatever you want to call it."

"Because of what happened to Scotty?"

"Yeah. Mr. Donlan told me he wished he could talk to him, to know if he's still suffering."

"Nobody really knows for sure what happens after you die, especially not this Aldous Watts guy."

"How would you know? You haven't read his book. But I did. You want to know what I learned?"

I didn't. But that didn't stop Alyssa from telling me, anyway.

"So that dream I keep having? Where I see that man in the water? It's not a dream at all. It's a memory."

My body tensed. A shiver shot through me.

"Listen to this." Alyssa flipped to a page she'd bookmarked and started reading. "'Subjects who had suffered from acute memory loss often reported having dreams related to their near-death experience. Upon further investigation, it appeared these dreams were actually buried memories related to the individual's cause of death.'" She closed the book and looked up at me. "So if that's true, it means the man from my dreams must have been at the lake when I drowned but I just can't remember him. Remind me who else was there that day."

"I already told you. Me, Trevor, and my mom. There were a few other locals out skating. Just strangers. The paramedics showed up after. You know, I bet that's who you've been seeing in your dream—Mr. Donlan."

"I don't think so."

"How do you know? You said you can't see the man's face, right?"

"Yeah . . . "

"Mr. Donlan brought you back to life. It has to be him."

"Maybe." She didn't sound convinced.

"I know you want to believe there's more to it, but there isn't. No matter what Aldous Watts wrote in his stupid book."

"Then I guess the only way I'll know for sure is to ask the man himself when I see him."

My breath caught in my throat. "You're going to meet him? When?"

"As soon as I can."

Alyssa explained how she had pulled out Aldous Watts's letter the day after she got home from the hospital. She found it crumpled up at the bottom of her mom's tote bag. She jotted down his address and wrote him a letter back, saying that she'd read his book and wanted to talk to him in person. She included her phone number and gave him a specific time to call when she knew her mom wouldn't be around. Then she snuck the letter into her dad's outgoing business mail.

If Alyssa spoke with Aldous Watts, it would set off a bomb of epic proportions. I had to stop it from going off, for Alyssa's protection.

"Even if this guy gets back to you, I don't think meeting him face to face it a great idea," I said.

"Why not?"

"What if he tries to kidnap you or something?"

"Why would he do that?"

"How do you even plan on seeing him without your parents knowing?"

"I'll figure it out. Just keep this between us, okay?"

"Fine, but I think you'd feel better if you stopped obsessing about all this death stuff."

"I want to know what happened to me when I died."

"Sometimes knowing just makes things worse. Or did you forget what happened on 'take your kid to work day'?"

"No. I definitely remember that . . . "

Alyssa had always known her father's job involved being around dead bodies and making funeral arrangements. But as a kid, she didn't understand exactly what that really meant. When we were in second grade, our class got a day off from school to visit where our parents worked. While I hung out in my dad's boring office building, Alyssa stayed home because that's where her dad worked. But when her father headed down to the basement, he told her to stay upstairs. He said his work wasn't for the eyes of little girls. That only fueled Alyssa's curiosity, and a little while later, she sneaked down the stairs.

Her eyes flicked around the embalming room, with its stainless steel tables and cabinets filled with jars, brushes, and other scary-looking tools. Her father stood beside his table, a dead woman's body lying on it. She was pretty young, like in her twenties. A deer had run out in front of her car and when she swerved to avoid it, she crashed into a tree. Totally random. But seeing the dead body wasn't what had the biggest impact on Alyssa.

She watched as her father delicately pulled down the woman's eyelids to swipe on eyeshadow and dabbed her cheeks with blush. He dressed the body in a floral print dress and adorned her with jewelry. Then he airbrushed the woman's pale face, adding back color before gently running his fingers across the cheek to smooth out any imperfections in the makeup. He painted red on her lips and delicately molded them into a peaceful smile.

Her father treated the woman's corpse with such love and tenderness. It was a side of her father she'd never seen or experienced before. He'd never treated her that way.

Alyssa ran to her room and buried herself under her covers and stayed there for the rest of the day, haunted by what she'd seen. She never went back into the basement and her father never knew she'd watched him.

"If you meet with Aldous Watts, it'll be like going into that basement all over again," I said.

"That's what you don't seem to get, Jack. I was glad I saw what my father did that day."

"You were?"

"Yes, because even though it upset me, it showed me how much we love the dead, sometimes more than the living."

BEFORE EVERYONE COULD EAT, we all held hands around the table while Mr. Sawyer bowed his head and said grace.

"Bless us, O Lord, and these thy gifts that we're about to receive from thy bounty through Christ, our Lord. Amen."

"Amen," everyone replied.

I stayed quiet. Of all the ways you could say grace, Mr. Sawyer's version was by-the-books. He didn't even try to make it personal. There was no mention of his daughter being resurrected or his family being back together or the smells of the lasagna on the table. It was kind of strange. Like being at a birthday party where no one sang "Happy Birthday."

During dinner, Allison and Althea told dumb kid knock-knock jokes, which the adults laughed at half-heartedly. Mom and the Sawyers made small talk about people in town and the weather and crap like that. No one spoke about the lake or "the incident," which was fine by me. If they could all pretend things were back to normal, so could I.

The whole time, I picked at my lasagna, trying to figure out a way to stop Alyssa from meeting Aldous Watts. It was possible the letter might get lost in the mail or that Aldous Watts wouldn't write back, but I couldn't count on either of those things.

Before dessert was served, Mr. Sawyer excused himself from the table and disappeared into the basement, saying he needed to get back to work. I noticed everyone else's plates were empty. I'd barely made a dent in my lasagna, which was cold by then.

"You didn't like it?" Mrs. Sawyer asked me as she began clearing the table.

"It was delicious," I said. "I'm just not that hungry, I guess."

I offered to help Mrs. Sawyer clean the dishes, which got me a suspicious look from Mom because I never offered to clean up anything at home.

While Allison and Althea entertained Mom with more jokes, I followed Mrs. Sawyer into the kitchen and stacked the dirty dishes in the sink.

"Thank you for helping," she said.

"No problem. I imagine everyone in the neighborhood has been stopping by to pitch in."

"Isn't it remarkable how the Holy Spirit works through community?"

"What about Mr. Donlan? Has he come by since Alyssa got home?"

"No, not yet. Why?"

"Because he got that book out of the library for Alyssa. He'll need to return it soon."

It wasn't the most natural way to alert Mrs. Sawyer that Alyssa was up to something, but it got the job done.

Mrs. Sawyer dropped a stack of dishes into the sink, almost breaking them. "What book?"

I lowered my voice and told her about how Alyssa found Aldous Watts's letter and planned to meet with him secretly. Mrs. Sawyer thanked me for telling her and assured me she'd handle the situation. Problem solved.

Afterward, Mrs. Sawyer brought out apple cobbler for dessert. As everyone ate, Alyssa glanced back and forth between me and her mom like she knew something was up.

Once dessert was over, I wanted out of there as fast as possible, but Mom kept chit-chatting with Mrs. Sawyer. I threw on my coat and told Mom I'd meet her in the car. But before I could get out, Alyssa blocked the door, arms crossed, glaring at me all suspiciously.

"What were you and my mom talking about in the kitchen?"

"Uh, she was just asking me about school," I said.

"Nothing about Aldous Watts?"

"No, I didn't mention him."

143

I could feel the doubt radiating from her piercing gaze, so I hurried out the door before she could interrogate me any further. I was drowning in a sea of my own lies and no one was coming to save me.

Chapter 18

On the day of my appointment with the shrink, Mom picked me up after school and we drove to a brick office building on Main Street. The tiny waiting room only had two folding chairs and a fake potted plant. Mom rang a buzzer on the wall by a door, and a minute later, a woman in a black skirt and glasses came out. She said good afternoon with a plastered-on smile and introduced herself as Mrs. Jenkins, but I already recognized her from TV. While Mom sat in the waiting room and filled out some forms, Mrs. Jenkins led me to a room down the hall.

Her office had an old wood desk and shelves full of books I'd never heard of, with titles about psychology and psychiatry. She told me to take a seat on the couch. My heart started racing. Looking for a way out of my situation, I pulled Renny's hundred-dollar bill out of my pocket and offered it to Mrs. Jenkins. "This is yours, if you want it."

She eyed the money, then me. "And what are you expecting in exchange?" she asked.

I told her I was hoping we could skip the session and Mrs. Jenkins could just let my mom know I was fine and that I didn't need therapy. Mrs. Jenkins stared at me like she was trying to figure out if I was serious.

"I'm not joking," I said.

"And I'm not going to take your money," she said.

I stuffed the hundred bucks back in my pocket and dropped onto the couch. "Fine. Let's get this over with."

Mrs. Jenkins picked up a notebook and pen and sat in a leather chair across from me. "Your mother told me about your family situation. I'm here to help you though this difficult time and to act as your ally. It's important for you to understand that all your feelings are valid. Sometimes it's hard to talk about your sadness and anger and worries, but in this office, it's all safe to share. So . . . how are you feeling today, Jack?"

I didn't know what to say. No one had ever really wanted to know about my feelings. Sure, Mom would ask, "How was school today?" Or "Did you have fun with Trevor at the mall?" But her questions always sounded parroted, like she'd gotten them from a parenting pamphlet about "how to talk to your teenager." So I could get away with saying "fine" and that would satisfy Mom. Mrs. Jenkins didn't seem like the type of lady who was going to take "fine" for an answer.

I tried anyway.

"I'm fine."

Mrs. Jenkins scribbled some notes, then asked, "Do you know why your mother wanted you to talk to me?"

"Not really."

More scribbles. I couldn't see what she was writing, but I figured it wasn't anything good.

"She told me what happened when your house was being sold. Can you tell me about that?"

"There's not much to tell."

Mrs. Jenkins didn't realize who she was dealing with.

Maybe I couldn't bribe her, but I could dodge her questions for forty-five minutes, easy. Just run out the clock.

"Transitions can be difficult," she said. "And it sounds like you've had a lot of changes in your life over the past year. What's been the hardest one?"

After about a minute of me not saying anything, Mrs. Jenkins let out a long sigh. *Good*, I thought, *I'm getting under her skin.*

"Jack, this only works if you talk to me. I know it can be hard and scary to open up about these kinds of things, but I promise you'll feel better once you do."

The tone of Mrs. Jenkins' voice was soothing. It sounded like she really cared. But that was impossible. She'd only known me for, like, five minutes. I kept quiet.

"Your mother mentioned that your father left quite suddenly last year to walk the Appalachian Trail. Is that right?"

"Mmm-hmm."

"I see . . . and how was that for you?"

"How was what?"

"Often when a loved one becomes absent, the loss can be profound and intense. How did you feel after your father left?"

"Abandoned," "devastated," and "worthless" were the words that came to mind. But if I gave Mrs. Jenkins an honest answer, it would only open me up to more scrutiny. She'd keep picking away at me, demanding to know more and more. And I wasn't ready to spill my guts. So I stuck with my standard response.

"Fine."

"Did you feel sad?"

"Maybe."

"Angry?"

"Sort of."

"And as we sit here today, are you still feeling sad or angry about your father leaving?"

147

"I don't know."

It went on like that for the rest of the session. Mrs. Jenkins would ask me questions about Dad or my home life or school and I'd reply with vague answers, hoping she'd eventually give up. She didn't.

Instead, every few minutes, she'd jot down another note on her pad. Like she was gathering evidence against me. I had to give the woman credit. She didn't lose her cool with me the way Mom usually did when I evaded her questions. Which meant I needed to throw Mrs. Jenkins a curveball and say something so off-the-wall that she'd consider me a lost cause and refuse to see me again.

With time almost up, Mrs. Jenkins asked if there was anything she didn't specifically ask that I wanted to talk about.

"Actually, there is," I said, shifting my imagination into overdrive.

She perked up and leaned forward in her chair. "Go ahead, I'm listening."

"So, there's some stuff going on in my family you should know about. With my mom. See, the thing is, I think she's a Russian spy. She's always sneaking out of the house at weird times, like in the middle of the night. One time, I followed her, and she went to this hidden underground bunker in the woods. I'm pretty sure she's sending her reports to Russia through video games. On the high-score screen there are players' initials, only they're not real initials—the letters are actually a code and only other Russian spies have the cypher."

Mrs. Jenkins stared at me blankly, then said, "That sounds very serious. Thank you for telling me."

And with that, the session was over.

On the way out to the car, Mom asked me how it went.

"Fine," I said.

IT TURNED out that my ploy to get out of seeing Mrs. Jenkins failed. After the appointment, Mrs. Jenkins called Mom to schedule another session as soon as possible so she could finish her assessment. Apparently she had "some concerns." So that Friday, Mom picked me up from school early and we headed back to Mrs. Jenkins's office. As we pulled into the parking lot, I told Mom I didn't want to go in because I didn't like the way Mrs. Jenkins had treated me the last time.

"What way?" she asked.

"Like I was some lab rat she was studying."

Mom put a hand on my knee and said she knew this was hard, but that she was proud of me for being so brave. She sounded sincere, but I wasn't buying it. She was just trying to get me to do what she wanted, which was to let Mrs. Jenkins observe me and write notes about how I behaved. Which is exactly what they do to lab rats. I saw a filmstrip about it in my seventh-grade science class.

When I got to her office, Mrs. Jenkins picked up our conversation exactly where we'd ended it.

"Last time, you told me a story about your mother being a Russian spy. What made you say that?"

"I don't know," I said.

Mrs. Jenkins nodded and jotted down a note.

"And what about your mood?"

"What about it?"

"Have you been sad lately?"

"I don't know."

Mrs. Jenkins said that sadness is a completely normal emotion, but sometimes when all we feel is sad, that can be a problem. I told her it was better to be real sad than fake happy,

149

like some people I knew—Mom, Trevor, Mrs. Sawyer, to name a few.

Then, out of nowhere, Mrs. Jenkins asked if I'd ever had thoughts about hurting myself. I never had. Not seriously, anyway. But there was one time when Alyssa wanted to play a game where you share a fantasy about killing yourself. The game didn't sound very fun, but I went along with it. I said I'd probably take my mom's sleeping pills because I wouldn't want to feel any pain. Alyssa's fantasy was way worse. She wanted to go into her basement where her father worked and lie on the table where he embalmed dead bodies. Then she would use one of his scalpels to slit her wrists. That way, when her father showed up to work and found Alyssa's dead body covered in blood, he'd be overcome with grief and guilt. I said it sounded pretty over-the-top. Alyssa thought it was the only way she'd ever really get her father's attention.

"Jack?" Mrs. Jenkins said.

"What?"

"You didn't answer my question. Have you ever considered hurting yourself?"

If I told Mrs. Jenkins about Alyssa's game, I was scared she'd call the guys in white coats and they'd drag me off to the nuthouse. Like the men who took Norma Desmond away in *Sunset Boulevard*. So, I told her that the thought of hurting myself had never crossed my mind. She kept bombarding me with questions, anyway.

"What were you just thinking about?"

"Nothing."

"You were staring off into the distance. Where did your mind go?"

"Nowhere."

For the rest of the session, Mrs. Jenkins badgered me with questions: "Do you have an appetite?" "Do you still enjoy doing the things you used to do, such as playing with your friends?" "How are you doing in school?"

I kept my responses short. "Sometimes." "Depends." "So-so."

I guess I didn't give her the right answers because after the session ended, Mrs. Jenkins summoned Mom into her office to talk to her alone. I sat in the waiting room, watching the clock as its hands slowly ticked by. When Mom finally came out, her eye makeup was a little runny, and she was wiping her nose with a tissue. She tucked a small piece of paper into her purse.

"We have to make a stop on the way back to the motel," she informed me.

THE SUN WAS DOWN by the time we got to the drugstore. Inside, Mom gave the piece of paper to a man in a white lab coat who worked at the pharmacy. She didn't tell me what was written on the paper, but I knew it was a prescription for something. I waited by the comic book rack and flipped open an issue of *X-Men* and pretended to read while I kept my eye on Mom. After a few minutes, the pharmacist came back to the counter and gave Mom a brown paper bag like the kind she packed my lunches in.

Mom bought me the comic book even though I didn't ask her to, which meant she wanted something in return.

When we got to our motel room, Mom pulled a yellowy-orange plastic bottle out of the bag and popped open the cap and plucked out a pill. She filled a glass with water from the bathroom sink and handed me the pill. It was purple and oval, like the candy that comes out of Pez dispensers.

"I need you to take this," Mom said.

"What is it?"

"Mrs. Jenkins told me it will help you start feeling better."

"But what is it?"

"Just take it, Jack."

"You can't make me take drugs." I realized how much I sounded like Renny.

"These aren't drugs, honey. They're medicine."

"But you got these pills from a *drug*store."

"The medicine is safe."

"Have you taken it before?"

"No."

"Then how would you know if it's safe?"

"Because a medical professional prescribed it for you. Please, help me out here."

She shoved the glass into my hand, determined to make me take it. Water sloshed out, splashing my arm. In retaliation, I pushed the glass back so hard that the rest of the water spilled out, soaking her blouse. It was an accident, but kind of not. I threw the pill on the floor.

The slap came like a lightning bolt, so fast that I didn't have time to react. A second later, the entire side of my face was on fire. Tears threatened to spill out, but I refused to give Mom the satisfaction, so I stuffed them back down. Mom's face turned red, and she started sweating. Her breathing was ragged and heavy, like she'd just run a mile. Her eyes were wide, and she pressed her hands to her mouth in shock.

"Jack . . . I didn't mean . . . " Her voice shook.

She reached for me and I swatted her hand away and screamed at her to leave me alone. To go away forever. Mom begged me to keep my voice down so I didn't disturb the other guests.

"You mean Mr. Donlan? Yeah, he probably won't want to date you when he finds out you beat your own son!"

"That's not what happened."

"You've been wanting to do that for weeks! You just needed an excuse!"

"It was an accident!"

"Then you won't mind if I mention this little 'accident' to Mrs. Jenkins during our next session."

"Please, Jack . . . honey . . . you know I would never hurt you. You know that, right?"

She kept sputtering apologies and going on and on about how that had never happened before and it would never happen again. I wanted to believe her, but my entire body tensed. And before I knew it, my vision started going blurry. Like when I'd panicked and bolted out of the Army Surplus store, but worse. I shut my eyes hard. Opened them again. I started getting dizzy and my body burned like a furnace and I thought I might pass out.

I heard Mom calling my name, but I was making a mad dash to the bathroom. I slammed the door and dropped to my knees, barely making it to the toilet.

I don't know how long I sat on the bathroom floor, but it was a while. After puking my guts out, I remember Mom talking to me through the door, trying to convince me to open it. I told her again to go away and leave me alone. I said I was fine, even though I obviously wasn't. She must have finally got the hint that I didn't want her around because, at some point, I heard her leave the room and slam the door.

Eventually I picked myself up and splashed some water on my face. I put my ear to the door and didn't hear Mom, so I went back into the room and curled up on the bed. That's when I heard sobbing through the wall. Mom had gone over to Mr. Donlan's room to cry on his shoulder. I didn't want to think about what else she was going to do over there, so I put on the TV and turned the volume way up.

I tried to focus on the screen, but my eyes kept drifting to

153

the prescription bottle on the bedside table. I grabbed it and dumped a pile of pills in my hand.

"What are you planning on doing with those?"

Dorothy Jackson was back, standing at the foot of my bed, microphone pointed at me.

"I was thinking about swallowing all of them."

"Aren't you concerned you could die?"

"Or they might just make me feel really, really happy."

"Are you willing to take the risk to find out?"

I took another look at the pills, then went into the bathroom and tossed them into the toilet. The tiny purple tablets splashed into the bowl like dozens of tiny high divers. I flushed, and the pills whirlpooled down the drain. As I slipped on my shoes and pulled on my jacket, Dorothy Jackson hit me with one last question.

"Where are you going?"

"To the one place I can hide from the world."

I shut the door on my imaginary interrogator, then hopped on my bike and rode like hell.

Chapter 19

B y the time I finally made it to Old Mill Road, I was out of breath, my legs spent. I headed up the path to Renny's cabin. The lights were off, so I assumed Renny was asleep inside. I ditched my bike next to one of his sculptures and crept past the cabin to the bunker.

The hatch doors groaned as I pulled them open. I held my breath, bracing for Renny to come barreling out, shotgun in hand. But he never did. Heart racing, I hurried to the bottom of the stairs and yanked on the door handle—locked. Frustrated, I was about to head up to the cabin for Renny's keys when I heard a low growl followed by a frantic scratching at the door. Terrified that a wolf was about to bust out of the bunker and eat me, I jumped back. But then Renny's voice called from inside.

"Whoever's out there, you should know I'm armed!" He sounded pissed.

"Don't shoot! It's me! Jack!"

It was quiet for a second, then Renny unlocked the door and swung it open. He flicked the lights on, blinding me for a moment. Renny stood there, in his long underwear, supporting himself with his shotgun instead of his crutches. The growling

I'd heard had been Seneca. He bounded out and jumped up to lick me.

"What the hell are you doing here?" Renny said, scowling. But there was a hint in his voice that he was happy to see me.

I gave him the answer that felt closest to the truth, because there were too many reasons to choose from. "I need somewhere to hide out for a little while. I didn't think you'd be down here."

"Wasn't planning to be. But I figured I should get some use out of it before I'm gone. So, a few days ago, I moved in. There are worse places to spend my remaining time on earth."

"Don't say that."

"Why not? It's a fact."

"Yeah, but you don't have to say it."

Renny gave me a long, silent stare while he decided my fate.

"Please," I said. "I don't have anywhere else to go."

Finally, Renny nodded and gestured toward the back of the room. "The top bunk's made up. You're welcome to it."

"Thanks."

"I'm only agreeing to this because I'm too damn tired to argue and I want to go back to bed. But you need to leave in the morning. Got it?"

"Okay."

Renny was snoring by the time I climbed into bed. Now that I had some distance from Mom, my entire body relaxed. All my pent-up anger and energy evaporated and before I knew it, I was asleep.

I woke up the next morning to the smell of something sweet. I peeled open my eyes. Renny was at the hotplate, flipping pancakes. I climbed down out of the top bunk and Seneca ran over and licked my hand.

"I think Seneca missed you," Renny said.

"I missed him, too."

"Hungry?"

"Starving."

Renny handed me a dish with a stack of pancakes, and I drowned them in maple syrup.

"After breakfast, you should be on your way."

"All right," I said. Even though I wanted to devour the pancakes, I paced myself, since I was in no rush to leave.

Renny lowered himself into his chair and stuffed a wedge of pancakes into his mouth, eyeing me. "Does your mom know you're out here?" Bits of pancake exploded out of his mouth as he spoke.

"Not exactly."

"You sneaked out on her?"

"Yeah."

"Don't you think she might be worried about you?"

"She doesn't care. Me being gone is probably a relief to her."

Renny pointed to my face with his fork. "Did she give you that bruise?"

I rubbed my cheek. It was still a little sore. "It was an accident. We got in an argument."

"About what?"

"Nothing. And everything."

"Sounds like most arguments I've had in my life. But hiding in a bunker won't solve your problems."

"Why not? That's what you're doing."

"It's not the same thing. Not by a long shot."

"If you say so," I said with a shrug.

We ate the rest of our breakfast in silence. When we finished, Renny picked up our plates and went to put them in the sink. But he'd barely made it two steps when he keeled over on his crutches and crashed to the floor. The plates shattered. I rushed over to him and pulled him up to sitting.

"Are you all right?"

"I'm fine. Still getting used to these damn crutches."

But the crutches weren't the problem. Renny was moving slower than the last time I'd seen him, even considering his busted knee. His face was paler than ever, his cheeks had become hollow pits, and his clothes hung looser. He looked like he'd aged ten years since leaving the hospital.

I picked Renny off the floor and got him to the chair, then swept up the broken dishes. Once I'd cleaned everything up, Renny nodded toward the door.

"It's best you head out now," he said without looking at me. "I can handle it from here."

I didn't move. I wasn't ready to go back to the motel and deal with Mom, but staying meant watching Renny waste away.

"Sure you don't need some extra help?" I said.

"There's nothing you can do to help me anymore."

He was right, but I wanted to believe that my staying would prevent the worst. Like, as long as I was keeping tabs on him, death couldn't snatch him away.

"If you want me to go, you'll have to drag me up the stairs yourself," I said. "And you're in no shape to do that."

Renny didn't respond. He just pointed to a coffeepot on the stove.

"Then make yourself useful and pour me a cup of joe, would ya?"

I grabbed a mug and poured. The coffee came out dense and dark, smelling like the woods. I handed Renny the steaming mug.

"Pour yourself a cup, too."

"I don't drink coffee."

"I'll make a deal with you," Renny said. "You drink a cup and I'll let you stay as long as you like."

"Won't it stunt my growth or something?"

"Where'd you hear that nonsense? I started drinking coffee when I was younger than you and I sprouted up just fine."

"All right." I poured myself a cup and took a sip. It was so bitter I could barely swallow it. I was coughing and making gagging noises.

"You gotta finish the whole cup."

"It's horrible. How can you drink this stuff?"

Renny chuckled. "It grows on you."

Why did Renny come up with the coffee-for-shelter deal? I think he wanted to prove that he was still calling the shots, even though he was sick. So I followed his orders and drank it all. At least he let me put some sugar in it, which helped with the flavor. By the time I took my last sip, my nerves were buzzing.

Renny smiled. "Looks like we're going to be roommates."

Mom's slap had been like an atomic bomb going off. So it only made sense to take refuge in the bunker while I waited out my emotional nuclear winter. Made sense to me, anyway. Other than letting Seneca out to run around and pee on all the trees, I stayed underground. There was something comforting about being in the bunker, being surrounded by the earth. It was like a cocoon. A safe place where my problems wouldn't find me. But I knew Renny's bunker couldn't protect me forever. Eventually I'd have to return to the real world and deal with the fallout.

After breakfast that first day, Renny and I did a puzzle. We ate baked beans from a can and some white bread for lunch and a whole chocolate bar for dessert. Who knew food from the Army Surplus store could taste so delicious?

Once our bellies were full, Renny asked if I played cards.

"Like go fish?" I asked.

"No. I'm talking about a proper card game. Texas Hold 'Em."

"There's a card game about Texas?"

"It's a poker game. You put down money and try to get the best hand."

Renny got out a deck of cards and started shuffling. I reached into my pocket and pulled out a handful of quarters from the last time I'd been at the arcade. "This is all I have."

"That'll work."

Renny had me stack the quarters, then made a stack of his own. "Normally you play with more than two people. But since we're not expecting any guests, we'll make do."

He insisted that poker was the greatest game in the world because of how complex it was. I told him I might be good at poker since I played a lot of chess, but Renny laughed. "The two games are nothing alike. Chess is all about strategy and patterns. It's very logical. Poker's a psychological game. The luck of the draw is just as important as looking in your opponent's eyes to tell if they're bluffing."

"So you can lie in poker?" I asked.

"It's more like . . . obscuring the truth."

It sounded like my kind of game.

Renny described the rules and the rankings of different hands. The best is a royal flush, where you have all face cards of the same suit, which is pretty rare. But the coolest part about poker is that you don't need to be holding the best cards. You just have to make everyone *think* you are. So even if you only have a pair of twos, you could beat someone with four kings. But if you bluff and someone calls you on it, you have to show your cards, and the jig is up. And if nobody calls your bluff, you keep your cards to yourself and the other players never find out if you were fooling them.

We played a couple of practice hands until I got a feel for the game. Then we played for real.

Renny tossed a quarter into the middle of the table, and I did the same. That was the ante. The cost of playing. Then he dealt two cards face down. We did one round of betting, then Renny dealt three more cards in the center of the table, face up. "The flop," he called it. Those cards were for both of us to use. Renny tossed another quarter into the pot.

"Raise."

There was an eight showing on the table. I had another eight in my hand. Two of a kind. It might not be enough to win, but I figured I had a good chance of bluffing Renny, so I matched his quarter and added another one.

"Raise," I said confidently.

Renny looked into my eyes, studying me. Then he dealt another card face up. He raised again. I matched him until I was out of quarters. Once he'd dealt the last card, Renny called and laid out his hand. A full house. I still only had the two eights. Not enough to win.

Renny raked the pile of quarters to his side of the table. That was the moment I realized the stakes were real, and that Renny wouldn't go easy on me. You can lose or win real money. Renny called it, "having skin in the game."

Since I was out of money, Renny loaned me five bucks in quarters, and we played a few more rounds. I kept getting terrible hands and trying to bluff, and Renny kept calling me out and winning.

"How do you know when I'm bluffing?" I asked.

"You have a tell."

"But I didn't tell you anything."

"Not with your words. With your actions. A tell is

something you do without realizing. Like an unconscious, nervous reaction."

My insides froze. "And I have one?"

"Sure do," Renny said with a chuckle. "It took me a few rounds to pick up on it, but it's clear as day."

"What is it?"

"If I point it out, then you'll stop doing it and I lose my advantage."

I tried to remember all the things I did during the game but I didn't have the first clue about what my tell was. I do a lot of things when I get nervous—sit on my hands, tug on my ear, scratch my chin, blink a lot, bounce my knee up and down, and crack my knuckles. It could've been any of those things, but I had no idea which one it was. And that's how I ended up owing Renny ten bucks by the end of the game.

SOMETIME LATER THAT AFTERNOON, while Renny was dozing on the couch, I checked out his bookshelf, which was fully stocked like his pantry. There was one book by Aristotle and another by Plato. They were names I'd heard before, old philosophers from like a million years ago. But I'd never read them and doubted I ever would. At the end of one row was a thick book with a gold cross on the binding. Renny had never struck me as a church-going guy, so it surprised me he owned a Bible. I pulled it out and was flipping through the tissue-thin pages when Renny woke up.

"Hands off," he snarled, snatching the Bible out of my hands.

"Do you believe in God?" I asked.

Renny shrugged. "The jury's still out on that, but I have a sense of curiosity about the matter. You?"

"Still mulling it over, too. But if there is a God, shouldn't there be a lot less pain and suffering?"

"What if I told you that pain and suffering are necessary parts of living?"

"I'd say living sounds like it sucks."

Renny nodded, like he'd expected me to say that. "Do you know why I named my dog Seneca?"

"Because it's a cool-sounding name?"

"Seneca was a philosopher. One of the Stoics."

"Did he and Thoreau hang out?"

"No, the Stoics were around a couple thousand years earlier, even before the Bible was written." Renny pulled out a book called *Letters from a Stoic*. He said that most people thought the Stoics weren't emotional. But it was the opposite. They were actually pretty happy. "Want to know their secret?"

"Sure."

"They didn't shy away from death, but reflected on it. Every morning when they woke up and every night before falling asleep. They didn't waste time worrying about if they were going to die because that was a given. Instead, they were grateful for every breath."

"What does that have to do with whether God's real?" I asked.

"I'm saying it doesn't matter if God's pulling the strings up in heaven or not. Either way, you have to live your life. Might as well enjoy it."

"But it does matter. Because if God isn't real, nothing in life means anything. And if he is real, then all the death and suffering are his fault."

"So you think life is unfair, and you want to blame God? You're exactly like Job." Renny patted the cover of his Bible. "He's got a story in here. You should hear it. Sit down."

I plopped down in the chair across from Renny as he

cracked open the book and flipped the pages. Inside, I noticed a piece of paper sticking out. I thought it was a bookmark, but Renny shoved it back between the pages, hiding it from view.

Seneca—the dog, not the philosopher—came over and I pet his head as Renny read from the Book of Job. It was like being back at Sunday Mass when Father Murray would read Bible passages and I'd get so bored I'd nod off. But this story was different. I mean, I didn't understand half of what Renny was saying, but Job's story was interesting and kept my attention. I really felt for the guy. But he had it way worse than I did. First off, his animals and servants all died. Then his kids died, too. So Job went to God and accused him of neglecting his responsibilities and blamed him for all the misery in his life. God took him on an adventure to explore the universe and showed Job all these amazing places and a creature called a Leviathan. God's point was that the universe is ordered and chaotic at the same time.

"But God never explains to Job why there's so much suffering in the world," I said after Renny finished reading.

"That's the whole point of the story," Renny said. "It explains why the universe wasn't designed to prevent suffering. Sometimes awful things happen for no damn good reason."

"But why do good people have to suffer? Shouldn't bad things only happen to bad people?"

"The world isn't like in your *Star Wars* movies. Nobody is a hundred percent good or bad. There are no perfect saints or evil villains."

"If there aren't villains, then why'd you have to fight in a war, huh?" But my attempt to stump Renny didn't rattle him one bit.

"The Viet Cong did horrible things, but the U.S. had plenty of blood on its hands, too. Both sides lied and killed innocent people. Our government claimed Agent Orange was harmless, which was a load of hogwash. I'm proof."

"Don't you hate them for dropping chemicals on you? For giving you cancer?"

"I'm not the first soldier who ever died because their own government screwed them over."

"How can you be so forgiving?"

"You misunderstand. I'm mad as hell for what happened to me and my buddies over there. I hate that I'm paying the price because a bunch of government bureaucrats got in a pissing contest with the Viet Cong. But what happened, happened. No one ever promised me life would be fair."

"Then why do you have the American flag hanging outside your cabin? And that prisoner of war one?"

"Because I can love my country and hate its policies and its actions. The world's full of contradictions, and the only way to make sense of it all is to learn to hold two conflicting ideas in your head at the same time."

He made it sound so simple and obvious, even though it wasn't. "And how am I supposed to do that?"

"Accept uncertainty while you keep living life, no matter what it throws your way."

I sat with Renny's words. I could tell he was trying to teach me some important wisdom, but I couldn't make sense of it yet. My brain ached from thinking so hard.

We only said a few words the rest of the day, and after dinner Renny turned in pretty early. He looked beat even though we'd spent all day in the bunker, just puttering around. I helped him into bed and turned out the lights. Since I had nothing else to do, I got in the top bunk and stared at the ceiling, which was a few inches from my face. I imagined all the dirt on the other side, pressing down. I pictured it breaking through and burying me and Renny.

A few hours later, the nightmares came. For both of us.

IN THE MIDDLE of the night, a piercing scream startled me awake. In my sleepy haze, I thought a crazed killer had sneaked into the bunker and stabbed Renny. Not wanting to be the next victim, I lay frozen and waited for the screaming to stop. I peered over the edge of the top bunk. No one else was there except Renny, tossing and turning, mumbling and moaning. I asked if he was all right, but he didn't respond. Seneca sat next to Renny's bed and let out a worried whine.

"It's okay, boy," I whispered. "Go back to sleep."

Seneca curled up on the floor and I pulled the covers to my chin. I don't think either of us slept much after that.

In the morning, Renny made lumpy oatmeal, and I devoured it. Despite Renny's lackluster cooking, something about living in the bunker had brought back my appetite. I was even getting a taste for coffee and poured myself a second cup.

"Sleep okay?" Renny asked.

"Yeah, until I got woken up by you screaming."

"Sorry," he said. "It's been a long time since I've had to share a room with someone."

He left it at that, but I wanted to know more. "Were you having a nightmare?"

"Yeah, I get them sometimes."

"What was it about? The war?"

"I'd rather not say." Renny took a swig of coffee. "Unless you're planning to tell me about your nightmare?"

"What are you talking about?"

"You weren't the only one who got woken up by someone screaming."

I thought Renny was just messing with me, but then my dream came back to me in a rush.

I glide across the frozen lake, skating with Alyssa and Renny. Suddenly, the ice groans ominously beneath us. My heart races as I shout at them to turn back, but it's too late. The ice gives way and splits open. Alyssa plunges into the water first, followed by Renny. I desperately scream for help, but my cries are drowned out by the sound of more ice cracking. I spin around to see Trevor, his parents, Mr. and Mrs. Sawyer, and my mom and dad skating, oblivious to the danger. Even weirder, Mrs. Jenkins, Dorothy Jackson, and Denim Dave from the Army Surplus store are there too. The ice opens up beneath them, and one by one, they disappear with a splash. I shut my eyes, bracing myself for death, but somehow the ice around me holds. When I finally dare to open my eyes, I realize I'm stranded on a small slab of ice, floating in the middle of the vast lake. Completely alone.

Renny's voice snapped me back to the bunker. "Any chance your nightmare had something to do with what happened to your friend out on Lake Trapper?" He leaned on the table with his elbows, his steaming coffee mug hovering below his lips, waiting for my answer.

"I'd rather not say."

"Fair enough."

We both sat there for a while, not saying a word, drinking our coffee. Even though I'd loaded mine with sugar, the flavor was suddenly a lot more bitter.

We spent the afternoon making another puzzle. It was a picture of a covered bridge in fall with a white church in the distance. The sections with the red, orange, and yellow leaves were the hardest. Renny worked on the river area, which had a small waterfall. We finished the roof of the bridge last. It looked peaceful there.

But when we got to the end, there was a piece missing—the

167

tip of the church steeple. I looked and looked, but I couldn't find that stupid missing piece.

———

BEFORE DINNER, I climbed the bunker stairs and took Seneca out to pee. Bits of orange sky appeared through the trees, and the air was cold. When we got back inside, Renny was already in bed, snoring away. I didn't want to have more nightmares, so I tried to stay awake as long as I could.

I flopped on the couch, wishing I could watch some TV. Hollywood should make a sitcom about God and Job, I thought. They'd share an apartment, like Oscar and Felix in *The Odd Couple*. There could be an episode where the plumbing breaks and floods the apartment and Job blames God for making his life miserable. God throws up his hands and says, "Hey, it's not my fault every time something breaks around here!" And they have a nosy neighbor named Noah who ends up fixing the plumbing and saving everyone in the building from the flood.

I'd watch that show.

Thinking about Job reminded me about the piece of paper I'd seen in Renny's Bible. I wondered if it had something to do with his nightmares.

It was a long shot, but I tiptoed over to the bookshelf, took out the Bible, and flipped through the pages. The paper fell out and drifted to the floor. I picked up the paper and brought it closer to the lamp. It was a black-and-white photo of a young family—a man and woman smiling at a baby in their arms. The man looked familiar. It took me a second because without the beard, wrinkles, and trucker hat, Renny was almost unrecognizable.

He looked about twenty in the photo, which meant the kid was probably all grown up by now. A million questions ran through my mind. Renny had a wife and kid? Why hadn't he mentioned this before? Did Renny ever talk to them? Visit them? My eyes moved back to the woman. She was really pretty, and looked like a hippie with her long, dark hair and flower-print dress.

I tucked the photo between the pages where I'd found it and slipped the Bible back on the shelf. Lying in bed, the image of Renny and his family kept coming back to me. It made me think of my own family. Or what was left of it. A couple of days had passed since I'd run away from the motel. Despite all the problems between me and Mom, I knew she was probably worried about me. I thought about going back, but I wasn't ready yet. Not until I got some answers from Renny.

Chapter 20

When I woke up, Renny was still snoring, so I climbed down from the top bunk and went to the kitchen. By the time he finally got out of bed, I had a bowl of oatmeal and buttered toast waiting for him at the table. He eyed the meal suspiciously, like he was worried it was poisoned or something.

"You made all this?"

"Coffee, too." I poured him a cup.

Renny settled into his chair. He took a sip and swallowed. Then nodded. "Not bad."

I sat across from him with the identical meal. "Sleep okay?"

"You tell me. Did you hear any screaming?"

"No."

"Then I must've slept the sleep of the just."

Seneca sat by my chair and whined. I tossed him the crust from my toast. "I've been meaning to ask, before you came to Ravensberg and started living in the cabin, where were you?"

"I told you. Vietnam."

"No, I mean even before that. Where are you originally from?"

"Why the third degree all of a sudden?"

"Just curious."

"Mmm-hmmm," Renny didn't sound convinced. "And this breakfast . . . you made it out of the goodness of your heart?"

"You need to eat."

"Seems to me you're itching to ask me something, but you're afraid to."

He was right. I was worried that if he found out I'd been snooping around his stuff, he would've kicked me out of the bunker immediately.

"Doesn't it bug you?" I said.

"What?"

I pointed to the puzzle that was still on the coffee table.

"That missing piece. Where the hell could it be?"

"Who cares? You enjoyed making the puzzle, right?"

"I guess so."

"Then leave it at that. Sometimes you don't get closure."

I sat with that one for a while and sipped my coffee, my mind reaching for Dad. "Do you think the people who are gone miss us?" I said.

"Hard to know. What does your friend Alyssa think?"

"What do you mean?"

"From what I gathered she's been to the other side. Experienced death for herself. You don't come back from that the same person. You ever ask her about what she went through?"

"She . . . she doesn't remember what happened."

"If she ever does, I bet she'll open your mind to a whole new way of seeing life and death."

After we finished eating, I cleaned up and took Seneca outside to pee. When I got back, Renny was standing at the bookshelf, staring at his books.

"I told you not to touch my Bible," he said.

"I didn't."

171

Renny showed how the Bible was sticking out from the other books. "I always line up the spines so they're flush."

"Okay, you caught me. I just wanted to read the story about God and Job again."

"You're bluffing."

My body froze. I still had no clue what my tell was, but Renny was on to me, so I had no choice but to confess. "I noticed you hiding something in your Bible yesterday, and I had to find out what. Sorry."

Renny sat in his chair and opened his Bible. He took out the photo and stared at it for a bit. "It's okay. I suppose it's a good thing you saw this. Hell, maybe I wanted you to see it."

"Who are the woman and the baby?" I asked.

"They were my entire universe . . . "

After a long silence, Renny began his story. "My old man walked out on me when I was a little older than you," he said. "I had to make some money to support my mom and two younger sisters, so I got a job working at an auto body shop. I started when I was fourteen, cleaning up the place. Eventually I learned how to fix engines from watching and helping the mechanics."

One day, when Renny was twenty-four, a woman came into the shop because her green VW Bug needed repairs. They got to talking and hit it off. Her name was Vivian and she was a senior at UMass Amherst studying literature. Renny hadn't gone to college, and he didn't make much money, so he didn't think someone like Vivian would ever go for a guy like him. But when Vivian picked up her car, she asked Renny out for drinks after he got off work. Renny said he'd be there at eight.

As soon as he clocked out, Renny rushed home, took a shower, and put on some clean clothes. He headed over to the bar—a place called Charlie's. He rushed in at two minutes past eight, but Vivian wasn't there. Renny felt like a fool, thinking he'd been stood up. But just as he was getting ready to drink away his sorrows, Vivian walked in wearing a green dress, her hair done up, looking stunning. She apologized for being late, and Renny acted like he'd hardly noticed the time.

They spent the entire night talking and getting to know each other. Renny learned that Vivian was a dreamer like he was. After she graduated, Vivian planned to travel the world and write. She wanted to be a famous author one day. Renny revealed his dream was to be a sculptor. Vivian thought that was terrific. Renny wasn't used to having people support his artistic goals. The few friends he'd told had laughed at the idea. They said Renny was a decent mechanic but a terrible artist who could barely draw a stick figure. What made him think he could be the next Picasso? Vivian thought people made insensitive comments like that because they were afraid to pursue their own ambitions. Renny appreciated Vivian's way of looking at the world because it made him feel less alone.

When Renny started telling me how they fell in love, I made him skip the sappy, romantic parts.

A month after Vivian graduated, she and Renny decided to get married. Her parents were against it so Renny and Vivian had to tell them what was really going on—Vivian was pregnant. Reluctantly, Vivian's father gave Renny his blessing. They officially tied the knot at City Hall in front of a small group of friends and family. For their honeymoon, they drove Vivian's VW Bug through New England for a week, camping out at night under the stars, sometimes in the pouring rain. It actually sounded pretty incredible.

When Renny and Vivian got back, they moved into an apartment in town. Renny kept working at the auto body shop while Vivian stayed home, writing stories and sending them off to magazines. After a few months, she'd collected a stack of rejection letters, but she kept trying until finally one of her stories got published. Their son was born in February, and they named him Charlie, after the bar where they'd had their first date.

Renny took being a dad seriously. He changed diapers and got up in the middle of the night to soothe Charlie when he was crying. He was determined to be there for his son, in the way his father had never been around for him.

Years earlier, on his eighteenth birthday, Renny had registered for the draft, because at the time that's what you had to do. The U.S. wasn't in any serious wars back then, so Renny had barely given it a thought. But a few years later, friends and neighbors started getting drafted and sent off to fight in Vietnam. Renny's name never got called up, and by the time Charlie came into his life, he was too old to be drafted. "I'd gotten lucky," Renny said. "Or at least I thought I had."

Soon after Charlie's third birthday, he started coughing and having trouble breathing. He had a fever, too. Renny and Vivian thought it was just a flu, but Charlie kept getting worse. So they took him to the hospital, and the doctors ran a bunch of tests. It turned out Charlie had cancer. Leukemia. Six months later, he was dead.

I sat there, stunned. "My friend Trevor . . . his little brother died of leukemia, too."

"No one's grief is unique," Renny said.

After cremating Charlie, Vivian and Renny spread his ashes in a creek where he used to play. Not long after, Vivian left. She told Renny she was going to the store, but never came home. He was worried something might've happened to her, so he called her parents. They told him that Vivian had moved on from her misguided marriage to Renny and needed time to heal after Charlie's death. They supported her decision. Renny went to their house to talk to Vivian, but she wasn't there and her parents refused to say where she'd gone. A few weeks later,

Renny got a postcard with a picture of the Eiffel Tower on it. Vivian wrote she was sorry for leaving so suddenly. She needed a fresh start, and it was time to follow her dreams. She urged Renny to do the same.

"So your son died, and she just takes off to Paris? Weren't you pissed off?"

"Furious," Renny said.

"What did you do?"

"Volunteered to fight in Vietnam."

"What? Why the hell would you do that?"

After his son died and his wife left him, Renny was in a dark place. Every day after work, he'd spend hours drinking at Charlie's. Some nights, he'd pass out right at the bar. After a while, he figured he had two choices. Either he could keep drinking until he died, or he could get killed on the battlefield. At least going off to war, his death might mean something. But the war didn't end up killing him. Instead, it strengthened him and helped him appreciate life in a whole new way.

After the war, he inherited his aunt and uncle's land and moved into the cabin. He did odd jobs around town, and that led to collecting scrap metal. After experimenting with the pieces and welding them together into different forms, he found his style. He didn't think his sculptures had any greater meaning. He just wanted to create something out of his pain and anger.

"Did making art help the pain go away?"

"The pain never goes away, it just changes," Renny said.

A few years after he got home from the war, Renny got a letter from Vivian. She let him know she'd gotten remarried, to some Italian guy she'd met during her travels. She lives in Tuscany now and is a pretty famous mystery writer. Renny had read one of her books, but it wasn't really up his alley. Still, he was glad she'd found happiness.

"What about you?" I asked. "Did you find happiness?"

"I got a roof over my head, plenty of food, my beautiful dog next to me, and a friend to talk to. Sometimes it's the simplest things that bring you joy."

Hearing Renny refer to me as a friend made me smile.

THAT NIGHT I had a dream about Renny. He was wandering through the woods, looking for something. Or someone. Seneca and I followed him, but when I called out, Renny didn't turn around or react at all. I don't think he was ignoring me. It was more like we were in two different realms and my voice couldn't reach him. Fog rolled in and Renny walked into it. I ran after him, trying to catch up, and lost him in the mist. I looked and looked, but there was no trace of him. He'd just . . . vanished.

When I woke up, the sadness I felt in my dream still weighed on me like a heavy blanket. I peered over the edge of the top bunk to check on Renny and didn't see him in his bed or anywhere else in the bunker. Seneca was gone too. But a shaft of light from the stairwell was visible through the half-open door.

Fear crept over my skin like a thousand spiders crawling in every direction. I tried to convince myself that Renny had just taken Seneca out for an early walk, but deep down I knew something was terribly wrong. I threw back the covers and jumped to the floor, my body shaking. *Maybe it's not real, maybe I'm in another nightmare,* I thought desperately as I got dressed and stumbled toward the door.

But as soon as my hand touched the doorknob, a distant howl snapped me back to reality. There was no question—it was Seneca's howl.

For a few minutes, I seriously thought about closing the

bunker door and locking myself in. I had enough food and supplies to last for a while. And no one knew to look for me there. I could've waited out the storm until everything settled down. In a few years, I'd go back up and start a new life, the way Vivian had. Sure, Mom would probably be sad, but she'd move on pretty fast. The way she moved on after Dad.

But the thought of staying in the bunker was unbearable; I had to see Renny for myself, even if it meant facing an uncertain future.

Get comfortable with being uncomfortable, I told myself.

My heart pounded against my ribs as I walked up the stairs and stepped outside.

Rays of morning sun were streaming through the trees. Dew sparkled on blades of grass. Birds sang. Despite the dread hanging in the air, it was actually kind of peaceful and beautiful.

Seneca howled again. Convinced he was calling for me, I put one foot in front of the other and walked toward the sound. Soon I was running, the trees blurring past. I shouted Seneca's name because I knew if I called for Renny, I wouldn't get an answer back. Just like in my dream.

I found them off the main trail, in a small, hidden grove Renny had never shown me before. I stumbled into the circle of trees, my heart pounding in my ears. A shiver of fear prickled down my spine when I saw Renny lying motionless on a bench, his arm hanging limply over the side. Seneca stood protectively in front of him, howling mournfully. The crutches lay on the ground nearby, forming a lonely cross. I nearly collapsed right there, but somehow forced myself over to Renny.

I remembered how Mr. Donlan had checked Alyssa's pulse after she'd been pulled from the water. I put my fingers on the side of Renny's neck. His skin felt ice cold. And there was no pulse.

But that doesn't prove he's dead, I thought. When Alyssa came out of the water, she didn't have a pulse either, and Mr. Donlan still somehow brought her back to life. What if Renny was floating in that in-between realm where Alyssa had been? What if he was waiting for me to bring him back?

But I'd never done CPR on anyone before, and when I tried to turn Renny on his back, his body was stiff and as heavy as a bag of cement. I didn't need a doctor to tell me he'd been lying there for a while. Probably hours. Alyssa had only been gone for twenty-three minutes.

Every part of me wanted to howl and wail like Seneca. But I couldn't and I didn't know why.

As I sat there with Renny's body, the cold air filled my lungs, and I looked around. One of Renny's metal sculptures stood in the center of the grove. But it was smaller than the ones I'd seen near the cabin. After staring at it for a little while, I made out a form. I got up and circled the sculpture. From most angles, it looked like a mess of metal curves and rods and plates, but when I stepped into a particular spot, the pieces magically lined up to create a figure. It was of a little boy with his arms reaching up to the sky. A shiver went through me. I took a few steps to my right, and the boy's form vanished.

A small, rusty plate was screwed to the base of the sculpture, etched with the words *Charlie's Grove.* I realized it wasn't just some random clearing. It was Renny's shrine to his son. That's why he'd dragged himself outside in the middle of the night to die there. He wanted to be with his son again.

Sometime later, sirens wailed in the distance. As the sounds got closer, I realized Mom must have gone to the police and they were coming to Renny's place looking for me. I heard tires skid to a stop, car doors slam, and a man yell, "Search the cabin!" The loud noises startled Seneca and he took off into the woods.

I begged him to come back but he didn't listen. Then Mom's voice rang out screaming my name.

I stayed with Renny, letting reality sink in. He was dead. Really, truly dead. And there was nothing I could do to change that. But even though I was sitting with his cold, lifeless body, I still couldn't cry about him being gone. Finally, I left the grove and headed toward the sound of Mom's voice.

WHEN I GOT BACK to the cabin, the cops had kicked the door open and were checking out the place. Renny wouldn't have been happy about them trespassing and since he wasn't there to defend his home, I did it for him. I shouted at the cops to get out and told them they had no right to be there. Mom heard me and came out from behind the cabin. She ran over and hugged me really hard, bursting into tears. She was angry, but mostly just relieved to see me. To my surprise, I was relieved to see her too and hugged her back.

Sheriff Winslow stepped out onto the porch. I'd met him once before at the lake, right after "the incident."

"Are you hurt?" he asked, looking me up and down.

"I'm fine," I insisted.

"Where's Mr. Laforge?"

I pointed in the direction of the grove, my hand trembling. "He's dead."

Sheriff Winslow sent two officers to check on the body while he stayed behind to interview me. I told him everything—how I'd first met Renny at the mall, found his dog, then ended up working for him after school doing odd jobs. I left out Renny's personal stuff because he would've hated a stranger knowing all about his past. But I made it super clear that Renny had nothing to do with me going missing. It had been my decision to run away.

"Ah, I see . . . " Sheriff Winslow said and nodded like he'd just solved some big mystery. He turned to my mom. "I'm guessing this has something to do with your husband?"

"It's been a difficult time." Mom didn't elaborate.

Satisfied that he'd done his job and the case was closed, the sheriff radioed for an ambulance. Twenty minutes later, it arrived. Mom gave Mr. Donlan a smile as he got out of the front, but he was all business. He and the other EMT wheeled a gurney out to the grove. A while later, they returned with Renny's body stuffed in a black bag, like they'd found a sack of garbage in the woods and not a person.

"Where are you taking him?" I asked.

"To the county morgue," Mr. Donlan said. "They'll do an autopsy and notify any family, so they can retrieve the body."

"He doesn't have any family anymore."

"Then the state will deal with his remains."

"What if I want to claim him?"

"It doesn't work that way. Sorry."

"Oh."

Mr. Donlan let down his professional exterior for a moment. "I'm glad to see you're okay, Jack. You had your mother really worried."

"Yeah," I said. "I know."

"Once you sort things out with her, talk to Trevor. He's been through a tough time, too. I think he'd like you two to be friends again, even though he won't come out and say it."

After losing Renny, I was happy to hear that. "Okay," I said.

On the ride back to the motel, Mom told me the story of how she'd found me.

"The other night, when I got back to the room and you weren't there . . . it was the worst feeling," she began.

"What time was it?"

"What do you mean?"

"What time did you get back to the room?"

"I don't see what that has to do with anything."

I dropped the subject. "Fine. You got back to the room. Then what happened?"

"I knocked on Steve's door and asked him to help find you. I was pretty upset, but he assured me you were probably fine. But then he looked around outside the motel and noticed your bike was missing. According to him, it was a good sign. 'It means Jack left of his own volition,' he said. Well, I didn't like hearing that you had run away but Steve assured me it's pretty common and that you probably just needed to blow off some steam. He thought you might have gone to Trevor's but when he called his house, Trevor's mother said you weren't there and that you and Trevor hadn't spoken in a while.

"Since you weren't with Trevor, I assumed you must be at the Sawyers so I called over there. But when Alyssa answered the phone, she said she hadn't seen you since the night of the dinner. I asked to talk to her mother, but she was out running errands. I gave Alyssa our number and said it was important that her mother call me as soon as possible because you were missing. Alyssa said she'd deliver the message and hung up but I didn't hear from Gayle that day. While I was trying to figure out where to look for you next, Steve asked me if anything had happened between us that might have made you run off."

"Did you tell him you hit me?"

"It was a slap, Jack. An accident. And no, I didn't tell him."

"Why not?"

"Because it wasn't one of my finer moments as a mother, okay?"

"So, what *did* you say?"

"That we'd had an argument. Which is the truth."

"Yeah, technically."

Mom clicked her fingernails on the steering wheel, eager to move the conversation along. "Anyway, we made a few more calls and looked around the motel for any signs of you, but we'd hit a dead end. And that's when Trevor and his mother drove up. It was Steve's weekend to take him. Diane wasn't very happy seeing us together, so she took off in a huff. Then Steve, Trevor, and I headed over to the police station so I could file a report that you were missing.

"I talked to Sheriff Winslow, and he said they couldn't send out an official alert for twenty-four hours. But since he knew our situation, he told his officers to keep an eye out for you. For the rest of the day, Steve drove us up and down every street in town. Later, while Steve and Trevor got dinner at the food court, I stood outside the mall showing people your old school photo. I hoped that someone might have seen you but no one had.

"Then, this morning, before I was even awake, the phone rang. It was Alyssa's mother. She apologized for calling so early and said she'd found a number scribbled on a kitchen notepad, written in Alyssa's handwriting. Gayle asked Alyssa about it, and Alyssa said she'd forgotten to give her the message that I'd called. Gayle wanted to make sure everything was all right. When I explained that you still hadn't turned up, she told me about running into you and Renny at the hospital. Well, I couldn't believe it. I told her she must have been mistaken, but Gayle said she spoke to you both. That you said you were part of some volunteer program? Why would you lie to her like that?"

I crossed my arms and stared out the window, refusing to answer the question.

"Well, after talking to Gayle," Mom continued, "I called Sheriff Winslow to tell him you were somewhere in the woods with that strange man. I was afraid he might have kidnapped you."

"I already explained, that's not what happened."

"What else was I supposed to think after all the lies you've been telling me?"

"Why are you making such a big deal of this? I was going to come back." I left out the part where I considered locking myself away in the bunker for a few years.

"Why is this such a big deal? Because you walked out on me! Just like your father did!" Mom slammed the brakes, and I flew forward as the car skidded to a stop in the middle of the road. Tires squealed behind us. We were lucky we didn't get rear-ended.

"What the hell, Mom?"

Horns started honking, and she just sat there with her hands on the wheel and stared ahead, not saying anything. It reminded me of the way Alyssa stared out her window after she woke up from her coma. How her body was there, but her mind was elsewhere. If Mom's goal was to scare me, it had worked.

"Mom? You okay?"

The honking got more intense. Finally, she snapped out of it. "All right, all right! We're going!" she yelled out the window at the other cars. Mom hit the gas and we took off.

183

Chapter 21

After Renny died, the last thing I wanted to do was go back to school, but Mom urged me to hang tough and push on. Plus, she had to go to work. And after everything that had just happened, she wasn't about to leave me alone, moping around the motel all day. I was too exhausted to argue with her, so off to school I went.

Turned out, my absence had gotten students talking, and a rumor had been going around the high school that someone had kidnapped me. I told everyone that it was a bunch of crap, but I still heard people whispering about me when I passed them in the hall. Mixed with those whispers was another rumor—about Trevor. People were saying that he'd gotten electrocuted while playing Pac-Man and almost died. It sounded like more crap, so when I saw Trevor sitting alone at lunch, I figured I'd ask him about it. What Mr. Donlan had told me was also lingering in the back of my mind. I hoped it was true that Trevor wanted to be friends again, but there was only one way to find out.

"Okay if I sit with you?" I nodded to the empty seat across from him.

Trevor shrugged. "It's a free country."

At least he hadn't told me to get lost, so that was an improvement. I slid my lunch tray on the table and took a seat. We both picked at our mac and cheese, each waiting for the other to start the conversation.

"So . . . " Trevor finally said.

"So."

"Were you ever going to clue me in?"

"About what?"

"What do you think? About your mom having an affair with my dad."

My stomach churned. I didn't want to lie to Trevor, not anymore. But he never would have talked to me again if I fessed up to knowing all along. So I gave him a half truth.

"I had a hunch. But I was afraid to say anything because I wasn't sure and I didn't want to freak you out."

"You still should have said something."

"I assumed you'd figure it out on your own. You really never noticed your dad getting home late?"

"He's an EMT. He works weird hours."

"Or talking on the phone late at night?"

Trevor thought about it for a second. "Huh . . . I asked him about that once. He said he was talking to his cousin in California."

"And I'm sure your parents were arguing way more than usual."

"Yeah, but I just thought they were upset over Scotty. They were falling apart. We all were."

Trevor said that after his brother died, his dad dealt with it by taking extra shifts at work, while his mom stayed in her room pretty much all day; Trevor started spending all his time at the arcade.

He waited for the tension at home to fizzle, but things only got more strained. His parents fought constantly, usually over

185

little things, like Mr. Donlan forgetting to take out the garbage. But there was one blow up that really stuck with Trevor. He was in his bedroom when he overheard his mom accusing his dad of not being sad enough about Scotty dying. Then his dad started yelling about how his mom had abandoned him and their family. After that, they could barely stand being in the same room.

"When did the affair start?" Trevor asked.

"I don't know, exactly. Sometime after Scotty died. But after my dad found out, my mom called it off."

"But now it's starting again."

"Yeah. When did you figure that part out?"

Trevor sighed and stared into his mac and cheese, stirring it with his plastic fork. "When you went missing, I was with your mom and my dad all day. We went to the police station and drove around looking for you. By the time we got back to the motel, I was wiped out, so my dad gave me the key to the room and went to the diner with your mom. I figured he'd be back in an hour or so. He didn't show until early the next morning. That's when I knew for sure."

"Where did he say he'd been?"

"He tried to pass it off like he'd gotten up super early and went out for coffee, so I asked him where his coffee cup was. He claimed he drank it on the way back, which was a total lie. I was so mad I couldn't even speak, so I got dressed and headed to GameZilla. It was early Sunday morning, so I had to wait outside until the mall opened. When it did, I was the first one in the arcade. I had the place to myself."

"Is that how you ended up getting electrocuted by Pac-Man?" I asked.

"What?"

"That's what people are saying."

"That's not exactly how it went down."

186

Here's what you need to do to get a perfect score in Pac-Man: eat every single dot, power pellet, fruit, and ghost. You can't miss even one and you can't lose a life while you're doing it. There's zero room for error. And you have to do this repeatedly. Not just on 10 boards or even 100 boards. But on all 256 boards. And there's no pause button. You can't take a snack break or a bathroom break. To play through all those levels takes over six hours.

That morning, Trevor dropped a quarter into Pac-Man and started gobbling pellets. All thoughts of the affair, the divorce, and his dead brother vanished amidst the arcade sounds. He was totally focused on the game, determined to beat it.

His first major hurdle was getting past the initial 20 boards. Each level got faster and faster, but Trevor had things under control. He devoured every piece of fruit and every ghost. But after board 20, the game reaches a whole other level.

Now, most people don't know what happens after board 20 because the average player can barely clear 10 or 15 screens. But I'd seen Trevor clear board 20 a bunch of times, so he was ready for what was to come. Once he hit board 21, the power pellets stopped working, which meant no more eating ghosts. But they could sure as hell still kill him. Trevor settled in for the long haul and put all his concentration on the game. He was in a war with his own mind and if he lost his focus, even for a second, he'd wind up dead.

It took Trevor a couple of hours to top his highest-ever score. That's when people in the arcade started taking notice. They crowded around, trying to glimpse Trevor in action, buzzing with amazement as Trevor breezed through board after board. When he made it past the 75th board, the crowd gasped in awe. They cheered when he cleared the 100th.

By the time Trevor's parents showed up at the arcade, Trevor was on board 150 and showed no signs of slowing down. Mrs. Donlan pushed through the crowd and told Trevor it was time to go home.

Trevor kept his eyes fixed on the screen. "I'm staying right here."

Mr. Donlan tried talking to him next, but Trevor refused to budge. Mr. Donlan grabbed Trevor's arm and tried to pull him away. It almost wrecked his winning streak, but Trevor kept his grip on the joystick and slipped out of his father's grip.

"Leave him be," Mrs. Donlan said.

"You're the one who didn't want him playing video games all day."

"He's only doing this because of you."

"What the hell is that supposed to mean?"

"I'm not discussing our personal problems in front of all these people," Mrs. Donlan said, motioning at everyone around them. She told Trevor that when he was ready to go home, she'd be waiting for him outside the arcade and made her way back through the crowd.

"You can't play Pac-Man forever," Mr. Donlan told Trevor.

"I can try," Trevor said.

And for the next few hours, he was unstoppable. The more boards he cleared, the bigger the crowd became, until it was spilling out of the arcade. Everyone wanted to get a glimpse of the Pac-Man Kid in action.

Around board number 200, Trevor started feeling faint. He was about to ask his father to grab him a hamburger, but in that moment of distraction, he turned his Pac-Man the wrong way and thought he was a goner. Luckily, his reflexes kicked in and he got back on track. Once he made it to the next level, he stopped thinking about food and remained focused on eating dots.

When he reached board 250, the crowd fell silent and all you could hear was Pac-Man's *waka waka waka* echoing through the mall.

He cleared the next 5 boards with no problem. But then on the final board—number 256—the game went berserk.

One second, he was gobbling dots and cruising through the maze, then suddenly, the screen split and his Pac-Man was gone. On the right side, letter and numbers appeared, like some kind of code. In that no-man's-land, the dots were hidden and so were the ghosts. Trevor was flying blind.

In one of his video game magazines, Trevor had read about a nineteen-year-old guy who had found a bug in Pac-Man, so he knew this glitch was possible. But he wasn't ready to accept defeat yet. As long as he could hear the *waka waka waka,* it meant his Pac-Man was still alive. With a spark of hope, Trevor moved the joystick, resurrecting Pac-Man on the left side of the screen, in the visible part of the maze. But the ghosts were on to him. Before Trevor knew it, they had him surrounded. He escaped back into no-man's-land, and Pac-Man vanished. A few seconds later, Pac-Man's death sound rang out. Trevor's stomach turned over. Even though he hadn't eaten all day, he thought he might throw up. The screen turned blurry. The last thing he remembered was feeling dizzy. Then the world went dark.

After maxing out, Trevor woke up lying on the floor. He heard screams and saw his parents leaning over him.

"What . . . what happened? Trevor said.

"You had a syncopal episode," his father told him.

"Huh?"

"You fainted, is all." Mr. Donlan ran his hand through Trevor's hair. "No blood. That's good. But we'd better get you to the hospital and let the doctors check you out."

He picked Trevor up and carried him outside, where Mrs. Donlan was waiting.

"Oh my God, oh my God," Mrs. Donlan kept saying as they drove him to the hospital. "You can't die on us, too."

"I'm going to be fine, Mom," Trevor kept reassuring her.

In the ER, Trevor got a bunch of tests to make sure his heart was okay and that his fall hadn't caused a head injury. The doctor came into the room and confirmed what Mr. Donlan already suspected. Trevor's blood pressure had dropped suddenly and caused him to faint. The tests all came back normal.

Mrs. Donlan asked the doctor what made Trevor pass out.

"A combination of dehydration and fatigue." The doctor looked at some papers on his clipboard. "It says here he was playing a video game for six hours. Is that right?"

"Yes," Mr. Donlan said, looking embarrassed. "But it won't happen again."

"Is your son under any other stressors?" the doctor asked. "Maybe at school . . . or at home?"

The Donlans said nothing.

"I mention it because stress can trigger a syncopal episode, like the one Trevor experienced. The body is like a machine and sometimes it reaches its limit and overloads."

Like Pac-Man going berserk.

The doctor sent Trevor home and told him to get plenty of rest and fluids and to stop playing those mind-rotting games.

The Donlans assured the doctor that Trevor would follow his orders. Trevor believed his problem wasn't Pac-Man, but his parents. He knew better than to bring that up, especially after the news interview fiasco.

Because they'd rushed Trevor to the hospital in Mrs. Donlan's car, Mr. Donlan's Volvo was still at the mall. Mrs. Donlan said she'd drive him over there the next morning to pick it up. She thought it would be a good idea if Mr. Donlan stayed over at the house to help observe Trevor. Just in case he fainted again. And only for one night. So, for the first time in months, the Donlans would be living under the same roof.

But the arguing started the second they walked in the front door. First, Mr. Donlan was upset that Mrs. Donlan had changed the locks without telling him—did she expect him to break into his own family's house? Then Mrs. Donlan got on Mr. Donlan's case for walking through the house with his dirty shoes on, which was one of his many habits that had always annoyed her.

While his parents kept arguing, Trevor retreated to his room. They yelled for a while, like they used to. Later, his mom came in to bring him a grilled cheese sandwich. Trevor said he knew what was going on with his dad and my mom. Mrs. Donlan told him not to worry about it.

"Get some rest," she said.

"I realize things haven't been the same since Scotty died," Trevor said.

Mrs. Donlan handed him the glass of water. "You need to drink."

"He's not here anymore, Mom."

"Drink."

"But I am."

Trevor noticed his mom fighting back tears. Mr. Donlan poked his head in the doorway. "How are you feeling, Trev?"

Mrs. Donlan got up and pushed past her soon-to-be ex-husband, who watched as she headed down the hall.

"What's her problem now?"

"*You* are, Dad."

"Excuse me?"

Trevor had never spoken to his father so bluntly. Mr. Donlan didn't look too happy about it.

191

"I think that doctor was right," Trevor said. "It's time to move on from Pac-Man. I'm done chasing those stupid ghosts."

"That's probably for the best," Mr. Donlan said.

Later that night, Trevor's parents talked in the kitchen. He couldn't pick up exactly what they were saying, but at least they weren't yelling at each other. Which seemed like progress.

As TREVOR FINISHED HIS STORY, his eyes met mine. "The next morning I woke up to the smell of pancakes. Me, Mom, and Dad ate breakfast together as a family, just like we used to. I figured it was the last time we'd probably do that, but I was okay with it."

I couldn't believe how relaxed Trevor looked. Seriously, he seemed totally fine with the fact that his life would never be the same. I was jealous.

"Dude, that's incredible," I said. "I mean, not the fainting part. The you-kicking-Pac-Man's-ass part."

"I think it was the other way around."

"No way. You made it to board two hundred fifty-six. How many people in the world can say they've done that?"

"Not that many."

"Exactly. You're amazing. Sorry I wasn't there to see it."

"Me too." Trevor sighed. "Why'd you run off, anyway?"

"I just needed to get away from my mom for a while."

Trevor nodded like he got it. "I just wish you'd told me. I thought we were best friends."

I smiled. "We still can be."

Chapter 22

You never know when you're going to get that call—the one that will change your life forever. I got the call one morning while I was getting ready for school.

"Hello, I'm looking for a Mrs. Finn," said a man's voice on the other end of the line.

"Who is this?" I asked.

"Is this Jack? Could I speak to your mother, please?"

"How do you know my name?"

Mom came out of the bathroom, putting on an earring. "Who is it?"

I held the phone out to her. "Some guy. He wants to talk to you."

Mom took the phone and sat on the edge of the bed. "Yes, hello?" After a moment, she started shaking her head. "I'm sorry. No, I don't need a lawyer."

My muscles clenched. Why was a lawyer calling? Was I in trouble?

The man on the other end said something that made her eyes widen. "Renny Laforge? Yes, my son knew him, but that doesn't make any sense."

Then it hit me—what if the hospital doctors found out I'd lied about being Renny's son and now they were coming after me? *Was that a thing that could happen?* I wondered. *Can someone sue you for being a phony?* If so, I'd be found guilty beyond all doubt and sentenced to life in prison.

"Mom, hold up. We might need that lawyer after all."

She held up a finger to tell me to wait and stayed on the line. After a couple of minutes of back and forth with the lawyer, Mom agreed that we'd meet him at his office later that afternoon. She hung up and looked at me. I couldn't read her expression.

"Am I in trouble?" I asked.

"It didn't sound like it."

My body relaxed. "Then what did he want?"

"Did Renny ever introduce you to a lawyer named Lincoln Emerson?"

It took me a second to remember how I knew that name. "No, I never met him."

"But you know who he is?"

"Yeah." I told her about how, after I picked up Renny from the hospital, we stopped by a lawyer's office but that Renny had me wait in the cab. "So what did he say?"

"He wouldn't give me all the details. He just said he's in charge of Mr. Laforge's will. Renny must have left you something."

The entire rest of the day at school, I couldn't concentrate. I kept wondering what Renny had left me and why he thought I was important enough to give it to. Even though he didn't have family around, we'd only known each other for a couple of months. I wasn't even sure he'd liked me very much. By the time Mom picked me up to go meet Lincoln Emerson, I'd convinced myself not to get my hopes up. Renny had probably just left me a few extra bucks for helping him out.

When we got to the minimall, Mom pulled into the exact parking spot where I'd waited in the cab. It was strange being back there without Renny.

We got out, and I followed Mom inside. The office was empty except for a few clownfish swimming in a gurgling fish tank.

"Hello?" Mom called out.

A couple of seconds later, a man with glasses and a bushy mustache popped out from behind a door in the hallway. He wore a tan suit that looked too big on him.

"Are you Mr. Emerson?" Mom asked.

"Guilty as charged." Mr. Emerson chuckled like he'd just invented that corny joke. He looked at me. "And you must be Jack."

"Yup."

He shook my hand and waved us into his office, which had a big, wooden desk and shelves filled with thick, fancy-looking law books. Lincoln Emerson took a seat in a leather chair behind his desk and Mom and I sat in two wooden ones facing him.

While he made some small talk about the weather, Lincoln Emerson rifled through a pile of folders on his desk. He pulled one out and opened it, then glanced up at me. "As I explained to your mother on the phone, Renny Laforge hired me to be executor of his will."

"What does that mean?" I asked.

"Simply that I'm authorized to make sure Mr. Laforge's last wishes are honored.

"You mean, like, who gets to take care of his dog? Because Seneca ran off and I'm not sure he's coming back."

Lincoln Emerson nodded. "Yes, this concerns his dog. Among other things."

"What other things?"

"All his other things. He left you everything, Jack."

"Everything?" Mom said, sounding excited. "What, exactly, is 'everything'?"

"Mr. Laforge was cash poor but land rich, as they say. He owned his cabin and two hundred acres of land surrounding it. It's been in the Laforge family for generations."

My mind started going fuzzy. I didn't believe what I'd heard.

"And he's giving it to Jack?" Mom asked.

"That's correct. Along with all possessions on the property, including sculptures, as well as his 1952 Ford F100."

It didn't make any sense. "He's giving me Big Charlie?"

Lincoln Emerson nodded and turned to Mom. "Now, since Jack isn't of age yet, Mrs. Finn, you'll oversee the assets until he turns eighteen. Any questions so far?"

"We wouldn't need all that land. If Jack wanted to sell it, how would that work?" Mom sounded like one of those lottery winners on the news who could barely wait to spend their new fortune.

"Before you get ahead of yourself, I need to inform you that Mr. Laforge instituted certain conditions."

"Like what?" Mom asked.

Lincoln Emerson read from one paper in the folder. "Jack must agree not to sell the land to a developer or tear down the cabin. It states here that he also must keep the bunker supplied."

"Bunker?" Mom glanced at me, confused.

"In case of nuclear winter," I said, like it should have been obvious.

Mom and Lincoln Emerson stared back like I was an alien. Which is how I felt sitting in a lawyer's office, being told I was inheriting Renny's land and everything that meant anything to him.

"Anyway, that's about it," Mr. Emerson said, handing Mom

a pen. "I'll just need your John Hancock on a few forms and I'll start working on transferring the property deed."

Mom took the cap off the pen, but before she could write her name, I snatched the pen out of her hand. "Stop."

"Give it back!" Mom snapped, and we started fighting over the pen.

"Don't sign!" I yelled. "I don't want any of it!"

"What in the world is wrong with you? Why not?"

"Because I don't deserve it!" I finally won the pen from Mom and collapsed back in the chair, victorious and defeated all at the same time.

The room was silent. Lincoln Emerson adjusted his tie. Mom's face flushed with embarrassment.

"I'm sorry, Mr. Emerson, it's just that, my son has been through a lot recently and this is a bit . . . overwhelming for him."

"I understand. It's quite all right." Mr. Emerson leaned forward across his desk and assured me that Renny wanted me to have this gift, to make sure my future was taken care of. "You may not think you deserve it, but Renny did."

Mom put a hand on my knee. "We could move out of the motel, Jack. Fix up the cabin and start a new life. This is like a gift from God."

That made me think of Job. At the end of his story, after all the crap that God put him through, God gave him a bunch of animals and money and a family. Job lived to be a happy old man. Did that mean if I turned down Renny's gift, I'd end up miserable?

"Sorry," I said. "But I don't want it."

"You can't turn down an inheritance," Mom said. "That's not how it works."

"Well, that's not technically accurate," Lincoln Emerson said. "A minor can legally refuse an inheritance, but—"

"Good," I said. "Then I refuse it."

"—but not until you reach the age of maturity," Lincoln Emerson finished.

I sagged against the back of the chair. "Oh. What does that mean, exactly?"

"All the assets would sit in a trust until you turn eighteen. At that time, you can officially disclaim the inheritance."

Mom perked up. "Then Jack still has time to change his mind?"

"Well, I'm not changing it," I said and got up. But before I could leave, Lincoln Emerson informed me there was one last item of business.

"Mr. Laforge insisted I deliver this to you personally." Lincoln Emerson pulled an envelope out of the folder and handed it to me. It had my name on it, written in Renny's blocky handwriting. "Do with it as you see fit."

I didn't open it. Not right then. I wasn't ready to read what I assumed were Renny's last words to me. I stuffed the envelope in my pocket and walked out of Mr. Emerson's office, positive I'd never set foot back there again.

Chapter 23

On our way back to the motel, we stopped for burgers and fries at the food court in the mall. While we ate, Mom kept subtly trying to change my mind about taking the inheritance. "I love how peaceful it is out in the woods," she'd say. Or, "I had a dog growing up. I loved him so much." And "I had no idea Renny was a sculptor. That's so interesting. I wonder if he sold his work anywhere."

I kept quiet, refusing to take the bait.

When Mom finished her meal, she got up to go to the bathroom.

"I won't run off while you're gone," I joked. She didn't find it funny.

As I watched Mom walk away, I noticed Alyssa across the food court, standing in line at the pizza place with her mother and sisters waiting to order. I slunk back into my seat, pretending to be invisible. But it was too late. She marched toward me, like a predator stalking its prey. She sat across from me, her fists planted on the table, eyes drilling into me.

"When were you planning on telling me the truth about the man from my nightmares?" Alyssa said.

Suddenly gravity stopped, and my body was floating. But the feeling didn't last long. A second later, I came crashing back down, the weight of the world squeezing the air out of me. I fought back.

"What . . . what are you talking about?"

"I know, Jack. Were you planning on lying to me forever? Why would you do that to me?"

"I don't . . . I don't know . . . " I tried to get up to leave, but Alyssa grabbed my arm and pulled me back into my seat. "You're going to stay there and hear everything I'm about to tell you. Got it?"

The fight went out of me. I nodded and listened.

IT TURNED out that Alyssa's letter to Aldous Watts didn't get lost in the mail, as I'd hoped. He had received it and called Alyssa to arrange a meeting. Alyssa told him the best time would be that Saturday morning at nine thirty.

Mrs. Sawyer normally went out grocery shopping with Allison and Althea then, and Mr. Sawyer would be working in the basement as usual. So Alyssa was confident she could meet alone with Aldous Watts for an hour and get the all the answers she was looking for.

At nine thirty on the dot, the doorbell rang. When Alyssa answered the door, her first thought was that Aldous Watts looked like a cool English professor. He was dressed like in his author photo, with the addition of a tweed blazer over his black turtleneck, a scarf, and a little more gray hair along the sides.

Aldous Watts introduced himself and Alyssa shook his hand, self-conscious of how cold and clammy hers were.

"Sorry, I'm a little nervous," she said. "You're like a celebrity to me. Come in."

Aldous Watts adjusted his glasses and assured her there was nothing to be nervous about.

"I'm delighted to meet you finally and hear your story." He looked around. "Where are your parents? I'm eager to speak to them as well."

"Oh, they're busy," Alyssa said.

"Maybe I should return later, when they're home?" Aldous Watts said.

Alyssa insisted he stay and ushered him into the living room, where they sat on opposite ends of the floral print couch. Aldous Watts wanted to get to know her and understand what her life was like prior to the accident. She didn't want to seem rude, so she answered his questions, but after twenty minutes, she interrupted him with her own questions.

"I read in your book that people who came back after a near-death event talked about their amazing mystical experiences. One person said she traveled through tunnels wrapped with every color in the universe, then emerged into a loving, accepting light, like a hug of warm energy. And she wasn't the only one. But it wasn't like that for me. I don't remember anything. It's just this blank void of aloneness."

"That must be scary. But I promise you, you're not alone. And not everyone who has crossed to the other side and returned, feels at peace. For some, it's a difficult transition."

Alyssa nodded, relieved she'd finally found someone who understood what she'd been through. Aldous Watts continued:

"If it's any reassurance, after an NDE, everything you thought you knew gets turned upside down. Many people feel mixed up, even if they have those clarifying experiences like I wrote about in my book."

"But why can't I remember?"

"I expect you will, in time. The brain is a mysterious organ, and we're only beginning to understand—"

201

The phone rang, interrupting him. Alyssa ignored it.

"Perhaps it's an important call?" Aldous Watts said.

Alyssa let out an annoyed sigh and rushed into the kitchen. She picked up, and it was my mom, looking for me. She said something about how I'd disappeared, but Alyssa was so focused on getting back to Aldous Watts that she didn't ask questions. My mom gave Alyssa a phone number that she quickly scribbled on the pad by the phone, then hung up and hurried back to the living room.

"Keep going," Alyssa said as she sat back down.

Aldous Watts explained recent advancements in brain science, including ways to encourage memory recovery. He knew about a kind of therapy that might help her remember the details of the accident and her near-death experience. Alyssa was ready to get started that second.

"If you wish to go down that road, I'm afraid you'll have to see a specialist in Boston or New York," Aldous Watts said. "And even with therapy, it sometimes takes years after a traumatic event for memories to return."

Alyssa slumped deeper into the couch. "So you can't help me?"

"In the short term, there is one thing you could try."

"What?"

"A few individuals I've spoken with over the years have been able to recall their near-death experience in vivid detail by visiting the place where they died."

"You mean if I go back to the lake, I'll remember?"

"There's no guarantee, but it's somewhere to start. Sometimes the closer we are to death, the clearer we see things." Aldous Watts must have noticed a look of worry in Alyssa's face. "Only when you're ready, of course."

Alyssa insisted she'd been ready to know the truth ever since she woke up from her coma. It was everyone around her who was scared to face it. She told Aldous Watts about how her mother had hidden the letter he'd sent, and how I had lied about his book being checked out from the library.

"It's like everyone is purposefully avoiding talking about what happened that day," Alyssa said.

"They don't understand what you went through or what it means. Uncertainty is a frightening place to live."

Alyssa saw his point. What parent wants to think of the day they almost lost their child? What friend wants to think back on the worst day of their life? She worried that if her memories suddenly came flooding back to her, they might be so disturbing that she'd want to forget them, too. Maybe losing her memory had been a blessing?

Alyssa was still full of questions, but then she heard the family car pull into the driveway sooner than she'd expected. Alyssa broke into a sweat as her mother walked through the door, arms full of grocery bags. Mrs. Sawyer was stunned to find her daughter sitting in the living room with a strange man. She calmly set the groceries down and sent Allison and Althea to their rooms. Once they were gone, Mrs. Sawyer's tone got more serious. She demanded to know "what on God's green earth was going on."

Aldous Watts stood and politely introduced himself. Mrs. Sawyer frowned, immediately recognizing his name. When he held out his hand, she didn't shake it.

Aldous Watts didn't get offended. He said it was nice to meet Mrs. Sawyer, and he was happy to explain more about his work and how it might help Alyssa cope with what she and her family were going through. Mrs. Sawyer refused to listen to a word of his "new age crap." She called him a charlatan who'd probably never attended a church service in his life. She said he wasn't welcome in their home and demanded he leave that instant.

Aldous Watts gave a nod and turned to Alyssa. "It was lovely speaking with you. Take to heart what I said, and I hope you feel better. Good-bye."

Alyssa felt a thickness in her throat. She wanted to speak out, to tell her mother that Aldous Watts was her guest and he was welcome to stay as long as he'd like. Instead, she watched helplessly as he walked to the door.

"Good-bye," Alyssa whispered.

As soon as the door shut behind Aldous Watts, Mrs. Sawyer laid into Alyssa. "I had a feeling something was up with you when I left this morning. Jack was right to be concerned."

"I knew he told you! He's such a liar."

"You're the one who's been lying and going behind my back. What were you thinking?"

"Mr. Watts was trying to help me."

"No, he's preying on you. I mean, what kind of man sends letters to a vulnerable young girl in the hospital and visits her unchaperoned?"

Alyssa insisted Aldous Watts wasn't a dangerous man. She'd been the one who invited him over. She'd been the one who insisted he stay. It was the only way she could get any answers.

"And did he give you these answers you were looking for?"

"He might have, if you hadn't been such a bitch to him!"

Mrs. Sawyer's face turned bright red. "How dare you speak to me like that! I ought to wash your mouth out with soap."

"I'm not five anymore!"

Alyssa stormed up to her room without mentioning that my mom had called looking for me. Maybe she forgot. Or maybe she wanted me to stay lost.

Alyssa stayed in her room that entire day and wouldn't come out, even for lunch or dinner. And the same night I was in the bunker, having nightmares about that day at the lake, Alyssa lay awake in her bed, thinking about her visit with Aldous

Watts. Her mother was right. He hadn't given her the answers she'd wanted, but maybe he had given her a way forward. A path to discover the answers for herself.

Sometimes the closer we are to death, the clearer we see things.

The thought kept looping in Alyssa's mind. She pictured the ice stretching out before her. The shock of plunging into the freezing water. Then it struck her—she didn't have to go to the lake to get close to death. Death was right there, in her own home.

It was past midnight. In her nightgown and slippers, Alyssa snuck out of her room and crept down the stairs, careful to avoid the creakiest steps. Her father was a light sleeper and she couldn't risk waking him.

She made her way into the drab, freezing basement. She kept the lights off and used a small flashlight she'd grabbed in the kitchen to light her way.

A body lay on the table, covered with a sheet. She moved closer and peeled it back. She recognized the man underneath. Everyone in town knew him. It was Mr. Reynolds, owner of Reynolds Grocery. He was the kind of guy who never stopped working, so customers were concerned when they hadn't seen him at the store in a few days. It turned out he'd slipped and fallen in the storeroom. He'd broken his hip, but the doctors expected him to make a full recovery. Unfortunately, while he was in the hospital recovering from his surgery, he'd gotten an infection. Three days later, he was dead, which was how he ended up in the basement of the Sawyer Family Funeral Home.

With his eyes closed and his lips pushed into a peaceful smile, Mr. Reynolds lay in that place between death and burial. The same place Alyssa had visited for twenty-three minutes after she fell through the ice. Which was why Alyssa believed she could use him to connect to the afterlife. His spirit was still floating out there, somewhere. All Alyssa had to do was tune into the right channel.

"Hi, Mr. Reynolds," she whispered from a safe distance from the table where his body lay. "It's me. Alyssa Sawyer. I don't know if you remember me. It's okay if you don't."

Alyssa didn't expect him to answer back, but she thought talking to him might make their connection stronger.

"My mom told me that when I was little and she'd push me in the shopping cart, that you'd always give me a high five and a lollipop. She didn't love that you gave me sugary treats, but she'd let me eat the lollipop on the ride home because she thought you were so nice. Like a real-life Mr. Rogers, she said. I used to love that show. Anyway, I was hoping you might help me remember."

Alyssa waited. Nothing happened. She tried to bring herself back to that day on the ice, but everything was still fuzzy in her mind. It was hard to tell what was really her memory versus what she'd been told about "the incident." She needed to get closer to death.

She glanced at the stairwell to make sure no one was coming. If her father ever discovered what she was up to, he'd never forgive her. Mr. Reynolds' family probably wouldn't be too happy about it either. But Alyssa had to try.

She reached out slowly. Which was silly because it wasn't like she would wake him up. Still, she wanted to be respectful. No sudden movements. Her hand hovered above Mr. Reynolds' forehead for a moment, then she touched it. His skin felt cold and waxy. Alyssa shut her eyes and cast her mind back to the day she woke up in the hospital. She went farther back, into the darkness.

She focused. Her breathing slowed. She went deeper . . .

Water rushed around her, like someone had thrown her into a pool. A freezing one. Her face went numb. She tried to swim up, but her clothes got heavy and pulled her even deeper. She gasped. Her lungs filled with water. She struggled and fought, but the water kept pouring into her . . .

And then she saw it—a tunnel filled with every color of light imaginable.

As she floated through it, an overwhelming sense of calm washed over her. She remembered the entire experience. Every feeling. Every thought.

Just as she was about to reach a bright, glowing light, someone grabbed the hood of her jacket and dragged her back through the tunnel—the man from her nightmares. As he pulled her toward the surface, she twisted her body around and got a clear look at his face. She instantly recognized the man—it was my father.

"I SNAPPED out of whatever trance I was in and ran up to my room as fast as I could," Alyssa said, finishing her story. "I buried myself under the covers, trying to convince myself that my memory wasn't real. That it was just my imagination filling the blanks. It was impossible for the man who saved me to be your father because, according to you, he'd gone missing on the Appalachian Trail. Both things can't have happened, right? So the next morning I asked my mother about it. At first she refused to talk about it, saying it would only make me more upset. But I wouldn't take no for an answer. I wanted the truth. Finally, she admitted what you, and everyone else, have been too scared to tell me—that when I fell through the ice, your father was the one who dove in after me. He died saving me. It was never my memory that was playing tricks on me, Jack. It was *you*."

My heart was racing. I felt like a cornered animal, one that still had some fight left in them.

"I warned you it was a bad idea to talk to that author guy. I knew he'd put a bunch of crazy ideas in your head."

"If anyone has crazy ideas in their head, it's you!"

"I'm not crazy! My father disappeared on the Appalachian Trail!"

It was around that point that Mom got back from the bathroom. I'm not sure how long she'd been standing there, but it was long enough. She stared at me, jaw dropped, eyes filled with worry. "Jack, honey, you know that's not true, right? Your father got back from the trail right after Halloween, remember? He was out on the ice with all of us that day."

Of course I remembered, I just refused to admit it. Because that would have meant admitting that I'd been lying to Alyssa—and myself—for weeks. There would be no saving our friendship after what I'd done. So I stayed stuck in denial. I convinced myself that everyone else had gone mad and that I was the sane one.

It was official—I'd gone full-on Norma Desmond.

Chapter 24

Once we were out of the public eye and in the car, I expected Mom to chew me out but she didn't say a word. She didn't have to. I could see it in her tight lips and clenched jaw and watery eyes. She was angry and confused and hurt, all at once.

We drove the few minutes back to the motel and when we pulled into the parking lot, a cop car was there waiting for us. Sheriff Winslow got out and waved to Mom. At first, I thought maybe Mom had called him to take me away to the nuthouse, but he wasn't there about me.

As we got out of the car, Sheriff Winslow came over. "Apologies for showing up out of the blue like this, but I wanted to tell you both in person."

"Tell us what?" Mom asked.

"Luckily, April's been warmer than usual, so the lake's good and thawed. We can finally send out a team of divers." He looked at me. "They're going to search the lake for your father's body. Once we find him, you and your mother can finally put him to rest and find some closure."

I stared at the sheriff. Did he really want me and Mom to find closure, or was it just a thing people say when someone dies because they're grasping for words? Was it even possible to move on and find closure? I doubted it. And dragging Dad up from the deep was only going to make my grief worse. Like opening up an old wound I'd covered with a pretty convincing scab.

I thanked the sheriff for stopping by, then asked Mom for the key to the room. On my way up, I heard Mom start to sob.

———

BACK IN THE ROOM, Dorothy Jackson was waiting for me, microphone in hand.

"That seems like it was quite a coincidence, wouldn't you say?"

"What?"

"Well, Alyssa finally confronts you about the lie you told her about your father and then the sheriff shows up to inform you about the search for his body?"

"I don't believe there's such a thing as coincidence anymore."

"So are you saying that some greater power worked behind the scenes to make these two events happen within an hour of each other?"

"Maybe."

"Why?"

"I don't know. To force me to deal with all the crap that happened, I guess."

"Are you talking about your father's death?"

"What do you think?"

"One last question before we go. Do you blame Alyssa for what happened to your father?"

"Yeah, maybe I do."

———

THAT NIGHT, Mom and I barely slept. All I could think about was Dad's frozen body somewhere at the bottom of Lake Trapper. What had gone through his mind in his last moments? Was he scared? Did he know he was dying? Did he think about me?

The next morning, Mom called in sick to work and got me excused from school. We ate breakfast at the diner, then drove out to the lake.

Sheriff Winslow and a few cops were already in the parking lot, drinking coffee by their police cars when we got there. A search and rescue boat floated in the water. A couple of guys were putting on diving suits. Sheriff Winslow came over and Mom rolled down her window.

"Good morning," the sheriff said with a tip of his hat, then leaned down to get a look at me. "How are you doing, Jack?"

My throat tightened and I couldn't get any words out, so I just nodded back.

The sheriff got right down to business. He explained the boat would head out to the site of the accident, near the mouth of the bay. The divers would start their search there. If nothing turned up, they'd widen their search radius.

He made everything sound so matter-of-fact. Like they were searching for a boat that had sunk, not a person who drowned, not my dad.

Sheriff Winslow told us it would be at least a few hours before he had any updates, so if we wanted to come back later, we wouldn't be missing anything. Mom refused to leave until they found Dad. Which meant I wasn't going anywhere, either.

The sheriff rejoined the other cops and gave the order to begin the search. The rescue boat with the divers headed into the bay, water churning in its wake.

Mom got out of the car and lit a cigarette. As soon as she finished sucking down one, she stamped the butt out in the gravel and lit up another, the whole time pacing the length of the parking lot. Back and forth, back and forth. She must have burned through three packs that day.

I stayed in the car, staring out at the tiny silhouette of the rescue boat bobbing on the lake. I'd catch glimpses of divers disappearing into the water, then after a while, their heads would pop up. Occasionally the sheriff's walkie-talkie crackled to life, and he'd get an update from the boat about the status of the search. After four hours, they still hadn't found him.

Word of the search must have traveled around town, because by the afternoon, the parking lot was full of cars. A bunch of people had gathered by the shore, pointing out at the rescue boat. Nobody I recognized. I doubted they even knew my father. They were just curious locals acting like it was leaf peeping season or something. I wanted to yell at them to get lost and to mind their own business.

But I stayed put.

A while later, a Channel 5 news van showed up. And who do you think got out? Dorothy Jackson. The real Dorothy Jackson, not the one from my imaginary interviews. She and her camera crew set up by the lake and started filming. Dorothy Jackson interviewed Sheriff Winslow about the recovery effort and talked to a few of the onlookers.

Eventually I spotted two familiar faces in the crowd—Mrs. Sawyer and Alyssa. They were talking to Mom, giving her hugs, their faces full of sadness. I remember Alyssa looking over at me. She didn't wave or smile. I just stared back through the windshield. She was the last person in the world I wanted to talk to.

Alyssa turned away and walked down the path toward the shore. The same path we'd walked that day. My mind drifted back to that morning . . . I saw Alyssa lace up her skates . . . watched her zoom out onto the ice, past me and Dad and Trevor . . . saw her vanish . . .

I shook myself out of the memory and looked at the keys dangling in the ignition. I climbed into the driver's seat and grabbed the wheel. All I had to do was start the car and step on the gas. Then take off somewhere, like Dad did. After wrangling Big Charlie, driving the station wagon would be a piece of cake. I had no clue where I'd go, but the idea of leaving Ravensberg and starting over in a new place where I didn't know anyone and they didn't know me sounded good in my head.

Instead, I got cold feet. There was no running away from this. Not anymore. So I got out of the car and marched over to Dorothy Jackson. I explained who I was and that I was ready to tell her everything.

Dorothy Jackson's face lit up, like she'd gotten the interview of a lifetime. She had me stand with the lake behind me and the cameraman framed the shot. Then she asked me to describe what happened that day, from the beginning.

Doing a real interview was a lot more nerve-racking than an imaginary one. But I tried to be as honest as I could. It was all kind of a blur.

I told her how, the day after Christmas, Mom and Dad brought me, Trevor, and Alyssa out to the lake to go ice skating. It was cold that morning and only a few other families were out on the ice. The lake looked frozen over, but my dad told us not to go out too far, just to be safe.

I told her how Trevor and I found a couple of long branches

and used them like hockey sticks to hit rocks across the ice like they were pucks. Alyssa wasn't interested. She went off to skate by herself and I lost track of her. At some point, I remember spotting her way out on the ice, zigzagging back and forth. It looked like she was trying to skate the entire way across.

I told her how I shouted Alyssa's name, over and over, and that she didn't answer. But I didn't know if she was too far away to hear me or if she was ignoring me.

I told her how one second Alyssa was there, and the next, she disappeared, like she'd dropped off the edge of a cliff.

I told her how I tried to scream, but my voice caught in my throat. How I tried to move, but it felt like my feet had stuck to the ice.

I told her how Dad had seen the whole thing and didn't hesitate. He looked like one of those speed skaters at the winter Olympics, body low, arms swinging. When he got to the spot where Alyssa had fallen in, he skidded to a stop and stared into the water. A second later, he jumped in like he was part of a polar bear plunge, except he had all his winter clothes on.

I told her how, by that point, the feeling had returned to my feet. I tried to skate out to help my dad, but Trevor grabbed my arm and jerked me back. He told me not to do anything stupid. That my mom was calling for help from the parking lot payphone.

I told her how Alyssa came out of the water first. How my dad shoved her onto the ice. How her body didn't move. How my dad tried to pull himself out, but he couldn't get a grip. How he slipped back into the water and didn't resurface. How I heard the sirens wailing in the distance.

How the whole time, I stood there, helpless to do anything.

The rest of "the incident" I only remembered in bits and pieces.

The ambulance, fire truck, and police car arrived. Sheriff

Winslow ordered everyone off the ice. The firefighters went out and brought Alyssa to shore, where the EMTs took over. Trevor's dad gave her CPR. They put her in the ambulance and took her away. I was sure she was dead. Mom grabbed me and hugged me so tightly I couldn't breathe. The firefighters stuck long poles in the water but they couldn't pull Dad out. The ice started cracking more, so Sheriff Winslow called off the rescue before anyone else fell in. Mom screamed at the sheriff to do something more, but he said they were out of options. He couldn't send divers into the freezing lake. They would have to wait until the temperatures warmed, and the lake thawed, which wouldn't happen for months. Until then, Dad would be lying at the bottom of the lake.

"That's a lot to handle for someone your age," Dorothy Jackson said. "How have you managed to deal with it all?"

I was completely honest with her. "I tried hard not to."

After the interview was done, I made my way over to Alyssa, who was still near the shore, staring out across the lake.

"So you know, I'm done lying about that day," I said.

Alyssa turned to me, her face covered in tears. "It's too late for that."

"I'm sorry."

"And it's too late for an apology."

RIGHT BEFORE DUSK, the divers finally found Dad. By the time the rescue boat came to shore, the crowd had thinned, but Channel 5's cameraman filmed the whole thing. Dad's body was wrapped in black plastic, the same as Renny's. The cops placed the body bag on a stretcher and wheeled it over to the coroner's van. Sheriff Winslow had told us they would do an autopsy on Dad's body, which seemed like a waste of time. You didn't need to be a coroner to know he died from drowning in freezing water.

As the van drove off, Mom burst into tears. I thought I would, too, but I felt strangely calm. Like I was watching a scene from a movie. Like none of it was real. I guess, despite my best efforts, I was still desperate to believe it wasn't.

Chapter 25

The morning of Dad's wake, Mom put on a long black dress and makeup and then went outside to smoke.

She'd laid a suit out for me at the foot of my bed. It was dark blue—not black—but close enough. The last time I'd worn it was for my confirmation. When Mom came back in, she instructed me to wash up and get dressed.

"I doubt that stupid suit even fits me anymore," I complained.

"These are the only nice clothes you have. Everything else is in storage," Mom said.

I dragged myself out of bed and took a long shower. I let the water get as hot as it could and stood under it until my skin burned. By the time I finished, my body was red, and the bathroom was so full of steam I could barely see the toilet.

When I put on the jacket and pants, sure enough, my arms and legs stretched a couple of inches past the cuffs. Mom made me wear the suit, anyway. At least she helped me tie the tie. Dad had never taught me how to do it on my own.

We drove to the Sawyers for the wake. Mr. Sawyer had donated his services for free. Maybe he was just being nice or maybe he felt guilty that Dad had died saving Alyssa, I'm not sure. If it had been up to me, we would've skipped the wake and gone straight to the burying Dad part. I just didn't see the point. Mr. Sawyer was good at his job, but even he couldn't fix up Dad's face nicely enough to make him presentable. The coroner had told Mom that Dad's body "exhibited advanced decomposition," which sounded like a fancy way of saying the fishes had gotten to him. Since Dad wasn't fit to be seen, Mr. Sawyer suggested we have a closed casket service. Which is how it should always be. I never understood why people wanted to look at someone who was dead, then hang around to have snacks.

Mom pulled up outside the Sawyers. We were the first ones there. Mr. Sawyer wanted us to arrive early, so we'd have time alone in the viewing room. Mom shut off the car and sighed. "Let's go."

"I'm gonna wait in the car."

"I know this is hard, but you have to do it."

"Who says?"

Mom leaned over and put her hand on my knee. "My grandmother was only in her fifties when she died. My parents thought I was too young to go to the funeral, so they sent me to stay with a friend of the family. I was only nine or ten, so I didn't really care. But as I got older, I always felt this hurt in my heart anytime someone mentioned Grammy or told a story about her. It still hurts . . . Anyway, I think my parents were just trying to protect me from all the emotional stuff, but it only dragged out the suffering."

"Your grammy was the one who died of lung cancer, right?"

Mom pulled her hand off my knee. "That's not the point. I just wish I'd had the chance to say good-bye."

"But maybe if she had quit smoking, you wouldn't have had to say good-bye."

Mom turned and stared out the window. "Please, Jack. I can't do this alone."

"You won't be alone. See?" I pointed across the street where Mr. Donlan had just parked.

"This isn't about Mr. Donlan, okay? This is about you and me. When you ran off . . . I've never felt so alone. Not even when your father left. After that happened, I was furious, but at least I still had you. I said to myself, as long as me and Jack are together, we'll get through this.

"But now your father's gone for real. So whether you like it or not, it's just you and me in this ridiculous world together. I need to know I can count on you."

There was pain in Mom's eyes. I wanted to promise her I'd never leave her alone again. But I would've been lying. And I was so tired of lying to people.

"Dad never showed up for me. Why should I show up for him?"

"Because that's what you do when someone you love dies. For a few days, you forget about all the not-so-great stuff they did and focus on the nice memories."

"I don't have any nice memories," I said.

Mom's face fell and her jaw tightened. For a second I thought she might slap me again, but she kept it together. Mostly. "Fine. Do whatever the hell you want. Skip the funeral tomorrow, too. I don't care anymore."

When she got out, she slammed the car door so hard I thought the window was going to shatter. Mr. Donlan came over to put his hand on her shoulder. They were talking, but I couldn't hear what they were saying. Mr. Donlan glanced at me in the car and it looked like he wanted to come over and talk to me, but Mom grabbed his hand and pulled him the other way. They headed inside, arm in arm.

A little while later, more cars arrived and people in their

black suits and dresses filed inside, looking somber. I slunk down in the seat, hoping no one would notice me. The last thing I needed was some well-meaning friend of the family to come over and tell me how sorry they were.

While I was crouched down in my seat hiding, I opened the glove compartment where Mom sometimes stashed extra cigarettes for emergencies. There was an old pack of Virginia Slims with two cigarettes left. I'd seen Mom smoke enough that I knew how to do it. I lit one with the car lighter and took a long drag. It tasted like trash and made me cough, but I kept puffing. I rolled down the window and blew out the smoke. Eventually a numbness seeped through me. I smoked the second one.

That's when I noticed something else stuffed inside the glove compartment—the envelope Renny had left me. I'd completely forgotten I'd shoved it in there after leaving Lincoln Emerson's office.

I pulled out the envelope and flattened it on my leg and stared at my name written on the front. I took the cigarette out of my mouth and held the burning tip close to the corner of the envelope. It smoldered. But a sadness came over me. I used my sleeve to snuff out the burning paper before it went up in flames.

I flicked the cigarette butt out the window and ripped open the envelope. Inside were two lined notebook pages filled with Renny's chunky handwriting.

DEAR JACK,

Right now, you're sitting in a cab wondering why the hell I'm meeting with a lawyer. Well, if you're reading this letter, that means Mr. Emerson has been in touch and you've gotten your answer. I hope you and your mother enjoy living in the cabin. I expect you'll find it's a pleasant life. Living in the woods can be really peaceful. Just ask Henry David Thoreau.

I appreciate you bringing me home from the hospital and getting me settled. It means a lot. I can be difficult to be around, especially lately, but I hope you realize that I'm grateful for your friendship.

I'm not sure how much time I have until death comes knocking, but I assume it's a matter of weeks now, not months. I can feel it in my bones. I sure wonder what's waiting for me on the other side.

Before things take a turn and I'm too weak to pick up a pen, I wanted to share some thoughts. If you don't want to hear them, you're welcome to tear up this letter and forget you ever received it. But my hope is, you won't. My hope is, these words will help you down the road.

I'm not exactly sure where to start, so how about the day I spotted you standing outside the mall. I hadn't planned on stopping, but I meant what I said to you that day. I took it as a sign that we were destined to meet. But more than that, you reminded me of him. Of Charlie. Or at least what I imagined he might have looked like at your age.

And seeing you out there, looking so lost and alone, I guess you also reminded me of myself when I was younger. Back then, it felt like nothing in this damn world made any sense. It was hard for me to appreciate the good in life because the bad was always lurking around the corner. I wanted to steer you in a better direction, assuming you'd let me help. I just didn't realize how lost you truly were.

I need to confess something. I wasn't completely honest with you. But I hope you'll understand on account of you not being completely honest with me. Hear me out.

A couple of days after you started working for me, I was reading the paper and there was a story about that girl who'd fallen through the ice on Lake Trapper. The article talked about how she'd woken up after being in a coma. And then it mentioned the man who died saving her life. A man named Mark Finn. That's when I realized who you were and all you'd been through.

Well, I nearly fell out of my chair. What were the chances I'd meet that man's son in the mall parking lot and offer him a job?

And here's another strange thing. Charlie died at the end of September of '68. Then I find out you were born a couple of weeks later. If there's such a thing as reincarnation, damn if that doesn't fit the description. Sure, you can call it just another coincidence. But eventually you pile up enough coincidences and it starts to mean something.

As the great Thoreau wrote, "The universe is wider than our views of it."

Anyway, I didn't want to pry into your personal business. But I could tell that losing your father . . . your friend almost dying . . . all that grief had you running from reality.

So, I confess. I brought you to the Army Surplus store on purpose. My buddy who works there, Dave, remembered you coming in with your old man when he was stocking up to hike the Appalachian Trail. After you bolted from the store, I knew I'd hit a nerve, but it was obvious you needed another nudge in the right direction. Which is why I led you out to the lake that day, so you might face what happened and come to terms with it. I knew if you didn't, all that heartache was going to destroy you. Most folks, when faced with death, run the other way. It's human nature, I suppose. But I can tell you from experience, the only way to deal with grief is to turn toward it and look it square in the eye.

When I was over in Vietnam, they stationed my unit in this little remote village. The only way in and out was by helicopter. We were there to protect the place, and to weed out any conspirators working with the Viet Cong against the Americans.

The thing was, these villagers had been through hell. People suffered from horrible burns, men were missing arms and legs, and kids were dying from starvation. Sadly, that village was nothing out of the ordinary. By that point in the war, the entire country was a giant pit of suffering and misery. But the villagers still took care of one another. If one mother fell sick, another mother watched over her kids until she got better. If a husband got killed in the fighting, his neighbor would step in and help his family.

I'll be honest, it was hard seeing all that pain, knowing my country was the cause of it and feeling like I couldn't do a damn thing about it. But I also witnessed joy. Every day, I'd catch a smile on a villager's face or hear the old women laughing or see children playing. It made me start to see life differently.

Somehow, the people in the community found the strength to collect all that loss and carry it with them as they went on living. There was hope even in the middle of darkness. And I glimpsed a path forward. If those villagers could endure all that grief, so could I.

And so can you.

You have a good heart, Jack. You're a good person. I wish I could promise life will get better, but it might not. But what I know for sure is that you're strong. Stronger than you realize. And I'm proud of you. Living in this world is complicated, but I have faith you'll make it. I'm sorry things turned out this way. I wish we'd had more time to get to know each other. You're a special kid. But whatever comes next, please don't give up.

One last thing. Keep an eye on Seneca after I'm gone. He can take care of himself, but he seems to like your company.

I love you, Jack. And I hope you remember me.

—Renny

AFTER READING Renny's letter for the third time, I folded the paper and slid it back in the envelope and put the envelope in my pocket. Then I carried it with me into the wake. I felt like I could face death as long as Renny's words were with me.

When I walked in, everyone turned to look at me. I tried to ignore the stares and the barrage of "I'm so sorrys." Mrs. Sawyer welcomed me and took me over to Mom, who looked surprised to see me.

She gave me a hug and whispered, "I'm glad you're here." She encouraged me to go up to the casket and be with Dad, but only if I was ready. No pressure. I sat in one of the folding chairs on the side of the room watching people file past the casket, kneeling and making the sign of the cross and whispering prayers. There were a lot of tears, but a lot of laughter and love, too.

When almost everyone had cleared out, I took my turn at the casket. I didn't kneel or say a prayer or do any of the religious stuff. I just stood there silently, bowed my head, and ran a hand over the smooth finish of the wood, picturing Dad inside.

The only words I could think to say were, "I miss you."

Chapter 26

The next day, Mom and I went to the church for the service. Dad's coffin had been placed by the altar. Father Murray greeted us and said something about how God was watching over him now. He ushered us to the pew in the front and we sat there while the congregation filled the rows behind us. It seemed like the whole town of Ravensberg had shown up. There were people I'd expected to see, like the Donlans and the Sawyers, along with some of our relatives, as well as a few faces I recognized from Dad's work. But there were a lot of unfamiliar faces, too. I was surprised so many people turned out to mourn my father.

On the wall behind the altar, Jesus stared down at me from his cross, his hands and feet all bloody, his crown of thorns digging into his head. I started getting all sweaty and pulled at my tie to loosen it. Now, I'm not saying I suddenly started believing in God again. But seeing Jesus' suffering made me think about how we're all suffering. Every day. We might not show it. It's not like we literally have nails through our hands and feet or blood trickling down our faces, but it can feel like that. Especially when someone dies. At least that's how it felt to me.

Father Murray came out in his white robes. He had married my parents, baptized me, and given me my first communion. He'd known my family a long time, so I hoped listening to him would give me some peace about Dad and Renny being gone. But he kept going on and on about how we have to trust in God's will and that God would bear our grief and other crap like that. I kept wringing my hands and couldn't keep still.

Once Father Murray finished, he asked others to give their tributes. I didn't know the first man who spoke, but he used to work with Dad. He told a story about how every time Dad went out to lunch with his fellow office workers, they'd pass a homeless guy on the street. My father's coworker said Dad always bought an extra meal at the restaurant so he could give it to the homeless guy. He called Dad one of the most generous men he'd ever met. Then he got a little choked up and sat back down.

Listening to the man talk, it sounded like he was describing some stranger. Not my father. But then I remembered this one time when I was six or seven. We were driving around doing errands, and Dad spotted a car by the side of the road with a flat tire. A woman and her two little kids were standing next to it. Dad didn't think twice. He hit the brakes and pulled over. He got out and pulled the spare from the trunk and changed the tire. Father Murray would have called him a good samaritan.

Aunt Beth stood next. She spoke about the day she got the call from my mom that her big brother, Mark, was dead. She said it was the worst day of her life because God had taken away her guardian angel. When my grandmother died—Dad and Aunt Beth's mom—Dad was the one who made all the arrangements. And when my grandfather started losing his

226

memory, Dad found an old folks' home that could take good care of him.

"He watched over all of us, Aunt Beth said. I miss you, Marky." She looked toward the sky and blew a kiss.

Mom sobbed and dabbed her eyes with a tissue. As Aunt Beth passed by, Mom got up to give her a big hug. Then it was time for Mom to give the eulogy.

She hadn't wanted to speak. She was afraid of standing in front of everyone and the words not coming. So she'd written her thoughts on a piece of paper. But as soon as she was at the podium, she sort of froze, just staring at the paper, totally silent. I wondered if I should to do something, but Father Murray walked over to Mom and whispered something in her ear. She waved him off and said she was all right. Then she took a deep breath and started talking.

First, Mom thanked everyone for coming. It meant a lot to her that the community showed up to support us. Then she told the story about the first time she and Dad met—which, by the way, I had never heard before, even after all those years living under the same roof.

In 1966, my parents were in college, but not at the same one. Mom went to an all-girls' school and Dad was at an all-boys' university the next town over. But every year, the boys and girls would meet up at a spring formal dance. That's where they first met. Dad caught Mom's eye, but she was too nervous to talk to him. Later, when he asked her to dance, Mom told him she already had a boyfriend. Dad slunk away, all disappointed.

When she got back to her dorm room that night, she lay awake, beating herself up for not dancing with Dad. Because she didn't have a boyfriend. She'd lied to him and couldn't explain why. Nerves, she guessed.

She figured she'd blown her chance, and that was the last she'd see of him. But then a few weekends later, she ran into

Dad again, at the local diner. This time she marched right up to him and said she'd broken up with her boyfriend and that she'd like to take him up on that dance. Dad smiled and put a quarter in the jukebox and they danced to the Beatles while everyone in the diner watched them like they were the most carefree couple in the world.

"Mark wasn't worried about what everyone else thought," she said. "And that was the moment I fell in love with him."

They got married right after graduation and bought the house I would eventually grew up in. The house she'd just sold.

Then Mom admitted she'd never told Dad she'd lied to him about her nonexistent boyfriend. "Mark went to his grave not knowing that the first words I'd ever spoken to him were untrue." She'd always wanted to tell him, but she'd always talk herself out of coming clean. It was so far in the past, and besides, what good would come of it, anyway? But in the end, she wished she'd told him and that there weren't any secrets left between them. "I'm sorry, Mark."

Then things took a turn, and Mom started laying into Dad. She said how challenging it was being married to him because he was gone so much, and when he was around, he acted really distant. She complained that he had a hard time expressing himself. I guess that was something me and Dad had in common.

The whole church went silent, and I could hear people shifting uncomfortably and coughing. But I leaned forward in the pew, wanting to hear more.

Mom looked up to the ceiling like she was talking to Dad up in heaven. Or wherever he was.

"I'm so mad at you, Mark. I've never known anyone who made me as angry as you did. But of all the infuriating things you've done over the years, abandoning me and Jack to walk that stupid trail was the most maddening. I figured you'd quit at some point, but you didn't. You stuck with it to the end and proved me wrong. Then you came back to us. When you walked through our front door after all those months, I could see in your eyes that you were a changed man. I took it as a sign. I told myself, 'If Mark could pull it together to finish the Appalachian Trail, then we could pull it together to be a family again.' And we almost did.

"But then you had to be the hero and dive into that lake and abandon me and Jack all over again. My heart broke that day because I knew you wouldn't be coming back a second time.

"But Alyssa did come back. She survived because of you. People have talked about your kindness toward strangers, and that's all true, but I knew you, Mark. And you were never the guy who'd run into a burning building to save someone. You didn't have it in you. So you're really putting me in a bind here. I want to hate you for being selfish and leaving our family. But I have a feeling that if you hadn't faced the challenges on the trail and come out stronger on the other end, we'd be here mourning Alyssa instead of you.

"Somehow, your selfishness gave you the courage to do the most selfless thing possible, to give up your life to save another's. You weren't a saint. God knows, neither am I. But you were a good man, Mark. One of the best. And I'll always love you."

Mom sat back down, and I put my arm around her. Over the congregation's sobs and nose blowing, Father Murray asked if anyone else would like to speak. After a long silence, someone called out.

"I'd like to say something."

It was Alyssa. The crowd murmured in surprise as she walked down the aisle to the podium. The Miracle Girl was front and center.

Alyssa started off by speaking to me and Mom. She thanked my father for saving her life and told us she would be eternally grateful to him. She apologized for him being gone on account of her. I could tell she meant it. Then she turned to everyone in the church.

"You all know the story of what happened that day, probably better than I do. Because until last week, I didn't remember the accident or what happened to me during the twenty-three minutes I was dead. I wasn't sure I wanted to tell you about what I went through because I can't prove it happened. I can only tell you what I experienced. Maybe you'll think I'm delusional." Alyssa's gaze found mine and our eyes locked. "But keeping it to myself . . . that won't help either."

I didn't think she was delusional. The only one who'd been guilty of holding on to a fantasy had been me. I nodded at her to say, *Go ahead. I'm listening.*

Alyssa nodded back and looked out at the congregation. She explained that when she was drowning, she didn't scream or panic, like you'd expect. She actually felt more alive than ever. Her spirit peeled away from her body and floated away, like a leaf in the wind, and traveled to another realm.

In that realm, she was greeted by spirits who were overjoyed to meet her, but she didn't recognize any of them. They took her on a pathway that exploded with every color in the universe. She experienced all of eternity in a second. She had a sense of being home.

At the same time, she could see her body back on earth was in danger, and she prepared to leave it behind. The spirits embraced her in warmth and love. It was the first time she felt acknowledged and really seen. But the spirits told her it wasn't her time and that she had to go back.

The next thing she remembered was waking up in the hospital.

Once Alyssa was able to recall her near-death experience, it totally changed how she saw the world. It taught her we can never know everything and that we have to live with uncertainty. Her knowledge came with a heaviness that weighed on her, but also an appreciation of life. She could now find beauty in places she never saw it before, like in a flower growing out of a crack in the sidewalk. And it changed how she thought of dying. How it's not the final word. It's not the end. The people we lose still survive, just in new forms, in a distant realm. And we'll see them again.

None of us had ever heard Alyssa talk like that before. She was always so quiet and reserved. But in that moment, she was brave and strong, like a wise soul who'd lived a thousand lifetimes.

Alyssa said death had always seemed like a big, terrifying unknown. She looked at me and Mom, then at Trevor and his parents.

"I understand how you feel and I know it's scary. But I promise you there is beauty and light on the other side. And that when Mark and Scotty died, they weren't scared. They were at peace. And they're surrounded by love."

People were emotional after Mom's eulogy, but it was double that after Alyssa finished.

That's when I lost it. The sadness I'd been fighting to hold back for so long all came out and I just collapsed in the pew, crying and crying. I tried to stop, but I couldn't. Mom wrapped her arms around me and held me and told me it was all right. To let it out.

The people in the church that day didn't look away or walk out, even though some of them probably wanted to. No, they stayed while I had a total breakdown. Someone even started singing a hymn, and one by one other people joined in until everyone's voices filled the church.

Chapter 27

I eventually ran out of tears—for Scotty, for Alyssa, for Renny, for Dad. Once I pulled myself together, Father Murray finished the service. Then we all went to the cemetery for the funeral. When they lowered Dad's coffin into the ground, another wave of sadness overcame me and I broke down again.

After the burial, people gathered at the Sawyers' for a reception. Mrs. Sawyer had offered to host it since we couldn't exactly invite a bunch of people over to our motel room.

As soon as Mom and I walked in, Mr. Sawyer was the first to greet us. He gave Mom a hug and said how sorry he was. Then he looked down at me and held out his hand, so I shook it. "If you ever need anything, let me know. All right, Jack?"

It was weird to have Mr. Sawyer talk to me like that. Or talk to me at all, really. Usually when I came over, he was so busy he'd just say a quick hi and disappear into the basement. But he held my hand longer than I expected and looked me in the eye, like he wanted me to take his words to heart.

"All right, Mr. Sawyer. Thanks."

Mom and I got some food on paper plates and sat on the

couch. I didn't eat. For the next hour, person after person came up to say how sorry they were for our loss and that it would get easier and to let them know if we needed anything. I winced whenever someone looked at me with pity. My cheeks burned with humiliation every time someone offered another condolence. And I swear, they all said almost the exact same things, like they'd been reading off a pamphlet that told them "the top five ways to tell the family of a dead person you care."

When the Donlans came over, it surprised me to see them together. But it showed that even in the face of grief, people can put aside their hurt feelings and lean on one another. Though there was one awkward moment. When Mr. Donlan hugged Mom, Mrs. Donlan tensed up and clenched her fist. She didn't make a scene or anything, but it was clear she wasn't happy with the situation.

Trevor asked if I wanted to go to the arcade after school the next day.

"Yeah, that'd be fun," I said. It seemed like things were cool with us again, which was a relief.

But things weren't cool between me and Alyssa. Every once in a while, I'd catch glimpses of her through the crowd, but the second we'd make eye contact, she'd turn away and disappear into another part of the house. I figured she was still angry with me for lying to her and I couldn't blame her.

Finally, I couldn't take all the tears and pity and condolences anymore and I looked for a way to escape people's relentless sympathy. I excused myself to use the bathroom, even though I didn't have to go. Wandering the halls, I eventually found Alyssa alone in her dad's study. She sat in a leather chair, staring at a chessboard. I walked over and sat in the chair across from her.

"Wanna play?" I asked.

Alyssa wouldn't even look at me. She just shrugged.

"What you talked about at church today . . . it was pretty incredible. You should write to Aldous Watts and tell him about your near-death experience."

"Maybe I will."

"He might want to put it in his next book."

"When did you become an Aldous Watts fan?"

"I'm not. But I realized . . . after what you went through . . . your story could really help people."

"Why are you trying to be nice to me? You must hate me."

"I thought you hated *me*."

"I guess we both have reasons to be mad at each other."

Even though that was true, I hoped my anger would melt away once Alyssa explained herself. "Why'd you skate out so far? My dad warned you not to."

Alyssa finally looked up, her eyes red and puffy, like she hadn't been crying just that day, but for the past week. "Why'd you tell me your dad was missing when, this whole time, you knew he saved my life?"

We stared at each other across the chessboard. Neither of us owned up to our mistakes or offered an apology.

"It's your move," Alyssa said.

I realized I was sitting on the side with the white pieces, so I slid a pawn into the center of the board. Alyssa moved her pawn to meet mine. While we played, my mind drifted back to the first time we'd met.

"Remember the first day of kindergarten?" I said. "After my parents dropped me off, I saw you and your mom going into the school. You wore a red dress with a white flower and you were holding a Snoopy lunchbox and your hair was in pigtails. Anyway, you were bawling your eyes out and your mom kept saying it was okay and not to cry and that she'd see you right after school. But nothing she said calmed you down. So I walked over and introduced myself and said that I liked your lunchbox and showed you mine."

"The Superman one?"

"Yeah. I asked if you wanted to go to class with me and you said yes and stopped crying. We ate lunch together every day after that."

Alyssa clicked her fingernails against the chessboard. "Is that supposed to explain why you lied to me?"

"Sort of. You were so upset that day. I wanted to help you not feel so scared. And I think that's what I was trying to do after you woke up from the coma—to make the world not feel so scary. For the both of us."

Alyssa nodded, taking it in. She moved her bishop and captured one of my pawns. "I wasn't crying on the first day of kindergarten because I was scared."

"You weren't?"

"No, it was because my dad had promised to drop me off with Mom. But on our way out the door, he said he couldn't come. And that's how it's been my whole life with him. He's never really been there. I mean, he was physically there, right down in the basement, but I barely ever saw him except for a few minutes at dinner sometimes. He was there, but not. I believed he enjoyed spending time with dead bodies more than he enjoyed being around me—his living, breathing daughter. So when I was out on the ice that day, I got this idea that if I skated out far enough . . . if I let myself sink into the water and disappear into the darkness forever, I could become one of his dead bodies. And that way, he'd have no choice but to spend time with me."

I sat stunned, unsure what to say, so I echoed the words I'd heard all day. "I'm so sorry."

"The strange thing is, my plan kind of worked," Alyssa continued. "There was a reason Mom sent my sisters to live with my aunt while she spent all her time at the hospital with me. It was so my dad could train an assistant to help with the funeral business. The accident made him realize he needed to spend more time with our family. I'm happy about it, but the cost of getting there was too high. I never meant for things to turn out this way."

"Neither did I," I said. "But what happens to us? Are we still going to be friends?"

"How would that even work? Every time I look at you now, I remember that day and how your father is dead because of me."

"I want to forgive you. It might take some time, but eventually . . . " Even as the words came out, I knew I was grasping for something that could never be recovered. There was no way to return to the friendship we'd once had. Alyssa had understood that sooner than I had.

"Even if you could forgive me, I don't know if I'll ever forgive myself," Alyssa said. "Turns out, the only thing worse than losing your memory is being forced to remember all the ways you've hurt the people you love."

The truth of her words hit me hard. "Are you saying we should forget that we know each other? That our friendship is over?"

"Maybe for now," she said quietly.

"At least can we finish this game?"

Alyssa calmly laid down her king and resigned. "Good-bye, Jack."

That was more than a year ago, and I haven't really talked to Alyssa since. I still see her around school, but she always keeps her distance. I've gotten used to our new reality.

When Trevor and I met up at the arcade, he told me that his parents' divorce was official. The family court judge had decided on joint custody. Four days a week he lived with his mom and the rest of the time he stayed with his dad at his new apartment.

"Are you glad it's finally all settled?" I asked.

Trevor shrugged. "At least I know where things stand now."

Even though no one was playing Pac-Man, Trevor walked past it and went over to Donkey Kong. It was his new obsession. He'd only been playing it a couple of weeks and his initials already had a spot on the high score screen. We popped our quarters into the game and Donkey Kong starting chucking barrels.

Trevor jerked the joystick up and down, right and left. Mario leaped over barrels and scaled ladders all the way to the top platform, where Donkey Kong held Mario's girlfriend captive. Trevor cleared three boards on his first turn. I didn't even get past one. A couple of kids put their quarters on the console and waited their turn. I told them they'd be waiting a while. The kids perked up when they realized who Trevor was.

"You're the Pac-Man Kid," one kid said.

Trevor smiled. "I used to be."

"Yeah, I was here when you beat the game," the other kid said. "It was amazing!"

"More like the game beat me."

While Trevor played, the kids asked if there was a trick to playing Donkey Kong, like there was with Pac-Man.

Trevor smashed a barrel with a hammer. "I haven't tried to figure out the pattern. I'm just trying to have fun."

A couple of nights later, I was lying in bed at the motel, watching TV while Mom was out with Mr. Donlan. They'd gone across the street to the diner for dinner. Another date, I figured.

I heard their footsteps outside when they came back. Mom sounded upset, so I turned the TV down and moved closer to the window to listen.

"I'm really sorry about this," Mr. Donlan said.

Mom sniffled, her voice tearful. "I just thought . . . now that the divorce was final, we could make this work."

"Pam, you're a wonderful woman."

"Not wonderful enough, apparently. I failed at my marriage, I failed with Jack, and now I failed with you."

"No, you're a great mother."

"Then why does my son hate me so much?"

"Because he's a fourteen-year-old boy. That's how they're wired. I remember hating my parents when I was his age."

Hearing Mom say that I hated her didn't feel good. She wasn't a bad person. Sure, I was mad at her for a lot of things she'd said and done. But I never stopped loving her. I mean, she is my mom, after all. And I hadn't been entirely fair to her. Some might say I'd been an asshole.

After Mom and Mr. Donlan parted ways, I unlocked the door. Mom just stood there, realizing I'd overheard everything.

"Well, this was what you wanted, right? No more Mr. Donlan." Her voice sounded weak and tired and sad.

Sure, I had wanted their relationship to be over, but I never wanted her to end up heartbroken. I hugged her.

"Looks like it's just you and me in this ridiculous world together," I said. "And I'm tired of living in this stupid motel. I'm ready to move out."

Mom wiped away her tears and smiled. "Me, too."

———

THE NEXT DAY, Mom and I drove to Lincoln Emerson's office, and I told him I'd decided to accept Renny's gift. Mr. Emerson explained there was one other condition to me getting the inheritance.

"It's regarding Mr. Laforge's remains." Mr. Emerson explained that Renny hated the idea of being buried in a graveyard so he had made arrangements to be cremated. "Someone from the crematorium will contact you soon about taking possession of the ashes."

Mom signed the papers, and a week later we packed up the car and said good riddance to the Treetop Motel.

Chapter 28

I was excited about moving into Renny's cabin, but I couldn't help feeling a little weird about the whole thing.

The gravel crunched under the tires as we drove up to the gate. I got out of the car to open it, but when I got back in, Mom didn't hit the gas. She sat in silence, staring out at the woods.

"Here we are," she said.

"Having second thoughts?" I asked.

"No. It's just . . . I never imagined my life turning out like this."

"Me either."

The station wagon bumped along the path until we reached the cabin. We pulled up next to Big Charlie and got out. I patted Big Charlie's hood and took a deep breath, inhaling the piney forest.

"It's so quiet out here," Mom said. "Almost too quiet."

"It grows on you," I said.

Mom opened the trunk, and we unpacked our boxes. We carried them inside the cabin and looked around. Specks of dust floated in a beam of sunlight coming through the window. All of Renny's furniture and belongings were still there. Off to the sides were wooden shelves cluttered with Renny's old books. Seneca's food and water bowls were still by the front door, empty. Flies buzzed around the foul-smelling kitchen sink, which was full of dirty dishes.

Mom opened a window to air out the place, then got to work, unpacking and organizing. "It'll take some elbow grease to get this place clean. But it'll be worth it."

I found myself drifting into the living room, passing by Renny's chair. Then something caught my eye through the window. It was the figure of a man. My breath caught. I know this'll sound like another one of my delusions, but I believe it was Renny, or his spirit. He stood by the door to the bunker, grinning. He gave a little wave and walked off into the forest.

I bolted outside, heart racing, but there was no sign of Renny, or anyone else. One second he'd been there and the next —gone. The woods had swallowed him whole. A shiver went through me. I blamed it on the cold. Maybe my mind was playing tricks on me, but after what Alyssa experienced, who knows? The barrier between life and death seems to be a lot thinner than we think.

In the distance, I heard tires crunching on dirt and an engine rumbling. A van approached and pulled up in front of the cabin. The logo on the side said, "Ashes to Ashes." A big guy with a bushy mustache got out and asked if this was the Finn residence.

"It is now," I said.

Mom came outside and stood on the porch.

"You folks sure are hard to find out here," the big guy said as he opened the back of the van and took out a box wrapped in brown kraft paper tied with twine. It looked like the world's most boring present. He held it out to me. "Sorry about your father."

"Oh, this isn't my father," I said, looking down at the box, picturing the ashes inside. "He was a friend."

I reached out and took the box. It was a lot heavier than I expected.

"My condolences," the big guy said, handing Mom a clipboard with a pen. Mom signed for the delivery and the big guy got back in his van and drove off.

"I don't get it," Mom said. "Renny could have had you sprinkle his ashes anywhere out in nature. Instead, he asked you to stick him in a bunker underground."

"How is it any different from Dad being buried in a coffin?"

Mom shrugged. "I guess it isn't."

"Want to come with me?"

"You go ahead. This is between you and Renny. I'm going to start cooking dinner. Come up when you're ready."

I waited until I was in the bunker to unwrap the box. I opened the lid and took out an urn. It was a simple clay container. Nothing fancy, which fit with Renny's style. I unscrewed the top and peered inside at the gray ashes. I reached in and touched them. They felt coarse, like sand. I stood there for a while, holding Renny's remains. It's bizarre how a whole human body can be reduced to a few pounds of ash.

I said a brief prayer, thanking Renny for being my friend when I felt all alone. Then I screwed the top back on and placed the urn on the bookshelf, as he'd requested. It sat between the Bible and *Letters from a Stoic*.

"I wish I could live down here with you," I said to the urn. "But Mom kinda needs me up there. Don't worry, though. I'll come visit a lot. Promise."

I took out the letter Renny had written to me and placed it underneath the urn. Whenever I hang out in the bunker now, I read it. It's not exactly like having Renny with me. But it's close enough.

The puzzle with the picture of the covered bridge was still laid out on the coffee table. I'd never found that missing piece, so the church steeple would forever be incomplete. But I was okay with it. The riddle of the lost piece was more beautiful than the answer could ever be.

———

THAT NIGHT, Mom cooked spaghetti and meatballs and we ate at Renny's rickety wooden table. I swear, it was the best meal of my life.

Mom had made the same dinner the night Dad finally showed up on our doorstep, a few weeks after my fourteenth birthday. His hair and beard were all grown out, he'd lost a lot of weight, and he was leaning on a crutch because he'd sprained his ankle. Mom stood there in shock for a minute before giving him an enormous hug. I didn't move from the couch. He told us both how much he loved us and that he was home for good. I desperately wanted to believe him.

After giving Mom a kiss, Dad came over to me and apologized for not making it back in time for my birthday. He hated himself for not keeping his promise, but he needed to see his journey through to the end.

"I know you're probably confused and angry with me right now," he said. "I don't blame you. But I needed to find myself to find my way back to you."

He told me I'd understand when I got older. Maybe someday I will.

While we ate, Dad told us bits and pieces about his adventure. Some of it sounded great—sleeping under the stars, watching amazing sunsets, living among nature. A lot of it sounded awful—almost getting bitten by a rattlesnake, surviving a lightning storm, and getting sick from drinking from a stream.

243

"I had good days and bad," Dad told us. "And it took everything I had to get up in the morning and keep moving. In a lot of ways, it wasn't so different from my regular life."

"How did it feel when you reached the end?" Mom asked.

"At first I felt nothing, just this emptiness. But as I sat on the summit of Mount Katahdin and looked out over the land, the emptiness filled with gratitude. I was grateful for my life, and for you and Jack. Grateful I could finally come home."

After Dad got back, he and Mom actually seemed to get along better. They didn't even argue much. But I wasn't so ready to accept everything was fine. Dad would ask me to go to the movies, or play chess, or take a bike ride. He even pulled the telescope out of the garage and suggested we go stargazing. I didn't want to do any of it. I was still so mad. Mad that Dad chose the trail over me. But since I couldn't put that feeling into words, I refused all of Dad's peace offerings and spent more and more time in my room.

Mom encouraged me to do something with Dad. She said that he was trying his best to make them all feel like a family again. So when he offered to take me and Trevor and Alyssa ice skating the day after Christmas, I agreed to go. And we all know how that turned out.

What if I'd said no that day and stayed in my room? Would Dad still be here? I still think about that a lot.

Now I wish I'd just enjoyed the time I'd had with Dad, instead of being angry about him leaving. At least I still have Mom. I can be grateful for her.

I was on my second helping of spaghetti and meatballs when I heard a bark in the distance. I told myself it was probably some hiker's dog. But then the barking got closer and closer. I headed out to the porch.

I saw a black dog bounding out of the woods. At first I

figured I was just seeing things again. Mom came up behind me and grabbed my shoulders, pulling me close to her.

"Stay back. That dog might have rabies or something."

"You see him, too?"

"Of course I can see him."

I ran down the steps, shouting Seneca's name. I dropped to my knees in the dirt and Seneca barreled into me, slobbering all over my face. I hugged him tightly.

I led him up the cabin steps to meet Mom.

"So that's Renny's dog?" she said.

"Don't worry, he's friendly."

Mom held out her hand and Seneca sniffed it, then nuzzled her leg. "Where in the world was he?" Mom asked.

"He probably just needed some time to figure stuff out," I said.

I filled his bowl with food, and he devoured it.

"We should probably put a leash on him," Mom said.

"Seneca doesn't like leashes," I explained.

"But what if he runs off again?"

"It's okay, Mom. Sometimes the things you love run off and they don't come back. That's just the way of the world."

ONCE WE MOVED into the cabin, Mom and I started getting along a lot better. She even quit smoking, which I was happy about, but she'd replaced cigarettes with nicotine gum. The constant chewing is really annoying, but at least it's not as stinky. And no matter how many packs she chews, at least the gum won't kill her.

After school, I like to take nature walks with Seneca. Sometimes Mom goes with us. And sometimes I take Renny. You probably think it's a little morbid to walk around the woods carrying an urn, but it's actually comforting. I can hear Renny reminding me to keep living life, no matter what it throws at me. And on our way back home, I bring Renny to Charlie's Grove and put his urn on the ground next to the sculpture of his son. I sit on the bench and let them spend time together.

It's not something Renny requested in his will, but I hope it brings them peace. Wherever they are.

Free eBook

Join my mailing list to receive a free copy of *Both Lost And Found*—a prequel novelette to *Both Here And Gone*.

What does it take to walk away from everything you know in search of what you truly need?

Bearing the weight of a life that no longer feels like his own, Mark Finn steps onto the Appalachian Trail with little more than a backpack and a heart heavy with regret.

Told through a series of journal entries, written in moments of solitude, *Both Lost And Found* follows Mark's quest for meaning. Through verdant forests and over mist-shrouded peaks, Mark confronts the raw forces of nature and the ghosts of his past. His failed marriage and strained relationship with his son haunt every step, but the trail offers unexpected companions, including a dog-eared copy of *Walden*.

Guided by the enduring wisdom of Henry David Thoreau, Mark discovers the strength it takes to follow one's own path and start anew. Embark on a journey of self-discovery and redemption that celebrates the unbreakable spirit within us all and the transformative power of human connection.

To join my mailing list and get your free ebook visit:
https://www.michaeldantedimartino.com/free-book

Please leave a review!

If you enjoyed this book's emotional journey, I would really appreciate it if you would leave a review.

Your review can help the book gain visibility and bring this story to the attention of other readers who might connect with its themes and message.

To leave a review, head over to Amazon or type the link below into your browser. Thank you!

https://geni.us/bothhereandgone

About the Author

Michael Dante DiMartino is the co-creator of the award-winning animated Nickelodeon series *Avatar: The Last Airbender* and its sequel, *The Legend of Korra*. He is also the writer of the graphic novels *Turf Wars* and *Ruins of the Empire*, the author of the fantasy novels *Rebel Genius* and *Warrior Genius*, and the creator and writer of the Audible audio drama *Sundown: A Time Capsule Society Mystery*.

For more information visit:
www.michaeldantedimartino.com

Made in the USA
Coppell, TX
25 July 2024

35178564R00152